CALL ME GRIM

Elizabeth Holloway

Month9Books

Month9Books

For Hana and Caleb.
Reach for the stars. Let no one tell you your dreams are too lofty, or not worth the trouble.

CALL ME GRIM

Elizabeth Holloway

1

I tap my fingers on my crossed arms and peer through the tinted front window of Carroll Falls High. At the top of the hill, a stripe of maroon paint flashes between the trees. I straighten up, hitching my purse over my shoulder. The car pulls into the school's parking lot, and I slump again. It's not Mom's Honda. It's just some old dude in a Camry.

Mom is ten minutes late to the art show, though I'm not surprised. She warned me. She tried to get out of working at the restaurant tonight, but her boss is an uncultured douchebag who doesn't understand how big of a deal this is for me.

"How long before we go in? I'm bored." Max's thumbs fly over the buttons of his handheld videogame. The cuffs of his dress shirt slip down over his hands. He lifts his arms and shakes the sleeves back while he continues his assault on the control buttons.

"I don't know." I tug on the collar of my blouse for what seems like the hundredth time and check to make sure my cleavage isn't trying to steal my thunder. "Whenever Mom gets here, I guess."

"That could be hours." Max sighs dramatically and leans against the wall beside me. "She said if she was late to go in without her."

"I know." I glance at the clock on the wall above Max's head. "But it's only been ten minutes, and she'd want us to wait."

That's true. No matter what Mom said, she'd want us to wait for her. It's not her fault her boss is a psycho control freak. But

I don't think I can wait much longer to find out if I've placed in this year's show. My heart might explode from anticipation.

I dig my phone out of my purse and flip it open. I would know if she texted me, my phone would have chimed and vibrated, but I check it anyway. Nothing.

Five more minutes. She has five minutes, then we're going in without her.

"Libbi!"

I tear my eyes from the steady stream of traffic at the top of the hill in front of the school and scan the sea of uncomfortably dressed people crowding the hallway. Haley's blond head bounces between the shoulders of two senior boys.

"Excuse me." She pushes one of the boys out of her way and ignores his indignant protest. "Libs!" She waves and almost walks right into the refreshments table. She skirts it with a grace only Haley Dennis could master, like a near collision with the table was something she meant to do.

"Hey, Haley," I say when she's close enough I don't have to shout. "Where's Kyle?"

"He's looking for you, silly." She grins, and her dark eyes sparkle with excitement. She knows something. Something really freaking good. "So...have you seen your display?"

My heart jumps up to high-five my teeth.

"Not yet," I say. It's hard to talk around the thumping in my throat.

"Oh my God, Libs. What are you waiting for?" She grabs my hand and yanks me from the window. "Come on!"

"Finally," Max mutters as he follows me and Haley through the crowd.

Haley's polka-dotted dress sways as she leads me down the hall to the gym. I'm sure Mom wanted us to wait, but I don't think I could if I tried. Haley has me in a death grip. Plus, I really don't want to wait anymore. Not after I saw that look on Haley's face. I have to know why she's grinning like the Joker as she practically drags me through the aisles of student artwork.

We round one last corner, and I yelp. Out loud. I smack my hand over my mouth as my eyes adjust to the bright blue of the ribbon hanging from my painting. *My* painting. Written in white calligraphy on the ribbon's center are the words "First Place."

A squeal builds inside me, and it takes all of my strength to keep it from squeezing out. I can't believe it. I not only placed, I first-placed.

As part of a program to promote the study of fine art in schools, the Philadelphia Museum of Art holds an annual show of work by students of Pennsylvania public schools. After applying for consideration every year for five years, Carroll Falls High School finally got the chance to host it. But the museum doesn't accept any old kid's work to display in their show. They want talent. I was one of only three from my school who they accepted.

And tonight, a representative from the freaking Philadelphia Museum of Art came and gave my painting first place. An actual art professional likes my work. If I wasn't so worried my boobs might spill out of my blouse, I'd jump up and down like the dork that I am.

"Congrats, Libs." Max sounds genuinely excited. Well, as excited as an eight-year-old kid forced to come to his big sister's art show can sound.

"See? I told you you'd place." Haley hooks her arm around my elbow. "You should never doubt me. I know all."

"I can't believe this." I run a shaky finger down the length of the blue ribbon. Yup. It's really there. "Where's that Philly art guy? I think I want to tackle hug him."

"Wait. What about me?" Kyle says behind me. "Without me, you wouldn't have that painting."

I turn and meet Kyle's smiling brown eyes. Considering Haley and Kyle are only fraternal twins, it's amazing how much they look alike, especially when they smile.

"I guess I owe you one too," I say as Kyle pulls me into one of his suffocating bear hugs. "Thanks for looking so damned awesome."

"Anytime." Kyle pats my back and lets me go. "What are friends for?"

My eyes drift over to my winning painting. It started off as a picture I took with my cellphone. Kyle had been upset at school that day, and I came over to the house to see if I could cheer him up. As expected, I found him in his garage beating the hell out of his drums.

He played so furiously he didn't hear me come in. After a few minutes, he stopped and dropped his hands to his sides. Sweat rolled down his cheeks and his arms glistened. Anger, hurt, defeat pulled at the tense angles of his face and his shoulders sagged.

I snapped the picture.

He never told me why he was so ticked off that day, but he liked the picture. He said it made him look like a badass, though I saw something different. To me, he looked broken. But he asked me to paint it for him anyway, as a gift. And I did.

***

The art show is supposed to last two hours, but by the one-hour mark the gym is pretty much empty.

Max ran off with a friend from school a while ago. The last I saw them they were sitting on the bleachers, heads together, with Max's videogame between them. Kyle and Haley left about five minutes ago. Kyle had to stop by his bandmate's house to drop off some equipment, and Haley insisted on hitting the books one last time.

"I can't get into Harvard if I don't study," she said, but I doubt one more night of studying will make a difference. Haley will ace that history final. She always does. I, on the other hand, need to cram. I actually studied for this exam—for once—but my brain is like a sieve when it comes to dates, and I could use a last minute refresher. But instead of heading home to turn my gray matter into historical mush, I wander up and down the aisles of student artwork and wait for Mom.

The restaurant must be slammed tonight. She's been late to events before—ten minutes here, twenty minutes there—but usually not a whole hour. Maybe I missed her and she's already here. Maybe she's waiting for me at my winning painting.

I find my way back to my work, hopeful that my hunch is right. I really do need to get home and study.

A boy I don't recognize stands at the opposite end of the aisle. He meets my eyes for a moment and smiles, then he crosses his arms over his chest and studies the still-life drawing in front of him. Other than him, the row is deserted. Mom still hasn't made it.

I touch my blue ribbon again, letting my fingers trail over the letters. First place. A thrill shoots through me. I can't wait for Mom to see it. She's going to be so proud of me, she might even cry.

The air around me changes, and the shiver of excitement shifts to a shiver of dread.

Someone is watching me.

I glance to the end of the aisle where that guy stood a few seconds ago, but he's not there. He must have moved to another aisle. I'm alone.

I'm being stupid. There's nothing to fear. There's nobody here except me and my artist's imagination. But I still feel it. Somebody's eyes are on me, scrutinizing me, looking through me. Either that or someone walked over my grave, as Gran would say.

"That's a beautiful piece," a smooth voice says behind me.

I jump and whirl around. My hand instinctively reaches for the inhaler in my back pocket.

"Holy Jesus! You scared the crap out of me." I hold my other hand over my galloping heart.

The boy who was checking out the still-life at the other end of the aisle is at my side. His faded blue eyes study me with interest.

"Sorry. I didn't mean to scare you." The guy's smile is warm, but I can't shake the cold feeling that settles in my stomach. He nods to my painting of Kyle and I follow his gaze. "I was just saying that's a beautiful painting. Great sense of composition."

Of course I'm proud of my work, but I'd hate to come off as a self-congratulatory jerk to a guy I just met, especially since he just scared the bejesus out of me.

"Yeah. It's okay." I pray the blood drains from my cheeks before he notices.

"It's more than okay. It's...I don't know." He touches his chin thoughtfully. "Passionate. Emotional. Just look at the use of color. This artist has talent."

Oh. He doesn't know it's my painting. Well, why would he? He doesn't know me, and I don't know him. As far as I know he could be the Philly museum guy, though I doubt it. He's only about my age. But it doesn't matter if he is. I'm not about to tell him it's my painting after he said such nice things. I feel weird enough as it is.

"So, are you an artist?" I ask to get his mind off my work.

"Ha! Unless you count origami, no." He shakes his head and his black hair feathers across his forehead. "I've tried, but I'm terrible. My sister's the artist in the family." A soft smile lights his face. "She's great."

Ah. Now it makes sense. His sister has a display in the show. He's here for her.

"Where's her display?" I say. "I'd like to see it."

"Oh." He shifts his weight and slips his hands into his pockets. "She's not in this show."

"She's not?" I ask, surprised. "Then, who are you here to see?"

"You, Libbi." His smile is friendly, but there's something more to that sparkle in his eyes. The hairs on my arms stand up like little soldiers.

The cold feeling I got when I first saw this guy never really went away, but now ice blasts through me like my blood has been replaced with Freon. I've never seen him before. Why would he say he's here to see me? My signature scrawled at the bottom of the canvas is barely legible to me, and I wrote it. So how does he know my name?

"Something bad is going to happen to you tomorrow," he says.

"What?" I say, because I'm shocked and my mind is too numb to think of anything else.

"Listen. What I'm about to say might sound crazy,

unbelievable even." He nervously twists a silver ring on his right thumb. "But I don't have a lot of time, and I need you to hear me out. It's important. Okay?"

"Okay." I swallow. What else can I say? He has me cornered.

The guy opens his mouth, but before he speaks, his eyes dart over my shoulder and his lips smack shut.

"Libbi?" Mom's voice drifts down the aisle behind me, and I sigh with relief. Saved by my mom.

"I'll talk to you later, when we can be alone." The guy turns and faces the painting opposite mine.

"Alone?" I ask, but he ignores me. He leans in close to the painting, so close he could count the brush strokes.

"Oh, honey, I'm so sorry I'm late." Mom slips one arm around me in a half-hug.

"It's okay." I give the creepy guy one last look. He said something bad was going to happen to me. Is he just crazy, or does he know something I don't? Maybe both. He might be crazy enough to have something bad planned for me.

A shiver passes down my body, but I shake it off. I'm letting my imagination get to me again.

"Was the restaurant busy?" I ask to get my mind off the guy and his insane prediction.

"Nuts." She tucks a loose strand of hair behind her ear. "But never mind about that. I'm here now, and I'm dying to see this award-winning painting of yours."

The guy glances over his shoulder at us, his eyes wide with surprise. Maybe he didn't think a girl could paint a winning piece. I ignore him.

"You know I placed?" Disappointment settles over me and kicks the creepy-crawly feeling the guy gave me to the curb. "Who told you?" I pout. I wanted to tell her myself.

"I ran into Max while I was looking for you." She points at my painting decorated with the blue ribbon. "Is that it? Oh my goodness, Libbi. You got first place?"

"Yeah," I say. At least Max didn't spoil that.

"That's so great." Tears swell in her eyes. Jackpot.

I can't help myself. I peek at the weirdo who complimented

my work. He's crazy, I'm sure, but I still sort of want him to know the painting he liked is mine. Maybe that makes me a little cuckoo myself, but I don't care.

He meets my eyes. His gaze slides back and forth between my painting and me, his face the definition of stunned disbelief. Yeah, he definitely knows it's my painting now.

Suddenly, his jaw clenches and his eyes harden. He mumbles something that sounds like "I can't do this," and then he turns and practically jogs away.

He can't do what? My brain fills in the answer with lots of awful, scary possibilities.

For the rest of our time at the show, I continuously glance over my shoulder for the creepy guy, but he's not anywhere.

Good. Take your insanity somewhere else. But part of me worries that he's waiting, out of sight. Biding his time until he can follow me home. Where I'll be in my room. Alone. Like he wanted.

2

The creep is back.

I may not be able to see him, but I know he's here, somewhere. Call it intuition. Or maybe it's just the eerie memory of when the guy stared me down last night. I don't know, but I'm not taking any chances.

I hunch over my history final and release my thick hair from behind my ears. It swings forward like a dark-brown curtain and hides my face.

Show's over, buddy.

I can't look around, not with Mr. Winkler on "cheater duty." Hopefully, the guy will get bored and go wherever the hell he went last night when he took off.

The final is what's important. I need to focus on this test.

I read the next question on the page, but the loser's gaze bores through my dark shield of hair and my arms erupt in gooseflesh. Before I can skim the multiple choice answers, my eyes betray me and shoot up to scan the classroom.

Mr. Winkler sits at his desk scratching at some poor schlub's paper with his red pen of doom. His bald head gleams in the harsh fluorescent light. God, I hope it's not my paper he's destroying. I can't afford another bad grade in this class.

I quickly scan the rest of the classroom through the part in my hair, but everyone is working. Eerie feeling or not, nobody's looking at me.

But I know someone is watching. Just like last night, I can feel his stalker stare.

This is ridiculous. I shake my head and rub my arms to dispel the goose bumps. This guy has freaked me out so much I'm imagining his eyes on me now. I don't have time for this. I have an exam to finish.

The tip of my pencil hovers over the letter C, and something in my peripheral vision shifts. I snap my head up and finally see him.

The guy I caught staring at me at the art show last night, the guy who warned me something bad was going to happen to me today, stands at the tiny rectangular window in the door. He tilts his head and his ice-blue eyes lock on mine, sending a shiver through my body.

Shake it off, Libbi, I tell myself. *He's just a crazy boy with a crush.*

Actually, with his tousled black hair and his nose pressed against the glass like that, he looks a little like a lost puppy. If he wasn't so creepy, I'd almost feel sorry for him. But couldn't he choose a better time than the middle of my history final to eyeball me? Plus, he said he wanted to talk to me alone, and this is most certainly not alone.

I point to my partially finished test and mouth, "Final exam."

He nods. A half-smile lifts the corners of his lips.

"Bye." I wave my hand.

"I need to talk to you," he mouths.

"No," I reply, but he continues to stand at the door.

Dude, catch a clue already. I spin away from the door, sneak a peek at Mr. Winkler, and shove the eraser of my pencil between my teeth. I yank the eraser out of its metal holder and flick it at the back of Haley's head. Her chair squeaks as she jumps and whips around to glare at me.

"What?" she whispers.

"Look." I point over my shoulder with my pencil to the classroom door. "That crazy guy I told you about is at the window."

We turn to the door together, but the window's empty. He must be a shy creeper.

"Where?" Haley says.

"Never mind. He's gone." I slump back in my chair. At least I can finish my test in peace.

"Is there a reason you and Haley are chit-chatting in the middle of the final, Libbi?" Mr. Winkler's cheeks flare as red as the pen he sets aside. He stands from his desk.

"Sorry, Mr. Winkler," I say. "We weren't cheating or anything. I thought I saw someone out in the hallway."

"Well, I'll be the judge of who's cheating." He stomps up the aisle toward us and snatches Haley's test off her desk as he passes.

"Hey, I'm not done," she protests.

"That's too bad, isn't it?" He seizes my test as well. "Maybe next time you'll keep your eyes on your own paper and your lips sealed."

Haley's eyes bulge and her face flushes crimson. She presses her lips together into a thin, pink line. I know just by looking at her that Haley is too pissed to defend herself. This is my fault. I should have just ignored my stalker and left her alone.

"That's not fair," I say.

"Cheating is not fair." Mr. Winkler sprays me with spittle. "Do I need to send you to the office to discuss this with Mrs. Greener?"

"No." I wipe his spit off my cheek. There's no way I'd willingly submit myself to Greener. I'll have to actually talk to Winkler after class, though that's not much better. Kyle calls Mr. Winkler "Mr. Sprinkler," and after sitting in the front row for nine months, he's earned the right to call him whatever he wants.

"Okay then." Winkler marches up to his desk with both of our tests clutched in his pudgy little hands. Once he's safely resumed his red pen massacre, Haley glances over her shoulder at me and gives me a look that makes me wish I could dissolve into the seat.

"Thanks a lot," she whispers and whips around to the chalkboard before I can say I'm sorry. Her curls bounce as she folds her arms over her chest.

Kyle turns in his seat and gives me a sympathetic glance. At least *he* isn't mad at me, but his sister is pissed. Haley would never cheat. And she'd never fail to finish a test. Haley never fails at anything. I'll have to make this up to her.

The bell rings a few seconds longer than usual, signaling the end of the school day. The scattered pile of papers on Winkler's desk grows as people deposit their exams and file out.

"Haley," I call, but she races out the door ahead of everyone. She doesn't even look at me. Okay, making it up to her might cost me more than a close encounter with Winkler the Sprinkler. I reach under my chair and grab my book bag by the straps.

"Don't worry, Libs." Kyle smacks his books down on my desk. "She'll get over it."

"Yeah, maybe. She's pretty ticked." I swing my bag over my shoulder and shrug. "Why don't you go on without me? I want to try and smooth things over with Winkler. If you wait, you'll be late for practice."

Kyle slips his drumsticks out of their home in his back pocket and taps a quick rhythm against my desk as he considers me. Any other day, he'd say, "I can be late," and wait for me anyway, but not today. Kyle's the drummer of the band Red Motive, and there's a huge Battle of the Bands at school tomorrow night. The winner gets to play three original songs at prom. Not even his huffy twin sister could keep him from band practice today.

"Are you sure?" He raises his eyebrows.

"I'm a big girl, Kyle. I can walk home by myself."

"Okay." Kyle scratches his cheek and smirks. "But I hope you realize that trying to convince Sprinkler to change his mind is like trying to convince the Pope he's not Catholic."

"Yeah, I know." I squeeze between him and my desk and into the aisle. "But Haley doesn't deserve to fail and I can't afford to. I have to try."

"Good luck with that." Kyle claps me on the shoulder on his way to the door. I lift my hand in a feeble good-bye and trudge up to Mr. Winkler's desk.

"Mr. Winkler, we weren't cheating. I swear. Haley would never—"

"Like I said, I'll decide that when I grade the exams." He stuffs the pile of tests and other papers into his briefcase. "You're wasting your time. And mine."

"But we really weren't—"

"I don't care. You were talking, and that's the same as cheating in my book." He snaps the clasps of his briefcase closed.

"But we weren't cheating." I slap my hands down on his desk in frustration. "And it wasn't even Haley's fault. I made her look at me."

"I know that." He levels me with his eyes. "I'm not stupid, Libbi. You need an A on this test to pass the class."

"That has nothing to do with this."

"Oh, really?" He crosses his arms over his chest.

"Well, maybe a little bit, but we weren't cheating."

"I'm not discussing this any further with you." He snatches his briefcase up and pushes his chair in with his knee.

That's it? He won't even hear me out? My nails dig into my palms. I take a deep breath and count to three.

"That's so unfair," I say instead of the four-letter-word tirade that presses against my teeth.

"Go home, Libbi."

"Fine." I barrel across the classroom and through the open door, yanking the doorknob as hard as I can. The door slams and the lockers on either side rattle. Good. I hope I broke Mr. Sprinkler's door.

What am I going to do? If I fail this test, I'll fail history. And if I fail history, I might fail the year. But if Haley fails, she'll never speak to me again. This is all my fault.

No. It's my freaky stalker's fault.

I turn the corner at the end of the hallway and charge directly into creepy-stare-boy's chest. A crunch sounds in my skull and tears spring to my eyes. I take a step back and rub my nose with my palm.

"Oh jeez. I'm sorry, Libbi." He places a hand on my shoulder to steady me. "Are you all right?"

I glance down at his hand on my shoulder then back up at him. A scowl pulls at the corners of my mouth.

He drops his hand from my shoulder and slips it back into his jeans pocket. His pale cheeks flush with color and I think he's about to apologize for touching me, but instead he pulls a rolled-up tissue out of his pocket.

"You're bleeding." He holds the balled up tissue out to me. "Take this."

"Uh..." I shake my head as I push by him. "No thanks."

After freaking me out and disappearing last night, the guy has decided this is the best time to talk to me? But instead of making me swoon with his stalker prowess, he's caused me to fail my final, piss off my best friend, and he's given me a bloody nose. Smooth. And now he wants me to use his nasty snot rag? Gross.

"I'm sorry about your nose and your test," he says as he follows me down the hall. "But I need to talk to you."

I ignore him.

The hallway echoes with the clang of slamming lockers and the squeak of sneakers. I don't need to stop at my locker, thankfully. It's the end of the school year; most of my books are already turned in. But even if I was having the worst asthma attack in history and the only inhaler in the world was in my locker, I wouldn't stop. I don't want to encourage conversation with this guy. He can ogle me from a distance if he wants, but I have to draw the line somewhere.

The double doors at the end of the hallway squeal when I shove them open. I squint as I step onto the green front lawn of the school. The sudden assault of sunlight makes me sneeze.

"Bless you," he says at my shoulder.

Great goodness. He doesn't get the hint.

I spin around, and he stops just short of slamming his chest into my nose for a second time. I take a step back and look up into his face.

His unruly black hair brushes his forehead and frames his angular face. A fine shadow of stubble darkens his chin and cheeks, but it's not bad. He's not a rug, or anything. And good Lord, those eyes. Azure blue and piercing. I'd love to paint him. It'd be a challenge to match that blue.

He's cute. He shouldn't need to chase any girl, much less me.

His full lips spread in a smile and my heart flutters, but only for a second. He is a crazy stalker, after all. Just because he's good looking doesn't mean he's not a creep.

"Who are you, anyway?" I plant my fists on my hips.

"Sorry. My name's Aaron." He wipes his palms on his shirt and reaches out to shake hands. I ignore the gesture. God, this guy is weird.

"Well, Aaron, thanks to you, I probably just failed history." I flick my hair out of my eyes. "So, I'm really not in the mood to talk right now. Why don't you go be crazy with someone else? Okay?"

"I said I was sorry about your test." A deep crease forms between his eyes. "And I'm not crazy."

"That's what all the crazy people say," I mutter. "Well, if you're not crazy, what was all of that crap last night? What were you doing outside my classroom? And why are you following me?"

"I'm trying to stop something bad from happening to you." He spreads his hands in frustration, palms to the sky. The sunlight glints off the silver ring on his thumb.

"Just leave me alone." I storm off across the grass.

"Wait, Libbi." He's at my heels. "Please."

"Go away." I start to jog up the hill to the street. A bit of distance grows between us, but not much.

Diablo Road isn't called "Hell's Highway" simply because of its devilish name. It's twisty and busy and at least one bad accident occurs per year. If I'm lucky and there's a break in traffic, I can get across the street before Aaron catches up. I can be at my front door and away from this creep in minutes.

I hear his slow, steady breathing behind me. His pants legs swoosh against each other as he climbs the hill. He's close. If I cross the street and go directly to my front door, he'll know where I live.

Okay. I'll run around the block and come in the back door. Maybe the traffic will be too heavy for him to follow. I cross my fingers and pray as I race up the hill, checking both ways for a break in the steady stream of cars.

I see one. A break in traffic. If I sprint, I can make it. I swear I hear angels singing.

I dart forward and step off the curb with just enough time to race across the street before the gap closes. It couldn't be any better. One foot grazes the blacktop and Aaron's fingers dig into my upper arm. He yanks me back onto the grass.

He touched me. I can't believe he touched me. Again. My hand balls into a fist and I swing around and slug him in the jaw. Hard. His teeth smack together with a pop.

"What is your problem?" I yell. People are looking at us. Someone mutters "freak," but nobody bothers to help me.

"What did you do that for?" Aaron massages his red, swelling jaw.

"Get a clue and leave me alone!"

"You know, you should be grateful."

"Grateful? Grateful for what? That you haven't murdered me yet?"

Aaron shakes his head and laughs.

"What's so funny?" I say, hands on my hips.

"I'm not trying to murder you, Libbi." He meets my gaze directly. "I'm trying to help you." His icy eyes penetrate mine and a chill prickles over my arms, despite the early summer heat. I don't believe in ESP or mind reading or crap like that, but there's something deep in his eyes. He knows something. More than he should.

"What the hell are you talking about?" I somehow manage not to stammer.

"I want to save your life and offer you a job." His hand is back on my elbow. "And believe me, Libbi, saving lives is not something I do often."

"Let go of me." I yank my arm from his grasp and stumble back.

"Please." He reaches for me. "Just wait a few more seconds before you cross. Please? Wait until it's safe."

"Safe?" I back away. "Until what's safe?"

"If you cross now, you'll get hit by a black pick-up truck and die."

My heels balance on the edge of the curb. One foot slips and Aaron rushes to me. He's too fast. He grips my shoulders and yanks me away from the curb. His arms wrap around me and he holds me against his body. My face presses into his chest and the smell of fresh dirt and dead roses overwhelms me. I yelp and struggle, but my balled fists are pinned at my sides.

"Three…" He whispers in my ear. "Two…" His warm breath brushes the back of my neck. "One…"

He lets go.

The shriek of tires against pavement startles me, and I twist around. A black pick-up truck takes the deadly turn in front of the school too fast and the backend fish-tails, sending the truck into an uncontrolled spin. It skids 180 degrees and crashes sideways into the parked Honda across the street from me. The Honda's car alarm screams to life.

"Holy shit!" I jump away from the scene of smoking, twisted metal.

"I'm all right." Jason, a senior and the driver of the pick-up, pushes his deflating airbag away from his face. The crumpled Honda he hit is in far worse shape, but at least it's empty.

If Aaron had let me cross the street when I wanted to, I would have been standing beside that Honda when the truck crashed into it. I'd be squished between the two vehicles right now, and I'd probably be dead.

"Oh my God." I turn back to Aaron with "WTF?" hovering on my tongue. "How did you know?" The colors blur and my heart pounds in my ears.

Aaron smiles down at me. He says something, but I don't hear it. The last things I see before the world goes black are his eyes.

Blue like the summer sky before a sudden storm.

3

"Shit!" a girl yells. "My parents are going to kill me." Her voice rolls around in my head, thick and garbled. I pry my eyes open and turn slightly. The owner of the voice, Salma Byrd, runs up the hill toward her mangled Honda. She's a junior, like me, but I never talk to her. Her friends are athletic and perfect. In other words, not me. She passes my sprawled body without a glance.

"Are you all right?" a different female voice says. "I think you fainted."

A wide-eyed girl I don't know, probably a freshman, kneels next to me and fans me with a pink piece of paper. A group has gathered behind her. Half of them watch as Salma flips a shit over her car. The rest watch me.

My foggy brain struggles to remember what happened. Did I have an asthma attack? Maybe, but I don't think so. I feel fine, other than dizziness and my missing memory. No tightness in my chest. No post-attack exhaustion. Something weirder than asthma happened before I passed out. What was it?

My stalker. Aaron.

Aaron was standing next to me. He grabbed me. Whatever weird thing happened, it had to do with him and the squished Honda.

He has to be here somewhere. I scan the group hovering over me for his face, but I can't see clearly. It's too bright. My eyes refuse to adjust to the harsh sunlight. I blink a few times and squint and realize the burning light isn't coming from the sun. It's coming from the girl fanning me. Her skin glows like someone stuffed her with neon lights. But it's not only her; her friends are blazing too. I'm surrounded by giant, human-shaped glow sticks.

I squeeze my eyes closed for a second and then refocus on the girl fanning me, but the glow is still there. What the heck? Did I have a stroke? Or maybe I hit my head when I fell. My head doesn't hurt, but there has to be some reasonable explanation for the shining people, unless a nuclear bomb went off while I was out. Maybe Aaron did something to me, brainwashed or drugged me.

I search through my foggy memory to see if I felt a pin prick before I fainted. I can't remember. Maybe I did. I push up from the ground into a sitting position, but I'm too dizzy to stand.

"Wow! Are you sure you should sit up like that?" the wide-eyed freshman says. "You look like crap."

"I'm fine," I say, more to convince myself than the concerned girl. At least I'm not slurring my words. "Where's Aaron?"

"Aaron?" She glances back at her friends. A boy in a black T-shirt printed with the picture of some band I've never heard of shrugs.

"Aaron," I say. "The guy who was with me when I fell."

The kid in the black tee frowns and says, "You were alone." He's the kid who said "freak" instead of helping me when I was yelling and running from Aaron.

"No, I wasn't." I shake my head. "There was a guy with me. He's tall and has black hair and blue eyes. He grabbed my shoulders and..." The memory rushes back and I gasp. "He stopped me from crossing the street. Holy crap! He saved my life."

"Um, I was right here," the boy insists. "There was no guy with you. You were alone. You were yelling and talking to yourself, and then you passed out."

"Fine." I pull my legs under me and get to my hands and knees. "Don't tell me where he went." My legs feel steady enough, so I stand. The dizziness is gone, but everyone still looks like their skin is on fire.

I swing my book bag over my shoulder and scan the accident scene for Aaron's bright blue eyes. Jason stands next to his crushed truck and shuffles his feet in the broken glass beside the open driver's side door. His mouth forms a perfect circle beneath his glassy eyes. He's glowing too.

"You ass!" Salma bellows. Strands of her chestnut hair come loose from her ponytail as she jabs her finger at his chest and then at her car. "You're gonna pay for that, you know!"

"I'm sorry, Sal." Jason backs up a few steps, holding his hands up to his chest, palms out. "I took the turn too fast."

A small crowd gawks at Jason and Salma and the Honda/pick-up pretzel. Aaron has to be among them. He was beside me seconds before the accident. I couldn't have been unconscious long enough for him to get far, but he's not here. If not for my nose—which still throbs from running into his chest—I would think I hallucinated him.

"Um, excuse me." A light touch on my elbow makes me jump.

"Sorry. You dropped this." The freshman who fanned me earlier holds an elaborately folded piece of origami out to me: a lily with four delicately folded petals. I've never seen anything like it. It's beautiful.

"It's not mine," I say.

"It fell out of your book bag." She steps closer and lifts the flower up to me. On one of the petals is my name written in unfamiliar, loopy handwriting, and there's more writing deep within the flower. It's a letter.

Didn't Aaron say something last night about liking origami?

I snatch the flower out of the girl's hand. It's from Aaron. It has to be.

"You're welcome." She frowns.

"Sorry," I say. "Thanks."

I grip one petal of the flower between thumb and forefinger so tightly my nail beds turn white. It's a short walk to an empty park bench, but something tells me I need to sit before I read this.

My fingers tremble as I disassemble the folded note and flatten it over my thigh.

Libbi,

Sorry I didn't talk to you sooner. I should have explained everything last night, but something came up. Anyway, now that I've saved your life there's someone important I need to see, and I can't stick around until you wake up. Things are going to get really strange for you now. Don't worry. I'll explain everything if you meet me at Oak Valley Assisted Living at six tonight. I need to talk to you and show you something.

Please, don't freak out. Just come. And don't be late.

Aaron Shepherd

I know that name: Aaron Shepherd. Where have I heard it?

I read the letter again and again, but I can't make any sense of it. What does he mean things are going to get strange? Is he talking about the light bulb people?

And why does his name sound so damn familiar?

I try to refold the letter, but give up when the first petal I fold pulls apart as I attempt to fold the second. I tuck the half-flower into my jeans pocket.

There's one thing I know for sure: even if I didn't have to babysit Max tonight, there's no way in hell I'd meet the crazy boy who chased me—and may have even drugged me—at a nursing home tonight. Even if he *did* magically save my life. Aaron Shepherd can suck it.

I swing my book bag over my shoulder. Traffic is stopped from the accident so I'm able to cross the street to my house easily.

Max stands on the front porch in his socks. His skin glows like everyone else's and when his copper hair flickers in the breeze, it looks like his head is on fire.

"Hey, Libs," he says around the straw of his juice box. "Nobody's dead, right?"

"Nope. No one's dead." I can't help but shiver. I could've been dead. I could have been a Libbi-and-metal sandwich. I swallow hard.

"Have you finished your homework?" I may as well wrap an apron around my waist and pin my hair in a bun. I hate pretending

21

I'm Mom, but Mom's at work and I'm in charge.

"No." Max rolls his eyes. "I've been out here watching the accident and stuff."

"Well, the party's over, buckaroo. Get back inside and do your homework." I place a hand on his shoulder and steer him toward the house, but he stops.

"What's that?" He points at my hip. I reflexively touch where he's pointing and find Aaron's letter hanging halfway out of my pocket. I shove it back in.

"It's a letter." I herd Max through the front door.

"From who?"

"A guy named Aaron." For some reason it feels like I've said something wrong, like I shouldn't be talking about him.

"A guy?" Max waggles his eyebrows at me. His straw makes an obnoxious sucking sound as he finishes his drink.

"Oh gross, Max!" I shut the door and drop my book bag on the floor next to his.

"Is this guy-named-Aaron cute?" he says in a sing-song voice.

"I am not discussing this with you." I grab his book bag and shove it at him. "Homework time."

The truth is, it doesn't matter if Aaron is cute. The guy is creepy. Something weird happened when he stopped me from walking out onto the street. I'm not sure what it is, but I have no intention of seeing Aaron Shepherd ever again. Not if I can help it.

4

I've never had a migraine before, but I'm sure I'm having
one now. It started with pressure at my temples while I was
making dinner, but by the time I sat Max's plate on the table
in front of him, the pain pounded behind my eyeballs and split
my head in two.

"Can I have more nuggets?" The shriek of his voice
reverberates in my ears and bounces around inside my skull.

Twenty-four hours ago I met Aaron Shepherd. Four hours
ago things started to get weird when the guy chased me down
and saved my life. And one hour ago I was supposed to meet my
creepy savior at an old folk's home.

I didn't go.

If Aaron slipped me a drug, the glowing-people thing should
have worn off by now. But it seems to be getting worse. This
headache is killer, and the light from Max's skin burns my eyes.
I can't look directly at him.

I glance at his plate. He ate all of his chicken nuggets, but the
stacks of broccoli and instant mashed potatoes stand untouched.
I nod, and my brain slams against the inside of my skull. I really
don't care if he eats his veggies. My head hurts too much to
pretend I'm Mom.

"Really?" Max says. "I can have more nuggets?"

It's me, Rosie...Rosie Benson.

"What did you say?" I squint at him.

"I said, 'Can I have more nuggets?'"

"No." I shake my head. My eyeballs are about to explode.

"You said something else. Something about Rosie Benson."

"Rosie Benson? Who's Rosie Benson?" Max scrunches up his face. "You're being really weird today."

"Forget it." I push back from the table and stand, knocking over the salt shaker. My fingers tremble as I set it upright and raise a hand to my clammy forehead.

"Are you all right?" Max sets his fork on his plate next to his forgotten potatoes and broccoli.

"I'm fine." I stumble out of the kitchen to the bathroom in the hallway. I need to be away from the light. Without flipping the switch on the wall, I turn on the faucet and splash my face with cool water. The door clicks closed behind me.

It should be pitch black in the bathroom with the door closed, but it's not.

I'm glowing too.

I hold my hand up in front of my stunned face and flex my fingers. The image in the mirror does the same.

I don't know why this surprises me, but it does. Brain tumor, concussion, or drugs—in the dark there shouldn't be enough light to trick my brain into seeing something that isn't there. Right? Can someone hallucinate light in the dark?

"Max?" I poke my head out of the bathroom door. "Can you come here for a second?"

"Why?"

"I want to see something. Are you still afraid of the dark?"

"I was never afraid of the dark." He struts into the hallway with his chest puffed out.

"Liar!" I say a bit too forcefully and my headache protests. "You're terrified of the dark," I whisper.

"Am not!"

"Well good, then you won't mind my experiment," I say.

"What experiment?" His eyes widen and his face pales.

"Don't worry, Max. I just want to see something. It'll take two seconds, and I'll be with you the whole time."

I take his hand and pull him toward the bathroom.

"Why do we need to be in the bathroom, in the dark, for your experiment?" His voice shakes.

"There's too much light out here and I need to see something."

"That makes no sense, Libbi," he says, but he comes with me anyway.

The door clicks closed, and the two of us stand in the bathroom with the lights off. We don't need the light. Max is enough. His skin blazes brilliant white. I glance in the mirror at our reflections and the difference between us is shocking.

"What the...?" I touch my fingers to my cheek. Yes, my skin glows. But I'm dull. Really dull. If Max is a bonfire, then I'm a tea candle about to flicker out.

"I'm not scared or anything." Max's sweaty hand grips mine. "But is your experiment almost done?"

"Do you see what I'm seeing?" This time *my* voice shakes.

"I can't see anything, Libs. It's pitch black in here."

The headache suddenly moves from behind my eyes to the center of my forehead and pulls, as if the pain is a rope attached to my brain and someone's playing tug-of-war. I open the bathroom door and stumble in the direction of the pull. The headache disappears. What the hell?

I'm here in this awful place, and I'm ready to go, the woman's voice in my head speaks up again. *Please, take me and make it stop. I'm ready.*

Soon, Rosie. Soon, a different voice says.

I stop walking and clutch my temples in my hands, praying for the agony to be gone for good, but it returns full force. A few more steps in the same direction and the headache disappears again. Weird. Aaron said in his letter that things would get weird. Is this what he meant? But this is beyond weird. This sucks.

Weird, sucktastic, or all of the above, I don't want the headache to come back, so I follow the pull down the hallway, through the living room to the front door. I rest my hand on the doorknob.

Where the heck do I think I'm going? I can't leave Max here alone just because my headache insists I leave the house.

Oh Bruce, it's so good to see you. I've missed you so much.

Pain explodes behind my eyes and I have to go, with or without Max. If I don't, the pain will kill me.

"Max, I'll be right back." I snatch my purse off the table beside the front door. "Eat as many chicken nuggets as you want, but don't touch the stove. Call my cell if anything happens. Don't call Mom. She'll kill me."

"Where are you going?" Max follows me down the hallway.

I don't answer. I have no clue where I'm going. I turn the knob and follow my headache out the door.

The cool breeze lifts the ends of my hair and covers my bare arms with chill bumps. I forgot my hoodie, but I don't care. There's no way I'm going back inside to face another blast of head-splitting pain.

I stop on the top step of the porch, unsure of what to do. Another torturous wave of pain hits me, and I double over. My stomach lurches and vomit threatens to color the stairs. I choke it down and stumble forward.

All right, all right, Headache, I think to myself. *You want me out here? Here I am. Do I need my car or should I walk?*

I know the answer before the thought fully forms in my head. Wherever I need to go, it's too far to walk. And I have to hurry.

I slip behind the wheel of my car, and the cracked pleather seat pinches my butt. Rosie speaks in my head again. She says something about how pleasant it is to spend time with Bruce— whoever Bruce is. Hell, whoever *Rosie* is. I ignore her.

Other than the occasional pair of headlights, Hell's Highway is deserted. It's seven thirty on a Thursday night. In a small town like Carroll Falls, people are home from work by now and are either eating supper or getting ready for bed. This is the time of night when Hell's Highway is the safest. It will stay fairly empty and safe for a while. Well, at least until the bars close.

I back out of the driveway and slam my foot on the accelerator. I have no idea where I'm going or even if I'm heading in the right direction, but my head feels better. It's still tugging at me, leading me forward, but the pain is almost completely gone. A nervous chuckle slips from my lips when it occurs to me I'm using a headache as a GPS system. I'm probably the most dangerous driver on Hell's Highway tonight.

5

The headache leads me across town to an oak-tree-lined driveway. I take the last turn, and my headlights sweep the brick facade of a large building. A well-lit sign in the carefully tended lawn reads: Oak Valley Assisted Living.

My head reels and spots burst in my vision. That can't be right. I blink and look again, but the sign remains the same. Keeping my eyes on the curving driveway, I slide my fingers into my pocket and remove the letter Aaron left for me. I almost rip the paper as my shaky fingers unfold the squished origami. I find what I'm looking for halfway down the page.

...Meet me at Oak Valley Assisted Living at six tonight.

He wanted me to come here. And somehow, despite my absolute refusal, he got me here. It's way past six, but I'm here. Tingles race over my skin. Who the hell is this guy?

I stop my car at the front entrance and shift into reverse. This is all too weird, in a bad, horror flick kind of way. I'm going home. Max has probably burned down the house by now anyway, and if he hasn't, he's at least wondering where the heck I disappeared to. I'll pop a few Motrin for the headache.

Pain seizes my brain, twisting it like a washrag, and I realize there is no amount of Motrin, or even morphine, that will dull it enough to ignore. My stomach heaves, and I swallow against the rising bile in my throat.

"Fine!" I slam the car door and trudge to the front entrance. The headache vanishes, but I'm too creeped out to be relieved.

The automatic doors slide open, and warm air envelops me.

The smell is the first thing I notice—a mixture of flowers and poop—and underlying that is another scent, something subtle and unpleasant. Something dark.

The tug in my head lurches me forward. I try not to appear crazy as I stumble past the front desk, but I must fail miserably.

"Excuse me, miss?" The tall, gray-haired woman behind the desk glares at me over her glasses. "Can I help you?"

I stop, and the pain brings tears to my eyes. Of course the headache is back. I stopped moving. I try not to wince as I turn around and face the woman.

"Um, yes." I have to think fast. How can I get by this woman before my head explodes? "I'm here to see Rosie." I cross my fingers and toes that there's a Rosie living at the home.

"Rosie?" She comes out from behind the desk and stands in front of me. "Well, first of all, there are more than a few Rosies here. And secondly, visiting hours are over at seven."

She points to a digital clock on the desk. Seven thirty.

"I'm sorry I'm so late, but I just got off work and I really wanted to tell her something. In person, you know. I want to see her reaction."

The woman's face remains hard. I'm not convincing her. I need to up the ante.

"I just got accepted to Harvard," I blurt out. It's a ridiculous thing to say and I have to stop myself from burying my face in my hands. Harvard is Haley's dream, not mine. My grades are so bad I've already resigned myself to a few years of community college. But my lie works. The woman's mouth drops open in astonishment.

"Wow. Harvard? That is an accomplishment." Her eyes soften and she whispers conspiratorially. "Okay, I'll let you in for fifteen minutes, but that's it. All right? Which Rosie are you here to see?"

"Um..." My mind searches through the pain for Rosie's last name. I know she said it. What was it? "Benson. Rosie Benson."

I say a silent prayer that there's a Rosie Benson living here. If not, and this woman sends me on my way, I'm sure my eyeballs will pop and blood will spew from my ears.

"Rosie Benson." She writes the name in a ledger, looks up at me, and smiles. She's all sugar and spice now. "And what's your name, sweetie?"

"Err...Tina...um...Benson," I say. I have no idea what's going on or why I'm here, but it seems best if I give the woman a fake name.

She scrawls the name next to "Rosie Benson" and looks back up at me.

"Do you know which room?"

"Yeah," I say.

It's a lie. I don't know where Rosie's room is, but I'm pretty sure my headache does.

***

I rap on the door at the end of the second-story hall and wait for a response. A small rectangular sign on the wall labels this room "R. Benson." A chill runs through me and my teeth chatter together, but the pain in my head is finally gone.

Something strange is about to happen, more strange than glowing people, a leading headache, or a crazy guy miraculously predicting my death and saving my life. I can feel the strangeness seeping through the closed door. But it's not in my head now, it's deeper than that.

There's no response to my knock, so I try again and press my ear to the door. Nothing. No talking. No TV. No soft snore of someone sleeping. Nada.

Then a thump and a small, feminine gasp. If I wasn't straining to hear, I would have missed it.

Whether it's Rosie in there or Aaron or both, the strange sensation in my head is leading me into that room. I turn the knob, nudge the door open with my elbow, and almost scream.

As soon as I see her I know the old woman on the bed is the Rosie I heard in my head. She's on her back with the blanket bunched at her feet, as if she was thrashing to wake herself from a nightmare. Her short white curls fan the pillow around her head like a halo, but the light I've seen on every other person since I met Aaron this afternoon is missing from her. It's as if someone came along and flipped her light switch off. Her wide blue eyes are fixed on the young man standing beside her, holding her hand.

Aaron Shepherd's skin is on fire, easily three times more brilliant than Max or anyone I've seen today. I can hardly look at him. His head snaps up at the squeak of the door, and his eyes find me.

"You're late," he says. "I thought I said to meet me at six."

He drops Rosie's hand. It flops to her chest and slowly slides across her body to dangle off the edge of the bed.

Dead. Rosie is dead.

I want to save your life. Aaron's words to me this afternoon replay in my memory. *And believe me, Libbi, saving lives is not something I do often.*

I stumble back, and my butt pushes the door behind me closed. Now I know why Aaron said he doesn't often save lives. He's the opposite of a lifesaver. He's a murderer.

"Oh," is all I can say as my hand scrambles for the doorknob. A scream builds in my throat.

"No, Libbi! Don't leave, and don't scream. I know this looks bad, but it isn't what you think it is." Other than the bruise from the punch I gave him earlier, Aaron's face is pale. I suddenly wish I'd punched him harder. Added a little more color to those white cheeks of his.

My stupid fingers scramble over the door behind me, but I can't find the doorknob. Aaron takes a step toward me with one hand raised. I yelp and leap away from him and the door—my only means of escape—like an idiot.

Aaron takes the opportunity my stupidity creates and blocks my exit. He raises both hands to the level of his chest, palms out, like my father used to do when he tried to calm Mom during a balls-out fight.

"Look," Aaron says, his eyes earnest. "There's no need to be scared. I'm just doing my job. If you had been here on time, you'd know that."

"Killing old people is your job?" I say. "What are you? Some freaky, psychic hit man to the elderly or something?" I scoot deeper into the room, moving closer to Rosie's dead body, but farther away from her killer. My fingers close around a glass of water on Rosie's table. He may be able to predict my death and psychically lead me around town with a headache, but I know I can hurt him if he's surprised. The greenish-purple mark on his chin is proof. Maybe Aaron will stumble away from the door if I throw the glass at him. Then I can rush out and sprint down the hallway, yelling for help the whole way.

"What? No! I didn't kill her," Aaron says. "She was dying. It was her time. Didn't you feel it? The headache? The pulling in your head?"

"Yeah, I know about the headache." I lift the glass off the table behind me and prepare to lob it at his head. "I'm not sure how you did it, but I felt it."

"I didn't do it, Libbi, but I'm the reason you had it." Aaron says this like the pounding explosion between my ears is some precious gift. "I can prove it."

"Oh yeah? You can prove you're the reason I had a headache? Well, I've pretty much had a headache since I met you."

"Rosie told me she was ready to go. She called me Bruce. You heard that inside your head, right? How would I know that?"

I don't know how he knows that, and I don't care. The guy can do a lot of freaky things; he can probably read minds too.

"Now, I won't keep you from leaving, if you want, but please don't interrupt me anymore. It's getting late and I need to finish this. Let me finish my job. Rosie has somewhere important to be, very soon."

I glance over at the still form on the bed. Rosie isn't going anywhere very soon, unless the morgue counts.

Aaron keeps his hands up in front of him as he steps away from the door, true to his word. The sleeve of his shirt brushes my arm as he returns to his place next to the bed, and chills roll over my body. It's as if the guy has an eerie force field surrounding him.

My fingers release the rim of the glass. I don't trust him—he totally creeps me out—but I no longer need to throw the glass at him. My escape route is clear.

And my curiosity is up to full throttle.

"Where does she have to be?" I say. "Where are you taking her?"

"Well, that's a little advanced for you." He scowls down at Rosie. "I'll show you that later. But you should really watch this part closely." His frown drifts back up to me. "I really wish you'd been here earlier. This would make more sense. But there's no time to explain now, so let's call this 'Lesson One.'"

"Lesson one? Are you teaching me something?"

"I'm offering you a job, if you want to learn it." He looks over his shoulder at me and raises his eyebrows. His blue eyes sparkle in his own unnatural light.

"What? If I want to learn what?"

"How to be a Grim Reaper."

"A what?"

Aaron opens his mouth, either to repeat what he just said or to say something else that's completely insane, but he doesn't get the chance. A quiet knock sounds, and the door creaks open.

"Mrs. Benson?" The tall, gray-haired woman from the front desk glides into the room to find me standing with Aaron, beside Rosie's dead body.

"Ah, you found her." She smiles at me. "I just wanted to make sure you didn't get lost. Mrs. Benson changed rooms a few days ago. You took off so fast I couldn't tell you, but I guess you already knew."

I don't know what to do. I feel like I've been caught taking the five-finger discount at the grocery store, except this involves a dead body and not a pack of gum. I'm not even sure what to say, so I just point at Rosie.

The good humor drains from the woman's eyes when she follows the direction of my finger. She takes three long strides and almost collides with Aaron, but he steps aside right before she would hit him. She doesn't even blink.

"She can't see you," I say.

"No, she can't." Aaron shuffles his feet and studies the secretary as she leans over Rosie's bed.

At the same time, the woman turns to me from the bed and says, "I know she can't see me, sweetie. I'm sorry, but I think she's passed away."

A light touch on my shoulder. Aaron is at my side. He leans in close, and his hair tickles my ear. I think he's about to kiss my cheek for some reason, and I'm surprised. Not that he would do such a thing, but that I would let him. My heart races in anticipation, but he doesn't kiss me.

"I'm running out of time, Libbi," he whispers. "Lesson one will have to wait. Do you want me to explain everything?"

I nod instead of answering. I don't want the woman to think I'm talking to her again.

"Go home and wait. Meet me at Jumpers' Bridge at midnight and I'll explain everything."

He walks around the secretary to the other side of Rosie's bed. The woman slowly turns and faces me. Black-mascara tears streak her cheeks.

"You know, I've worked here for twenty years, and I can never get used to seeing the residents pass on." She swipes at the black tracks with the palm of her hand. "Rosie didn't want to be resuscitated, but I'll go get the nurse anyway. You can stay here, if you'd like."

"Okay," I say.

She touches my arm as she passes.

"I'm really sorry for your loss, honey. But I'm sure she knows you're going to Harvard now. And I bet she's very proud of you."

Warmth flushes my cheeks at the reminder of my little white lie, but she doesn't see my blush. She's already scurried out of the room.

Aaron hurries to the bed and grasps both of Rosie's hands in his. The silver ring on his right thumb blazes with fiery light when his hands touch hers. He leans back as if he's helping Rosie out of bed, but her body doesn't move. Her hands remain completely still, as if she's made of stone, one arm draped across her abdomen and the other dangling off the bed.

He pulls harder. Tendrils of light shoot out of the ring and wrap Rosie's wrist. The muscles in Aaron's arms flex, and his overly brilliant aura dims as the light that was missing from Rosie's skin when I first walked in the door surges. The aura surrounding her dangling arm separates and comes away from her body in a bright and fully formed hand and arm. Young, feminine, glowing fingers curl around Aaron's hand. The light surrounding the arm draped across her abdomen separates as well, making Rosie appear to have four arms: two wrinkled, dead, and unmoving, and two young, alive, and held firmly in Aaron's hands.

He steps back and pulls the glowing arms with him, and a young woman sits up out of Rosie's old body. She looks up at Aaron with shimmery eyes and smiles.

"Bruce," she sighs.

"It's time to go, Rosie. Are you ready?"

Young Rosie looks back at the body of the old woman she had become. She gives a small nod then turns back to Aaron and nods again.

"I'm ready. Will it hurt?"

"It shouldn't."

Young Rosie considers him and cocks her head to one side.

"You're not my Bruce, are you?"

"No, I'm not Bruce."

"Can you show me who you really are?" Rosie shivers and her eyes grow wide. "Or is the real you too frightening?"

The image of a skeleton draped in a black shroud carrying a blood-stained sickle intrudes upon my thoughts. I shiver along with Rosie.

Aaron agrees with a shrug.

A moment later Rosie gasps, but I don't see anything different. Aaron looks exactly the same to me: tall with dark, black hair and faded-blue eyes. Even the bright light surrounding him stays the same, but Rosie's eyes brighten, and her lips curl into a smile.

"Oh. Well, you're not frightening at all." She giggles. "You're quite handsome, actually."

"Thank you." Aaron meets my gaze for a brief moment, and

his cheeks redden. He looks away. "Okay, Rosie, we have to go."

He helps her step out of her body and leads her around the bed to the closed door. Her eyes lock on mine as she passes me, and she stops.

"I guess you're not Kate, either."

"Um, no," I say. My slick hands tremble.

"Are you joining us?"

I look up at Aaron. There's a part of me that's dying for him to say yes, but a larger part of me hopes he says no. I need more time to digest all of this before I scamper off into the moonlight with the Grim Reaper and his newly acquired soul.

"Not this time." He shakes his head, and I try not to sigh too loudly.

"Well, I guess you don't have to show me what you really look like then." Rosie pats my arm with her icy, glowing hand and lets Aaron lead her to the door.

"Tonight. Jumpers' Bridge. Midnight. You'll be there?" Aaron asks.

I whisper, "I'll be there."

I may not be ready to join him and Rosie on a moonlit trek to wherever the hell they're going, but I'm sure ready for some answers. And I don't care if I have to go to the creepiest place in town, in the dark, to get them. This has got to be the strangest thing that has ever happened to me in my life. But it's also the most exciting. Adrenaline tingles in my fingertips.

Aaron nods and then steps through the closed door without opening it, taking Rosie with him.

6

"Libbi Piper, where have you been?" Mom stands in the archway separating the living room from the foyer with her fists planted firmly on her hips. Her green eyes burn into me, and I freeze, one hand on the doorknob.

Less than twenty minutes ago, I watched the Grim Reaper collect a soul and take it God knows where (literally). That was scary as hell, but when I see my mother's face, I momentarily forget it all. She's livid, and her furious eyes are set on me.

"I thought you were at work," I say, as if it's a valid argument that will get me out of this mountain of trouble.

"I was." Strands of auburn hair fall out of her hairclip and brush her angry-red cheeks. "I came home when Max called me, scared out of his mind, and told me you left him home alone."

I glance to the top of the stairs. A shock of red hair disappears behind the banister.

Thanks for ratting me out, traitor.

"He was supposed to call me on my cell if he had any trouble. I specifically told him not to call you." Jeez. I can't stop digging myself into a deeper and dirtier hole with every word.

"I guess you had a fool-proof plan then, didn't you? Except your cell phone's turned off."

"What?" I rummage through my purse for my phone and flip it open. She's right. The battery's dead. "I didn't know."

"Obviously. So where were you? Max says you've been acting weird today." Her face shifts from seriously pissed to concerned. "Are you taking drugs?"

"No!" I can't believe she would think that. What kind of a girl does she think I am? "I went out with a friend."

"Is that so?" She crosses her arms over her middle. "Which friend? Because you weren't with the twins. I called the Dennises' and could hear Kyle and Haley in the background."

"I have other friends, you know." It's not true, and she knows it. Sure, I talk to other kids at school—I'm not a complete dork—but none of them are really friends. Acquaintances, maybe, but not friends. I slip my hands in my pockets. My fingers brush Aaron's crumpled origami flower, and I get an idea. "Actually, I had a date."

"A date?" A stray piece of hair blows away from her purple face with the force of her words. "You left your eight-year-old brother alone in this house to go out with some boy on a date? Are you insane?"

"No. It was just a date, and I wasn't gone that long. Max is fine."

"I don't care. You can't do that, Libbi! What if something happened to him? He's your responsibility when I'm not here."

"Max is always my responsibility." My face is hot and my hands ball at my sides. "You're never here."

Her cheeks drain of color as she stares, opened-mouthed, at me.

"You know I can't help that," she whispers. "I have to work."

"Well, just so you know, I *do* have friends, but I never get to see them unless I'm in school because I'm *always*. Responsible. For Max." I blink away the angry tears that spring to my eyes. "And just because you can't get over Dad and date someone doesn't mean I can't. I have a life."

Mom opens her mouth to speak then snaps it closed again. The vein in her left temple pulses as she fixes me with narrowed eyes. She juts her finger at the stairs.

"Go to your room," she growls. "I can't look at you right now."

"Fine!" I storm up the stairs and glare at Max as I pass him in the hallway.

"Thanks a lot, pal."

"I'm sorry." His cheeks blaze, making his freckles stand out. "I was worried about you."

"Whatever." I slam my bedroom door.

The floorboards groan as I pace beside my bed. It's my fault; I know that. I shouldn't have left Max alone, no matter how badly my head hurt. And Mom was just worried about me, but I'm still pissed off. What I said was true, even if I pushed a few of Mom's buttons to say it. I *am* always stuck with Max. I love him, but he's my little redheaded ball-and-chain. It's not fair.

Kyle and Haley get to do things after school. Kyle has Red Motive, and Haley has student council and debate team. They don't even have curfews, not that Haley needs one. She's always home early. But me? I don't have a curfew either, because I never go out.

The red numbers of the alarm clock on my nightstand glow five minutes after nine. I settle on the edge of my bed, tapping my feet and listening to the house. Max plunks something— probably his tennis ball—against the wall he and I share. My Metric poster vibrates with each *plunk, plunk, plunk.*

The drone of Mom's voice floats up from the kitchen. She's on the phone, most likely with Dad. The two of them are kaput, but she can't stop herself from calling him whenever we fight.

My gaze drifts to the mirror over my dresser. My bloodshot eyes make the green of my irises seem unnaturally bright. Add in the pink cheeks and insane hair and I can't decide if I look more frightened or frightening. All I know is I look like shit. I rub my hands over my wet cheeks and smooth my hair down.

I grab my sketchbook off my desk and flip to an empty page. The white paper stares up at me, challenges me. Between failing the history final, pissing Haley off, creepy Aaron, this Grim Reaper stuff, and fighting with Mom, I want to make the page black. I want to cover every inch of it with angry streaks of charcoal.

My pencil darts across the page, and I let the familiar motions take me away. Sketch, shade, smooth. The drawing takes shape almost on its own, and the soft lines I create bring my boiling blood down to a simmer.

Drawing has always had this effect on me. That's probably why I like it so much. It's as if my emotions live on the tips of my pencils and as I lay down line after line, they channel my feelings, no matter how ugly, and make something beautiful.

The finished sketch isn't the angry mess of black lines I originally planned. Like always, my pencils took control. I hold up the page to see Aaron's beautiful, piercing eyes gazing back at me.

I want to save your life, Aaron said. *And believe me, Libbi, saving lives is not something I do often.*

Since Aaron is the Grim Reaper, I guess it makes sense he doesn't save lives often. But why me? What's so special about me?

Plunk, plunk, plunk.

I stand up from the bed, wrap my black hoodie around my waist, and hitch my purse over my shoulder. I can't listen to Max thunk his ball against the wall and Mom whine to Dad about me anymore. I have to get out of here.

The window squeals as I shimmy it up. The noise sounds like a freight train, and I freeze, breath caught in my throat.

Plunk, plunk, plunk from Max's wall.

Blah, blah, blah from the kitchen.

I heave a sigh and slide the window open all the way.

A cool breeze billows my curtains and caresses my cheeks and hair. The air feels good. The house is stuffy, suffocating. I straddle the windowpane and search with my foot for the roof of the front porch. When I find it, I swing my other leg over the windowsill and jump down onto the roof. I close my window and crouch-walk to the end of the roof.

Six intricately designed, wrought iron pillars hold up the overhang of the front porch, like six black ladders. On warm summer days, I've sat on the porch swing and worried about how easily a psychopathic murderer could climb those pillars and break in. It never crossed my mind I would use them to sneak out.

The wind chime in the backyard makes a lonely ting in the breeze as I climb down the closest pillar and step over the railing onto the front porch, behind the swing. As I tiptoe by the front door, I almost lose my nerve.

I can see Mom through the lace of the curtain. She's finished her phone conversation and sits at the kitchen table with her head propped in one hand. Wisps of her hair tuft out between her fingers. Purple smudges have appeared under her eyes, and the soft wrinkles she likes to call "crow's feet" look harsh and deep.

Even though I have Dad's dark, wavy hair, I have Mom's green eyes and round face. Strangers sometimes ask us if we're sisters, but I don't think they'd have trouble figuring out our relationship tonight. She's obviously the worried mother, and I'm the screwed up daughter.

A small part of me wants to walk in there, place my hand on her shoulder, and tell her it's going to be okay. I even take a step toward the front door, but I can't go in. If I moseyed in the front door after she sent me to my room, I could pretty much kiss my scrawny butt good-bye.

I could climb back up the pillar to my room, but the thought of breathing that stale air and listening to Max's ball hit the wall until I finally fall asleep makes my stomach turn.

Instead, I turn away from the door and my Mom and face Hell's Highway for the second time this evening with the same question: should I bring my car? It might be handy, but it's noisy. If I start it, it will be like announcing with a bullhorn that I'm sneaking out.

Jumpers' Bridge isn't far from my house, within walking distance, and half of that walk is on the railroad tracks. So I really don't need my car. I'm more than a little nervous to keep my word and meet Aaron—petrified, actually—but tonight I'm in a daring mood. I'll be there earlier than midnight, but I can wait.

It's not like I have a curfew.

7

My tennis shoes crunch the gravel between the ties of the railroad tracks.

The breeze that felt so nice at my bedroom window bites into my cheeks, and my breath billows in a white cloud in front of my face. I yank my hood up, tuck my hands in my sleeves, and shove them into my hoodie pockets.

The rails glitter in the moonlight as they curve gently away. Maybe they lead south to Florida or west to California. I don't know, and it really doesn't matter. The rails lead to Jumpers' Bridge. They lead to answers.

The truss of Jumpers' Bridge grows out of the darkness like a spiny, ancient dragon; the roar of Carroll Falls his warning growl. Mom says Carroll Falls Bridge picked up its morbid nickname after countless suicidal people jumped off the bridge to their deaths. I like to think the nickname came from stupid, bungee-cord-carrying thrill seekers, but maybe I'm being optimistic.

Tonight, there are no idiot thrill-seekers or suicidals clinging to the cold steel of the truss, working up the nerve to take the plunge. Nor is there a certain Grim Reaper. I'm early, as I knew I would be, and the skeletal bridge is deserted.

I hum a nervous melody, and it drops to the bottom of the ravine. The bright moonlight illuminates the ties and the rails, but it's still too dark to see the white water of the river below. I offer up a silent thank you for that miracle. I've never been fond of heights, and if I could see the long drop to the river I don't think I'd be able to breathe, much less stand around waiting for Aaron.

To distract myself from the thought of plunging to my death, I face the bridge's namesake: Carroll Falls. The water spills over the lip of the cliff above me and shimmers in the moonlight as it cascades down. The spray drifts up from below, adding to the chill. I shiver, cross my arms over my chest, and turn away from the waterfall.

A light as bright as a police car's searchlight shines from the other side of the bridge. I would think it's the headlight of a train, but it's moving too slow, there's no rumble of the tracks under my feet, and there was no warning whistle. As trains approach the bridge, regardless of the time of day, they're supposed to sound their whistles. The shrill noise often stirs me from a deep sleep and makes me want to sever the whistle-pulling arm of every engineer alive.

No whistle, not a train.

The light takes on a human shape as it gets closer, and as it approaches the bridge's midpoint, I recognize it as Aaron. He raises one hand in greeting.

"You came," he says with a bright smile. "I was a little worried you wouldn't."

"Of course I came." I shrug. "I told you I would. Not to mention, I had a fight with my mom and needed some fresh air anyway."

"I just thought, after you were late to the nursing home..."

"Well, I didn't want to go to the nursing home. Your headache sort of made me go. Not to be insulting, Aaron, but you're a little creepy." I rub my arms and look over his head at the dark ribs of the bridge. "And so is this bridge."

Aaron chuckles. "This place is a bit eerie, but *I'm* not so bad...once you get to know me."

I disagree. The more I get to know Aaron Shepherd, the creepier he becomes.

"So why here?" I ask.

"Well, I live close to this bridge, and it's a place I knew you'd know. Plus it's away from town and prying eyes."

"It's probably a busy place for you, too. All those suicides."

"Um." Aaron runs a hand through his hair. "Well, that has

something to do with it too, I guess. Let's get away from the bridge. It's freezing."

He strolls the last few feet of the bridge, jumping from tie to tie like he could cross it in his sleep. He meets me at the entrance, and then motions for me to follow him. I have to jog to keep up with his long strides. We step out of the wind tunnel created by the ravine, and the chilly breeze disappears. Away from the bridge, my tightly coiled muscles relax.

I lower my hood. Even in the dark, I don't want hoodie hair. I use my fingertips to comb through the tangled mop on top of my head and glance up at Aaron.

His cheeks flush a deep crimson as he drops his gaze to the ground at his feet. Whatever he's searching for in the gravel must be hard to see, because it takes him a while to look up and meet my eyes again. When he does, he peeks at me through his lashes and smiles.

My stomach summersaults, and I restrain a stupid, middle-school giggle. Now it's my turn to blush but, thankfully, he doesn't see it. He's turned away.

"So, you can feel cold?"

"I felt your punch, didn't I?" He rubs his chin and winces. "I have a bruise."

"Yeah, but you're the Grim Reaper," I say. "Aren't you, like, supernatural and all-powerful and stuff?"

"Ha! I'm powerful, but not *all*-powerful. And I'm not *the* Grim Reaper. That's Abaddon. I'm *a* Grim Reaper. There's a big difference."

"What? There's more than one?"

"Oh, yes. I don't know exactly how many, but there has to be a ton of us. We each work a small territory." He picks a dry leaf off of his sleeve. "I work Carroll Falls, plus a few miles outside of town."

"Still, even as *a* Grim Reaper, and not *the* Grim Reaper, you were invisible to that secretary. And you walked through the freaking door." I almost add his ability to predict my impending death, but that's an area I'm not quite ready to face. "That counts as supernatural and all-powerful to me."

"Well, trust me, it's not." His eyes grow dark for a fraction of a second, then his lips spread in a bright smile. "I have those powers so I can do my job. I'm invisible so I can escort a soul to the Gateway without being seen. I can walk through walls because some people, a lot of people, die where it's not easy to reach them."

A thought flickers through my mind: me, dead and cold and squished between a smoking pick-up truck and a twisted Honda. I bet it would have been hard to reach me there. I shudder.

"Oh, and I can run really fast too," he adds with a wink.

"So you're not all-powerful, but you have supernatural powers?"

"That sounds about right." Aaron's perpetual grin falters for a moment as he crumples the leaf he pulled off his shirt and flicks it to the ground. "My powers are the tools I need to do my job."

"Yeah, tools for your job," I say dismissively. "And you bruise and feel cold, so you're not dead."

"Nope. I eat and sleep and everything. I'm as alive as you are."

Something slinks through the tall grass at the edge of the woods. I follow the light emanating from the small animal until it disappears in the underbrush. Geesh. Even raccoons glow now.

"Okay, what's the deal with the glowing people? Everyone looks like they drank radioactive Kool-Aid or something. Even that raccoon." I point into the underbrush where the shape of the animal glows through the leaves. "And you're the brightest of everyone. I almost need sunglasses to look at you."

I look up into his faded blue eyes. Good Lord, he's cute. He's also scary and weird, but if I had met him at school—well, if I'd met him at school the *normal* way—Haley and I would have drooled over him. Maybe it's the "tall, dark, and dangerous" thing.

"The glow you're seeing is the soul," he says patiently.

"You collect the souls of animals too?"

"No. I don't know what happens to them. I can't touch their souls." He shakes his head dismissively and switches back to teacher mode. "For a Reaper, the brightness of the *human* soul is a gauge, like a measure. The intensity of that light tells us approximately how much time a person has left before their scheduled death. The brighter the soul, the more time. Does that make sense?"

His words drift on the air between us. Slowly, I nod. It makes perfect sense.

"I'm not as bright as everyone else. Actually, I'm not bright at all." I'm speaking more to myself than to Aaron, but he nods in agreement. "My time is out, isn't it? That's why Max is so much brighter than me. I was supposed to die today. I was supposed to be squashed by Jason's truck."

"That's right." He beams as if I figured out a complex calculus problem he didn't think I'd ever understand. "You would be dead right now if I hadn't stepped in. Your death has been rescheduled to tomorrow, exactly twenty-four hours from when you were supposed to die today."

"What?" I stagger back a step. "I'm scheduled to die tomorrow?" I thought when he saved my life today that was it. I didn't think I'd have to worry about tomorrow.

"Yes." He bends and plucks a long blade of grass growing between the ties of the tracks. "I don't know how it will happen— it depends on where you are and what you're doing—but it will come." He looks up at me, and he must see the panic in my eyes because he smiles and says, "Don't worry. I'll be there to stop it."

"Why?" It's a stupid question to ask. He's offering to save my life. Again. And I'm scared as hell to hear his answer, but I have to know. "Why didn't you let that truck pulverize me today, Aaron? Why did you save my life? And why would you save it again tomorrow?"

"You're a smart girl. I thought you'd have figured it out by now."

"Maybe I want to hear you say it." I give him the scorching glare Kyle calls my "no-bullshit stare."

Aaron twists the grass around his finger and sighs. "I need a replacement. There's something I need to do that I can't do without a replacement, and I thought you might want the job."

"Why would you think that?" I ask. It's not like I'm emo. I don't need an entire drawer dedicated to my various shades of black lipstick.

"It's just good timing." He shrugs.

"Good timing? That's it?" I cross my arms and glare at him. "Maybe I don't want your job. What if I say you can shove it up your—"

"If that's your decision," he cuts me off. "Then tomorrow, at 3:12 p.m., you'll die and there will be nothing I can do about it."

My legs jiggle under me, and I almost collapse at his feet. I lock my knees before I topple over onto the tracks like a melodramatic damsel in distress.

"Are you okay?" Aaron grips my shoulder. "You look like you're gonna puke."

"Yeah," I mumble. "I'm fine. Let go of me." I shrug him off, but his eyes bore into me.

I don't want his job. It sounds morbid and scary and better suited for a chick with dyed black hair. I can't even watch a horror flick without my hand over my eyes half of the time. But I don't want to die either. And Aaron doesn't strike me as the kind of guy who would mess around with something like this. He is Death, after all.

"So, what if I say I'll do it?" I'm still light-headed, but at least I'm not in danger of going face-first into the railroad tracks.

"Then we start your training." Aaron's eyes twinkle with excitement. "The sooner the better. Once you say you'll take the job, you only have a week to learn how to do it. And there's a lot to learn."

"Fine. I'll take the—"

"Shhh." He places a finger over my lips. "Before you say it, I'm obligated to tell you what it's like being a Reaper. It's part of the rules. But remember this: I can only save your life twice. Your death will be rescheduled each time. And if you don't decide before the last rescheduled time, you'll die."

"The accident counted as the first?"

"Yes. And at 3:12 p.m. tomorrow I can save your life for the second time. Which means, if you decide not to take the job, you will die on Saturday—"

"At 3:12, sharp. I get it." My knees turn to rubber again, but I manage to hold myself up. "So I have until 3:12 on Saturday to decide."

"Exactly." He's giving me the proud teacher look again, and I feel like I'm about to hurl all over his shoes.

In just a few hours, my life has changed. Forever. No matter what I decide, it will never be the same. Everything I've wanted. All of my hopes, dreams, and plans for the future. Gone.

"Just one more question before you start your sales pitch." I keep the vomit where it belongs and try to rub some warmth into my arms. Wind or no wind, I'm shivering. "I already asked you this, but you didn't answer. Why me? Why not ask one of the other dim bulbs in this town? I can't be the only one who's about to burn out. There must be dozens. Why not ask Rosie?"

"Because she's too old. Abaddon only accepts Reapers who are eighteen or younger." He shrugs. "There aren't any other kids scheduled to die soon. So, it has to be you or I don't know how much longer I'll have to wait."

"For what? What do you need to do?"

"Never mind," Aaron says. "It's personal." He yanks at the hem of his navy blue T-shirt. It's a shirt I'd expect Kyle to wear, not Death.

A high-pitched whistle cuts through the night. My right foot rests on the rail. It's been vibrating for a while, but I just now notice. The train that sometimes startles me out of sleep is about to make an appearance. Right on schedule.

I move my foot off the rail and take a few steps back. The gravel slips out from under me and I skid down the incline backwards, arms wind-milling. Aaron catches my hand and steadies me. His skin is warm, his grip solid. He leads me to a pile of old railroad ties at the edge of the woods, far enough away from the tracks to be safe from the speeding train, but still a little too close for me to feel comfortable.

The whistle pierces my skull again. The train is close. The tracks rumble as the headlight rounds the corner. The blast of wind from the engine as it passes blows me back into the pile of old wood, and I sit down hard. Something stabs the back of my leg, but I'm not about to grope my own butt for splinters in front of Aaron.

"So, what was the fight with your mom about?" Aaron yells over the roar of the train. He settles next to me on the plank as if the hurricane-force wind is a light breeze.

"I don't know. Stuff." I'm not paying attention to him. I've never been this close to a speeding train before, and I'm focused on the wind, the rails, and the solid wall of metal moving in front of me. Anything to distract me from the insanity Aaron just told me, even if it's only for a few minutes. I stretch my neck to look for the caboose.

"Like what stuff?" he says, and I stop looking for the end of the train to frown at him.

"My life sucks right now, okay?" If he can cry "too personal," so can I. "I don't want to talk about it."

The caboose finally turns the corner and the engine's lonely whistle sounds in the distance.

"It can't be that bad."

"Well, it is." I cross my arms over my chest. My jaw aches. I'm gritting my teeth. "And it's none of your business, really."

"You have friends, a brother, and a mother who care for you. Plus, you just won first place in the school art show." He scratches at a spot on his jeans and then meets my eyes. "I wanted to tell you last night that I think you're really talented, Libbi. I mean, amazingly talented. I'd like to see more of your work."

"Thanks," I say, but he can't win me over that easily.

The train is gone, but the after-breeze ruffles Aaron's hair. The moonlight accentuates the sharp angles of his face, and I briefly imagine sketching those lines. He drags a long finger across my pale knuckles.

"So tight," he says, and I reflexively loosen my fist. The cool metal of his thumb ring chills my skin as he curls his fingers around my hand and squeezes. I'm surprised when I squeeze him back.

"I'm sorry," he says. "You're right. I shouldn't assume your life is good."

"Yeah, well, remember that." I pull my hand out from under his. "So, are you gonna tell me the wonders of being a Reaper, or what?"

He stands from the pile of wood and offers me his hand. I push up without taking it.

"Actually, it is a pretty awesome gig." That shit-eating grin returns to his face. "But there are a few things that might not appeal to everyone. And before you say you'll take the job, I have to tell you about it."

"Fine. Enlighten me." I look up at his bruised chin, his full lips, his pale blue eyes. He starts to walk and I follow.

"Well, first of all, you'll see somebody die, several times a week, and sometimes more than once a day, like today with you and Rosie. Some deaths are peaceful and quiet, like Rosie's. But some aren't. And sometimes, if you could change one little thing, you could save their lives." Aaron shakes his head. "But you can't."

"Why not? You did with me." I turn to face him. We're back on the train tracks again.

"Yeah, because you can take over for me. That's the exception to the rule. I can only save the life of someone who can take over for me. Abaddon's rules are very strict, and I'm not about to take it up with him." A shadow passes over Aaron's face.

"That bad, huh?"

The dark look disappears instantly, and Aaron chuckles. "Nah, not too bad. Abaddon can be a tough boss sometimes, but he's almost never around."

"Okay, so as a Reaper, I'll see lots of death. Check." I nod, though I'm still not convinced that's something I can deal with. But it's better than dying myself, I suppose. "I can't say I was totally shocked by that one, honestly."

Aaron laughs. The sound echoes off the trees, and something rustles in the underbrush, probably that glowing raccoon.

"No, I guess that's not surprising," he says. "But you'll also have to witness the deaths of people you love, Libbi. And some of those people might…"

He stops talking and turns toward the bridge, shoving his hands in his pockets.

I touch his shoulder. It's a gentle touch, meant to comfort him like his holding my hand comforted me, but he jumps. "Might what?" I say.

He faces me with the smile, but his eyes are careful, flat, emotionless. "Well, let's just say this work can be scary sometimes."

"Okay, I'll see people I love die." My mother's face pops into my head. Then Haley's and Kyle's. Then Max's. I push the thoughts away. "And the job gets scary. Check and check."

"And you'll be stuck in Carroll Falls. No career as an artist." Aaron keeps his eyes focused on a point over my shoulder. "Not that you'd be able to do that anyway, if you were dead," he says, like he's trying to convince himself.

That gives me a moment's pause. I shake it off. Being stuck in Carroll Falls might only be slightly less awful than a death sentence, but I can't think too much about that. I need my pencils to help me sort it out.

"But at least I'll be alive." I whisper the words. "If I die tomorrow, I'll be gone for good, right? There's no coming back."

"Right, there's no coming back. And if you take the job, you could live forever, if you wanted. Think of all the cool things you could see. And you could stay with your friends and family. You could see their grandchildren's grandchildren."

"Okay," I say. "I've made my decision." The choice is simple, really.

"Wait." He holds up his hand. "Before you say it, there's one more thing."

His feet shuffle the gravel. I impatiently motion for him to continue.

"This is the hardest thing, I think. After your training, when I...I mean, when you take over for me, you'll become invisible. The living won't be able to see you or hear you unless they're about to die." Aaron takes my hand again, and I don't pull away this time. I only partially notice he's holding it. "You'll lose all contact with the living. It'll be like you're a ghost. A living ghost.

"But I can write letters, right? You wrote me a letter."

"You should be dead right now. Only you and the dead can read that letter. To anyone living, it will be a blank page. Anything I do, any change I make in this world at all, is forgotten immediately or invisible to them."

"But, how will I—? What will happen to me?"

"You'll disappear. Your family will search for you, and they'll cry for you, and eventually they'll get used to you being gone and forget you. Sure, you can stay with them, if they stay in town. You can eat dinner with them and watch TV with them at night. You can attend your brother's graduation and his wedding, but no one will see you there. You'll be with them, Libbi, but you'll be alone."

His words cut me deeper than anything he has said tonight. He's speaking from experience. It's in his hollow eyes and the tight set of his lips. He may try to pretend his job is awesome, but Aaron is a boy who knows loneliness.

"Oh my God." I want to put my arms around him. Pull him close. Tell him he's not alone anymore. But I don't. "How long has it been since you've spoken to a living person?"

"I talk to living people almost every day. They die within twenty-four hours, but..." Aaron shrugs like it doesn't bother him, but I know it does. "Other than that? Forty years. They're either dead or about to be dead. And most of them think I'm someone else." His voice becomes hushed and I have to lean in to hear him. "I think my sister can hear me in her sleep—she talks to me sometimes—but she doesn't remember when she wakes up."

I shake my head. "I thought you were trying to convince me to take the job."

"I am." He blinks a few times, like he just woke up in the middle of sleep-talking. He gives me a sheepish smile. "I'm sorry. It really is great. Did I tell you I can fly?"

It feels like I'm spinning. I need to sit down. I walk away from Aaron and the hulking shadow of Jumpers' Bridge and stumble back to the pile of railroad ties. My knees give out as I try to sit, and I plop down on the piled wood. Aaron slowly walks over with his head down and sits next to me. He grips his knees and turns his face to the full moon.

"So, I know you said it wasn't my business, but maybe you should make up with your mom. If you decide to take the job, you'll have a whole week left with her. But, if you decide not to, you only have about..." He counts on his fingers. "Thirty-nine hours. That's not a lot of time."

"Then I have to make a decision."

"Unless you know your answer now."

"I—I don't know anymore." My fingers tremble as I brush a wisp of hair from my eyes. "I need more time to think."

How can I make a decision like this? Either I die tomorrow and miss out on everything, like I was supposed to, or I live a lonely life as a Grim Reaper, watching everyone live their lives without me. Both choices suck. There's no way I can decide. Not now. I'm too overwhelmed. Maybe my pencils can help, but probably not. This feels too big, even for them.

8

The moon skims the treetops and ducks behind the large Victorian house on the corner. Diablo Road is deserted, and my footfalls sound hollow against the pavement.

When I told Aaron I needed time to think, he tried to tell me how awesome his stupid job is again, but I told him to stop. Eventually, he nodded and said he understood. Without another word, he got up and crossed Jumpers' Bridge, leaving me more alone than I've ever felt in my life.

I'm almost home now, but I don't feel any less lonely. I don't want to stare at the cracked ceiling over my bed. And my sketchpad and pencils will just remind me of what I'll lose. If I take the job, anything I make will disappear. The sheer waste of that makes my body ache.

I don't want to see the drawings on my walls as much as I don't want to see the photos propped on my dresser and taped to my mirror: Kyle, Haley, and me at the beach with humongous sunglasses and goofy grins; Max and Dad covered in pink silly string and laughing so hard I can almost hear them through the glossy paper; me and Mom after I won first place in the art show, her arm around my shoulder, tears shimmering in her eyes.

A tear trickles down my cheek now, and I wipe it away with the back of my hand. If I take Aaron's dumb job, I only have a week left with my family. And I don't care how great Aaron thinks being a Reaper is, what happens after I take over for him is awful. How can I sit back and watch Max grow up without me? He needs me. Mom needs me. And what about Haley and

Kyle? They'll get to go off to college and have careers and lives while I'm stuck in this shit town, a perpetual teenager, with no future except death, death, and more death.

But if I tell Aaron no, this will be the last day and a half I'll have with them at all.

The floorboards creak as I step onto the porch. I stop at the front door and peer through the lacy curtain. The kitchen chair Mom sat in a few hours ago is askew but empty. Weights pull at my limbs, and I'm suddenly very tired.

The climb up to my window is almost as easy as the climb down, but I won't worry about a psychopathic killer having easy access to me tonight.

I'm already a goner.

***

There's too much light. I can't sleep. I lie awake in bed with the covers pulled up to my chin and watch the dull halo on the ceiling—the halo that measures my life. I'm used to total darkness in my room, and even though my aura is dull, it's still too bright for me to fall asleep.

Most of the night, I stay this way. I watch my halo ripple over the cracks in the ceiling to avoid the pictures. I cry a little, but mostly I just stare.

The screech of the alarm clock in the room down the hall signals Mom's awake. Ever since Dad left us, she's worked two jobs, and she leaves for her day job about an hour before I wake Max up for school.

I sit up in bed, overcome with the desire to talk to her. Mom can be my sounding board. She can help me make sense of all this crap. If anyone can help me make a scary, life or death decision like this, my mother can. And even if she can't, she'll know exactly what to say to make me feel better.

I swing my bare feet over the edge of the bed and knock over my book bag. It thumps to the floor, and I freeze. The one-inch gap under my bedroom door blazes with the bright light of my mother's soul. The beam moves across the hardwood floor as she draws closer.

"Libbi?" Mom whispers from the other side of the door. "Are you awake?"

I want to answer her, but I can't force the air out of my lungs. I shift on my bed and the bedsprings creak, but I keep my mouth closed.

"Well, if you are awake and you're listening, I want to say I'm sorry for the stuff I said last night. I love you. You just scared me." She breathes a shaky sigh. "Just promise me you won't disappear like that again. Okay?"

After a few seconds of silence, she steps away from my door. I draw my legs up and tuck them under me. I don't want to talk to her anymore. I don't think I can face her, not if she wants me to promise that. Whether I decide to take Aaron's job or choose to die, I'm going to disappear.

9

Daylight and the normal routine of the school day make my problem a little easier to ignore. The sun's warm rays overpower the glow of the souls a little. That alone almost convinces me last night was a nightmare, and the glow that I'm seeing on everyone is just a symptom of a concussion which, for some reason, is more comforting. But my stiff muscles and grainy eyes remind me that I didn't sleep last night. Not one bit. It wasn't a dream. Last night was real.

"Libbi?"

Startled, I swing around in my chair and face Kyle. I hadn't noticed him sitting there. He studies me from behind his open calculus book, which stands upright on his desk. His skin illuminates the pages like a reading lamp and I restrain a shudder. That glow is definitely real.

"Damn, Libs." He bounces the eraser of his pencil against the desk in an intricate pattern only a skilled drummer could accomplish. "You look like you've seen a ghost or something."

Well, Aaron's too solid to be a ghost, but that's a good start.

"Have you ever heard of a guy named Aaron Shepherd?" I say.

"Aaron Shepherd?" Kyle bites the end of his pencil. "Maybe. The name sounds familiar."

I knew it. I knew I'd heard his name before. I grip the end of my desk with both hands.

"Do you remember where you heard it?"

"Um, not really. Why?" He frowns, and his hand slips down

to his side, closer to the sticks in his back pocket. If we weren't in class, he'd have them out, I'm sure.

"Never mind." I loosen my fingers, half-expecting to see my handprints pressed into the wood. "So, what time is the Battle of the Bands tonight?"

"Eight." He raises his eyebrows. "You're coming, right?"

"How could I miss it?"

"You know, you're my lucky charm." He beams at me.

"Then I'll be there."

His deep brown eyes sparkle under his mop of curly blond hair. I return his grin, but I wish mine felt as genuine as his looks.

Kyle goes back to his drum solo on his open calculus book, and I return to my doodle-covered paper and thoughts of Aaron Shepherd. After a few minutes of silence, I nudge Kyle with my elbow.

"Hey, do you think you could do me a favor?"

"What favor?" He puts down his pencil and looks at me.

"Could you watch Max after school for a little bit? I have detention with Winkler." I roll my eyes for dramatic effect.

"Really? Isn't flunking history enough of a punishment? That guy is such a tool," he growls. "Actually, he's a sprinkler." He flashes a big, cheesy grin.

"Will you just watch him for me, please?" I ask again, trying to keep the impatience out of my voice, but I don't think I succeed.

"Yeah." Kyle frowns. Then he shakes his head and says, "I mean, sure. Anytime. You know I love Max."

The bell rings. I stand and grab my book bag from the floor, and Kyle touches my arm softly, like a caress.

"Are you sure you're all right, Libs?" His deep brown eyes search mine. "I mean, there isn't something you need to tell me, is there?" His voice lowers. "This guy Aaron? Do I need to..." He smacks his drumsticks into his open palm and raises his eyebrows.

"No, I'm fine." I chuckle for the first time since yesterday. "Really. No need to bloody your sticks. You'll need them good and clean for tonight."

Kyle frowns, and I know what he's thinking. He's thinking of Will. In the seventh grade, I told him how Weird Will Collins cornered me behind the stage, groped me, and kissed me. Kyle flipped out. He had a "talk" with Weird Will and the creep never tried that stunt again.

"It's not like Will," I say seriously.

"Okay, then. No blood." He tucks his sticks back in his pocket. "But I'm here for you if you need me."

"I know, Kyle. But I don't have anything to talk about. Okay?"

"Okay, okay. I get it." He holds his hands up in surrender. "It's a girly thing. You don't want to talk about it with your guy friend."

"It's not like that either," I say.

"All right, Libs." He smirks.

At the end of the day Mrs. Kraus lets us out fifteen minutes early. Even the teachers get a little antsy for sunshine and warm breezes near the end of the school year.

I didn't lie to Kyle—well, not completely. I do have to stay after school, but not for Winkler.

I was right. I've heard Aaron's name before, and now that I know Kyle has too, I need to go to the computer lab to do some research. I would do it at home, but I don't want to risk Max walking in on me. I don't know what I'm going to find, and Max overheard me tell Mom I went on a date with the guy.

The heavy, floral scent of perfume assaults me as the computer lab door swings open. It clings to the back of my throat and nose, and I sneeze. I take a few deep breaths through my mouth. I don't need an asthma attack today. I have enough going on.

"Can I help you, Libbi?" Mrs. Lutz watches me over the frame of her black-rimmed glasses as I approach her desk.

I notice the difference in her soul immediately. A fine, dark line divides the light of her face like a crack in a porcelain doll. It starts above her left eye, zigzags over the bridge of her nose, and ends on her right cheek. A fracture in the light of her soul.

Without realizing it, I bend over the desk for a closer look, and she leans away, eyes wide.

"Can I help you?" she repeats, but this time she's less bored and more irritated.

"Um, yes." I straighten up and clear my itchy throat. I feel like I'm drowning in a pool of her perfume, but I ignore it. "I just need a computer for resear—"

"Research?" She cuts me off with her squeaky, grating voice. "Is it for a new painting? You know, I never told you congratulations on your win the other night. You deserved first place." She smiles brightly and I can't help but smile back. "Anything I can help you with?"

"No, I don't think so." My tongue sticks to the top of my dry mouth. "Unless you know something about Aaron Shepherd."

Mrs. Lutz's hand thumps to her desk and caramel liquid sloshes over the lip of her mug. The coffee's sweet aroma overpowers the floral perfume for a moment, but not long enough for me to catch my breath. She holds me with her gaze, and I force myself not to gawk at the crack in her face.

"Who?" she says.

"Aaron Shepherd?" I repeat and swallow. If I don't get away from her perfume soon, I will have an asthma attack, no matter how hard I try not to have one. I restrain a cough.

"Aaron Shepherd, huh?"

"Yeah."

Her eyes dart to the window then back to me. She leans across the desk and I can almost see sickening pink tendrils of odor wafting off her skin. My vision blurs as my eyes fill with water.

"Uh-huh." She taps her temple with her forefinger, leans back in her chair, and crosses her arms over her ample chest. She thinks I'm screwing with her. "You know, I knew him."

"You knew him?" I swallow against the itching in my throat.

"Yeah, I knew him before he disappeared. We were in the same class." She leans over the desk toward me and lowers her voice to a whisper. "I don't care what the stories say; I know he didn't do it. Aaron couldn't have done something so awful."

Preparing to ask what Aaron didn't do, I suck heavily perfumed air into my lungs. I can't get the question out. My throat's too dry and itchy.

I have to leave. Right now. If I don't get away from Mrs. Lutz's obnoxious perfume, the itching and dryness will turn into a full-blown asthma attack.

My legs wobble like they're made of noodles, but I manage to turn around and rush out of the computer lab. I drop down on the wooden bench outside the door and hungrily inhale several clean breaths of air. The tightness in my chest eases a little, and I'm able to focus on what Mrs. Lutz said.

She knew Aaron. She knew him before he disappeared and became a Grim Reaper. But what did he do? Even if Mrs. Lutz is convinced he didn't do it, it must have been pretty awful for his name to sound familiar to both Kyle and me, forty years later. Was that the reason he took his job? Was the Grim Reaper path a good way for Aaron to hide?

I shake my head to clear my thoughts. I have to go back in there and talk to Mrs. Lutz. She knows something and I need to find out what it is. Screw her fractured face and toxic perfume.

Determined not to let my asthma control me, I stand up and march into the computer lab. I take one breath of the floral-scented death air, turn around, and march right back out. I can't do it. There has to be another way to get the information I need.

The library.

It's directly across the hall. I blame my stupidity on the perfume clouding my brain and cross the hall to the door. I hope the school keeps records from that long ago. If they don't, I'll have to wait and go to the community library tomorrow morning. Between babysitting Max and Kyle's show, I won't have time to go tonight.

Ms. Weese looks up from her computer when I walk into the room, but my eyes automatically glance up to the striking still-life oil painting over her head.

Ever since Ms. Weese hung it a few months ago, I've envied the artist. On first glance, it's a simple still-life of a group of apples. Two of the apples are red and sliced into quarters. Offset from those two, another apple sits by itself. It's whole and green and has a paring knife jammed into it up to its hilt. The last apple, a yellow one, is mostly hidden under a black cloth in the background.

When I get up close and really look at the painting, however, it becomes more than a still-life. It tells a story. The paint strokes on the red apples are sharp and angry, and the color used is as deep as blood. In contrast, the paint strokes on the green apple are soft and careful. A single drop of juice trickles down the side of this apple, like a teardrop, from where the knife has penetrated the flesh. The apple covered by the black drape is too hidden to see much more than its shape, but there's an almost unfinished quality to the small, yellow sliver peeking out from under the cloth.

I shiver like I always do when I see this painting. I just can't understand how the artist managed to convey such raw, dark emotions using only fruit.

"Can I help you?" Ms. Weese's smile is as bright as her non-cracked soul.

"Yeah. Do you keep newspapers from, like, forty years ago?"

"Well, I know we have current newspapers." She tucks her bangs behind her ear. "But I don't know about forty years ago. Are you looking for something in particular?"

"Yes. I'm trying to find the story of a boy from this school who disappeared forty years ago. Aaron Shepherd?"

"Oh, yeah," she says and slowly nods. "I think I know what you're talking about."

"You do?" My stomach lurches. "Did you know him too?"

She looks too young to have known him forty years ago. But who am I to talk? I'm too young to have met him yesterday.

"No. My mom did. She tried to scare me with the story one Halloween, when I was about your age." Ms. Weese smiles fondly. "Her big finale was that it was all true and she knew it was true because she knew him." She chuckles. "But you're in luck. We probably have a copy of that paper. Mr. Boyd kept any papers that mentioned the school by name, even for messed up stories like that."

Mr. Boyd was the previous librarian. He passed away last summer. This woman, with her wispy blond hair and bohemian dress, took his place.

She waves for me to follow her into the deserted library. There are only a few days left of the school year, so most people have finished their book reports and research projects. The few that haven't would probably rather be caught at prom dressed in drag than holding a book in the library.

She leads me to the back of the library. A table and four chairs block a tall, dark wood door. The librarian heaves the table away from the door and I set my book bag on one of the chairs.

"There's just not enough space in this library," she says as she withdraws a set of keys from her pocket.

The door jams when she tries to open it. She jiggles the handle a few times, mumbles something I can't understand, then rams the door with her shoulder. A crack sounds when the door comes unglued from the jamb and swings into the cool, dark space. She reaches in and switches the overhead light on.

"Well, here you are. I'm sure it's in there somewhere, but you'll have to look for it. It shouldn't be too hard to find. I'd help you look, but I can't stay after today. I have an appointment." Her eyes suddenly widen in comic surprise and she whispers, "You won't steal anything, will you?"

"No. I just want to see the article. I won't even take it out of the room. I promise."

"All right. Just don't tell anyone I left you in here alone, okay? And make sure you're out by five. That's when they lock the doors." She graces me with her beaming smile. "Good luck," she says as the heavy door drifts closed behind her.

"Okay then," I mutter to myself. With the door closed, the rectangular room feels like a coffin.

I turn in a circle and read the bronze-plate markers above each chest of drawers. *The Baltimore Sun. The New York Times.* The chest labeled *The Carroll Falls Tribune* is at the far end, but the narrow room is so small it only takes me five steps to reach it.

The drawer marked 1960-79 is close to the floor. I stoop, lean back on my heels, and yank it open.

Dust and the dry scent of old paper waft out of the drawer. I sneeze, cover my nose and mouth with my hand, and cough. My vision clouds and tears spill down my cheeks. The next breath fills my lungs with another gust of old paper particles and dust.

The heavy, drowning-in-floral-perfume feeling I had in the computer lab hasn't really gone away yet. I'd only wrestled it under control. But now it's back, full force.

I turn my head away from the drawer and take three deep breaths through my mouth. *Asthma does not control me. I am the asthma master.* I hold the last breath and turn back to the drawer.

The newspaper on top of the pile is from December 10, 1979. I don't bother to read anything else. It's not what I'm looking for. This paper isn't old enough. I lift it and several others out of the drawer, scan them over one by one, and then drop them to the floor beside me. Dust clouds the air and I peer through the plume—careful not to breathe it in—to the next newspaper in the stack.

Aaron stares up at me from the drawer. His black hair—tousled and unkempt last night —is smooth and parted to one side. The worn, older-than-his-years pinch is absent from his face and he's smiling. I pull my eyes away from the photo and read the headline.

"Alleged Teen Murderer, Aaron Shepherd, Missing"

As much as I don't want to, I gasp, and dust-peppered air fills my lungs. I stumble back, land on my butt, and kick the drawer closed, but it's too late. My chest already feels like a boa constrictor has wrapped its coils around me. The next laborious breath rumbles with a deep wheeze.

My hands flutter over my pockets. My inhaler. Where is my inhaler?

It's in my book bag.

My book bag is on the chair, outside the door. I scramble to my feet. Beads of stinging sweat drip into my eyes. The door is so far away.

Using the chests of newspapers as support, I stagger to the door. The knob slips in my slick palms and I wipe my hands on my shirt and try again. My chest is on fire. The wheezing crackles in my ears. My hands grip on the knob this time and it turns, but the door refuses to open.

It's jammed. I shake the knob and jerk it as hard as I can, but the door won't budge. Oh God, why won't the door open? It feels like I'm breathing through a coffee straw. I need my inhaler.

The tips of my fingers transition from pale white to blue. I ball my hands into fists and pound on the door. I cry out for help, but I don't have enough air in my lungs to make any sounds other than grunts and wheezes.

"Do you need this?" a calm voice says in my ear.

I swing around and meet Aaron's cold, blue eyes. He smiles and holds something out to me.

My inhaler.

There's a small part of me that almost doesn't take the inhaler. That part of me wants to fling it across the room and run as far from Aaron as the cramped space will allow. But I can't run, even if I really wanted to. I can't breathe.

I glance at the inhaler, then back to his calm, collected face and rip the inhaler from his hand. Then he does something even more out of place than smile as I struggle for air.

He laughs at me. Jerk.

My breath rattles as I shake the silver canister, depress the plunger, and breathe in the life-saving medication. It stings the back of my throat, but I hold the medicine in for the count of sixty and let it out. The vise that grips my chest slowly loosens and air rushes in. The room spins, and I slide down the jammed door to the floor. Aaron crouches in front of me and places his hands on my shoulders. I flinch, but I'm too weak and woozy to do much else.

"Are you feeling better, now?" he asks.

I nod as I take another puff of my inhaler. The mist goes deeper this time. My fingertips tingle and my heart races, but I can breathe.

"You k-killed someone?" I stammer. It's probably not the best time to say this, since I'm trapped in a coffin-shaped room with him, but it comes out anyway.

Aaron looks over his shoulder at the file cabinet behind him and then back at me with narrowed eyes and a clenched jaw.

"That's not important." His features soften, but I'm sure his sympathy is fake. If I look closely, I know I'll see an angry, cold monster under that mask. "Let's not talk about my past right now, Libbi. It's not 3:12 yet. You still have a few minutes before you're supposed to die. So why don't we make sure you stay alive, okay?"

I try to meet his eyes. I want to see the monster, the murderer underneath, but my bangs obscure my vision.

Aaron brushes the hair behind my ear. His soft, warm fingertips graze my cheek, and the line of skin where he touches me tingles. The cool hue of his eyes, which struck me as monstrous and cold only seconds ago, relaxes me now. As does his smile.

"What are you doing to me?" I want to sound angry, indignant at this violation of my emotions, but instead I sound like Max when he's asking something stupid, like why dogs sniff each other's butts.

"You feel better, right?" His hand drops to his lap. "I just relaxed you, that's all. Like I said, we haven't passed the time of your death yet. You can't afford to be upset right now."

"Let me guess…another one of your awesome superpowers?"

"Yes." He gives me his big, you're-such-a-smart-student grin.

"Do me a favor, Aaron." Though my body remains loose and relaxed, I can hear the anger slowly creeping back into my voice. "Don't you *ever* use that on me again. Got it?"

The goofball grin vanishes from his face.

"Look. I'm just trying to help you," he says.

"Yeah? Well, thanks, but no thanks."

He stands as I push myself up from the floor and holds both of his hands out to me. I guess he wants me to take them, but I don't. Instead I level him with my gaze. Still feeling light-headed from the lack of oxygen and asthma medication, I tip slightly and lean against the closest file cabinet.

He reaches for me, probably to steady me, but I slap his hand away.

"Don't touch me," I say, and his arm falls to his side.

He may be cute and he may have saved my life, twice, and maybe last night I felt sorry for him for a minute, but Grim Reaper business aside, I always knew there was something off about him. And now I know what it is.

"How many people did you kill, Aaron? I didn't get to read the article."

He takes a step back and his face turns paper-white. Other than the greenish-purple bruise I left on his chin yesterday, he looks like a ghost.

"It doesn't matter," he says.

"Hell yes, it matters!" The woozy effect of the medicine is wearing off and so is Aaron's relaxation thing. I can breathe and now I need answers. "How many? Or was it so many you can't remember? Maybe you don't have enough fingers and toes to count on."

"It doesn't matter. None of it matters." His eyes flash with anger. "What matters is what's happening right now. And right now it's 3:13 and I've just saved your life. Again. So, have you made your decision?"

"No." I cross my arms over my chest and glare at him. "I won't decide until I know what happened."

"Look it up then." He sweeps his hand wide, inviting me to go back to the evil, dust-filled file cabinet. "But if you haven't made up your mind, then I have to go. I have someone important I need to see."

"They can wait," I assure him.

"No, Libbi. Abaddon cannot wait. He's expecting your soul and I need to tell him why I haven't brought you to him yet." He grips my shoulders and locks me in his stare. "Drop this thing, okay? You only have twenty-four hours now. You're wasting time searching for something you can't change. Go home. Think about all the cool things you'll be able to see and do as a Reaper and forget about all of this"—he tips his head toward the file cabinet behind him—"stuff."

"Fat chance of that happening," I say.

"Please, Libbi." His eyebrows bunch together. "And please, keep all of this Reaper stuff to yourself, okay? It will be easier for you in the long run. Believe me."

He faces the jammed door and without looking back at me, he walks through it. The last thing I see of him is the sole of his tennis shoe as it melts into the wood. I'm alone again.

"Wait," I say, mostly to myself. I figure Aaron's gone. "Don't leave me stuck in here."

"I'm not." I hear his voice on the other side of the door. "Step back or the door will hit you."

I take a big step back. Something solid thumps against the other side of the door and dust drifts down from the frame. With a loud pop, the door flings open and crashes against a chest of old newspapers.

Aaron turns away as I step out of the dark, coffin-like room and into the bright library.

"You're welcome for saving your life, by the way," he says over his shoulder as he heads to the front of the library and the exit.

Through the window in front of him, I see Mrs. Lutz closing the door to the computer lab across the hall.

"Wait!" I jog to catch up to him. "I have a question."

He stops with one leg halfway through the solid wood of the library door and glances back at me.

"Make it quick, Libbi. I can't be late."

"What's wrong with Mrs. Lutz's face? It looks like her soul is broken or something."

"That's because her soul *is* broken." He turns back to the door and his next words are so soft I hardly hear them. "Margie Lutz is marked."

"Marked?" I say, but he doesn't answer me. He's already walked through the door and out of sight.

I slowly turn and weave through the bookshelves, back to the door at the back of the library. The door to the newspaper room has drifted closed on its own. The doorknob twists in my hand, but when I push against the door, it's as stuck as it was when I was trapped inside. I don't have enough energy to force it open, like Ms. Weese and Aaron did. Asthma attacks really knock me on my ass.

So instead of ramming the door, I gather my stuff and head home. It looks like I'll be taking a trip to the community library in the morning.

I don't care if Aaron wants me to forget his past. I need to know what happened. It might be important. If he's a murderer, he's probably not someone I can trust.

10

Max and Kyle rock on the porch swing with their heads together, like they're sharing a big secret or a joke. The unintelligible low hum of Kyle's voice drifts to me as I trudge up the front walkway to my house. Max giggles and says something back. It's probably just my overactive imagination, but I could swear I heard the name Aaron.

As I top the steps, they both look up at me, eyes wide. Max's slack jaw and pale cheeks make him look like I caught him stealing. Kyle looks less guilty, though he's twirling one of his drumsticks about a mile a minute. The corners of his mouth dip down and for a brief moment his eyes are sharp, accusatory. Then he gives me his normal, best-friend smile and I relax.

"How was detention?" Kyle says, a little too enthusiastically.

"Good, I guess." I force a smile. "How was babysitting?"

"Fine." Kyle looks me up and down like he's just seeing me for the first time. Finally, he says, "Wow, Libs. You look like shit." He moves to stand up, but I stop him.

"Asthma attack. I'm fine now," I say. "What were you two talking about?"

"Oh, you know. Guy stuff." Kyle smiles easily, but it doesn't go past his lips. "So, are you ready to tell me why you've been acting so weird?"

"Um…" I frown and abruptly turn to my brother. "Max, are you done with your homework?"

His pale, freckled cheeks suddenly blaze. He doesn't need to say anything; his red face is all the answer I need. "Go inside and get it done or Mom'll be pissed."

That's true, but what's more true is I don't want him out here. I need to talk to someone about Aaron, and Kyle's the perfect person. But what I have to say will worry Max, if not scare him.

"Fine." Max slips off the porch swing and glowers at me as he passes.

"See ya later, Kyle," Max calls over his shoulder. I take his empty place on the swing.

"Yeah, buddy. I'll see you later," Kyle says and then he lowers his voice. "All right, what's going on, Libs? Why did you get rid of Max?"

"What do you mean?" I pull a string on the hem of my shirt, avoiding his eyes. "He has homework to do. Mom's not here, so it's my job to make sure he does it. You know that." I was totally ready to tell him everything a minute ago, but now I don't know where to start.

"Come on! What's going on with you? Is it Haley? Because if it is, she's being stupid about that test. I'll talk to her."

"It's not Haley." The string on my shirt unravels and makes a small hole. I twist it around my finger, tug, and break it off.

Haley avoided me all day today, but I understand why. It's physically painful for her to get less than an A on anything, and she blames me for the history final disaster. I'll give her until tonight to cool off, then I'll talk to her.

"What is it then?" Kyle touches my knee.

"I'm either going to die," I mumble. "Or I'm going nuts."

"I vote for going nuts." He laughs and mimes a punch-line drum roll in the air. Ba-da-boom-tish.

"I'm being seri—" I meet his eyes and stop, mid-word. The way his hair moves in the soft breeze casts a shadow across his face, and for a moment I think I see a hairline crack in the surface of his soul. Then the wind changes direction and it's gone. I blink twice and look again, but if the line was ever there, it's disappeared now.

"I'm being serious, Kyle," I say again. Maybe it's the way I look at him or the tone of my voice, but he stops laughing and his face straightens.

"All right. You're being serious," he says.

I stare down at my hands and try to think of the best way to begin. *Well, Kyle, everybody glows and I'm seeing an invisible guy who's the Grim Reaper and also a murderer and he wants me to take over his job, which he says is really great, but it sounds pretty shitty to me. What do you think I should do?* It sounds stupid and, well, crazy. So I chicken out.

"Never mind," I say. "Forget it. I really should get inside. Max might need help with his homework."

The swing creaks as I stand, and Kyle grabs my hand.

"Why won't you tell me, Libs?"

"It doesn't matter. None of it matters." I shiver when I realize I've just repeated what Aaron said when I asked him about the murders. I yank my hand from Kyle's closed fingers. "You'll just say, 'You're right, Libs. You *are* crazy,' and it will be a big joke for you and Max to laugh about and that'll be the end of it."

"No, I won't." He scowls.

"Well, like I said, it doesn't matter. I don't want to talk about it." I cross my arms over my chest. "Actually, I don't want to talk about anything right now. Maybe you should go."

Kyle's mouth hangs open. The breeze kicks up, and a few strands of his hair drift into his eyes. The thin line reappears across the bridge of his nose, but I'm too confused and scared to lean in and make sure it's not a break in his soul.

"Fine." He blinks a few times. "If you don't want to tell me, I'll go home." He stands from the swing and crosses my front porch, dragging his drumsticks along the spokes of the railing. The wrought iron spokes bong like a series of funeral bells.

"Hey, and no problem watching Max for you, by the way," he says before stomping down the stairs.

Shit. I hurt his feelings. I didn't mean to do that. I actually really want to talk to him. I just don't know how to say it without it coming out all weird.

"Kyle!" I call to his back as he stalks down the street toward his house. He turns, but his mouth is set, his eyes hurt and angry. "I'll see you tonight, okay. Let me get my head on straight and I'll talk to you after the show. I promise."

He nods and lifts his hand, as if to say "Whatever." But at the end of the street he whacks the stop sign with his drumstick so hard the stick splinters and a piece of wood flies into the grass.

***

I stand on Jumpers' Bridge with the midpoint of the truss arching over me. Sunlight streams through the trees and encrusts the waterfall with sparkling diamonds. The spray cools my face.

Something cold and slimy slips across my palm then wraps around my hand. I glance down at the skeletal fingers gripping mine. Fat drops of blood hang from the boney fingertips. I smile and look up at Aaron, but I can't see his pale blue eyes or his full lips. A tattered black hood casts his face in shadows.

"You've made your decision?" A voice crackles and wheezes from the black hole where his face should be. I chuckle and squeeze the bones of his hand reassuringly.

"Yes." Gore oozes between my fingers and drips to the wood at our feet. "I'll do it, Aaron. I'll take your job."

Laughter and the sound of voices. I turn and let go of Aaron's hand, my palm slick with blood.

Kyle and Haley step onto Jumpers' Bridge and stop laughing instantly. Their backs straighten and their blank eyes stare straight ahead as they walk hand in hand. With each slow, synchronized step I notice Kyle's hair graying. Haley's smooth face wrinkles and sags.

A crack pierces the silence. A few feet ahead of them, a large chunk of aged wood falls away from the floor of the bridge and spirals to the rapids below. They don't even blink. And together, they take another step.

"No! Stop!" I run to them. "You're going to fall through. Wait."

They ignore me. I stand in front of Haley and wave my hands in her face frantically. Nothing.

"They can't hear you." Dry, like the crackle of old parchment.

"They're going to fall through, Aaron! Look!" I jut a blood-soaked finger at the gaping hole in the bridge.

"All you can do is let them go. It's your job."

"Haley! Kyle! Wake up!" I scream into their faces. Both lift their left foot in unison and dangle them over the edge of the hole. Haley teeters back for a moment, but Kyle pitches forward. I reach for him, but my hand slides through his chest, as if I'm made of mist. He looks up as his other foot skids off the wood and he sees me, actually sees me. For that brief moment I know his fear. He doesn't want to fall through the hole, but he has no choice.

"Libbi!" he yells as he tumbles through the gap. "Help me!"

Haley loses her balance and follows Kyle over the edge. She doesn't see me as I grasp at the back of her shirt. Her scream echoes around me as she tumbles through the hole and is gone.

Hot tears spring in my eyes. Aaron's cold fingers caress the back of my neck, and a drop of blood trickles over my shoulder and down the curve of my chest.

"You'll get used to it after a while," he says. But I don't want to.

A gust of wind billows around us, bringing with it the scent of chicken nuggets and fruit juice. I pull my eyes from the swirling rapids below us and gasp. Standing at the end of Jumpers' Bridge are Mom and Max, lost in a trance. Their fingers intertwine as they each lift their right foot in unison.

"I can't do this! I can't, Aaron! I can't do it!"

I'm screaming into my pillow. My eyes pop open and tears tumble down my cheeks. I roll onto my back and kick my blankets to the floor.

I can't be a Reaper. No way. I don't care how fantastically awesome Aaron says it is, I can't do it. Even with the cool superpowers, when given the two choices, I'd rather die myself than watch powerlessly as my friends and family die.

I run my palms over my face, smearing my tears. I have to tell Aaron that I want to die tomorrow. He'll have to wait a little longer for his replacement, because it's not going to be me. He won't be happy, but he'll get over it.

11

The mouthwatering scent of fried eggs, bacon, and coffee wakes me. I rub my eyes and peek at my Hello Kitty alarm clock.

Crap. 10:36. How could I have slept in? I know I was tired yesterday, so tired I fell asleep on the couch and don't remember how I got up to my room, but now I have less than five hours left of my life. That's not enough time.

I untangle the blankets from my legs and bolt out of bed. I'm still wearing my clothes from yesterday, but I don't care if they're wrinkled. I straighten them as best I can and bound down the stairs to the kitchen.

Mom stands at the stove with a spatula in one hand and an oven mitt on the other. She looks over her shoulder at me and gives me an all-is-forgiven smile. Amazingly, I don't turn into a blubbery mess right there. Instead, I walk up behind her and wrap my arms around her waist.

"What's this all about?" She giggles. Her shirt smells like mountain-fresh fabric softener. It smells like home.

"I'm sorry," I say. "I'm sorry for leaving Max the other night and for what I said about you and Dad and, well, everything else." There's so much more I want to say, but if I start, I won't be able to stop the tears from flowing.

"It's all right, Libs. And I'm sorry for putting so much responsibility on you." She pats my arm with her oven-mitted hand. "I thought about what you said, and you're right. It's not fair for you to never have time to yourself."

"Mom, you don't have to…"

She places the spatula and the oven mitt on the stovetop and twists around. Her eyes glisten as she takes my face in both hands and kisses my forehead, like she used to when I was a little kid.

"No, I do," she says. "You're such a good kid, Libbi, and I've heaped a lot on you this last year. I think it's about time you had a little freedom. And so…" Her bright smile beams. "Miss Lena said she'll take Max anytime you need her. All you need to do is call. Her number's on the fridge."

She tips her head toward a yellow Post-it on the refrigerator and I lose it. I bury my face in her neck and sob, my whole body heaving and shaking.

"Oh Libs, it's all right." She pulls me close and strokes my hair, which causes another body quake followed by a watery eruption. I'm going to die in a few hours and she went and got Max a babysitter so I can enjoy more of my life. It's ironic in the worst possible way.

"No, Mom, it's not all right. It's not!" I pull away from her. My tears have left wet streaks on her purple T-shirt.

I sink into a kitchen chair and cover my face with my hands. She sits in the chair next to mine; her warm, reassuring hand heavy on my shoulder.

"What's going on?"

I open my mouth to tell her. It would be nice to talk to someone about it, especially my Mom. Just the thought of telling her makes it an easier burden to bear. I can almost feel the weight of the last two days lighten.

But what am I supposed to say? "Hey, Mom! Guess what? I'm gonna die today." I can't do that. I can't ruin our last few hours together with that kind of talk. I rub my palms over my eyes and sniff away the tears.

"Nothing, Mom. I'm glad you're not mad at me." My fingers find her hand. "I love you." I stop myself from adding, "I'm going to miss you."

"Aw, I love you too." She brings my hand to her lips and plants a kiss in the middle of my palm. "Are you hungry?"

"Yeah." I force a smile. "Where's Max?" I need to apologize to him, too.

"He's at camp, remember?" She pushes up from the chair, wrangles her disheveled hair back into her hair clip, and returns to the stove. "He left with one of the scout moms and a bunch of his friends this morning."

Camp. Right. I forgot.

My stomach turns sour and the familiar lines of the kitchen blur through my tears. As awful as I treated Max, I won't be able to say good-bye or even tell him I'm sorry. Unless—

"Where are they camping?"

"Oh, some place outside town. Camp Constance, I think. Why?"

"No reason. Just curious."

My stomach settles as much as the stomach of a person scheduled to die in a few hours can settle. I know the camp she's talking about, and it's not far away. About a twenty-minute drive outside of town.

***

I check my cell phone. 11:28. A little less than four hours left. Plenty of time.

My disjointed mind skitters between driving out to Camp Constance to say good-bye to Max and telling Aaron I'd rather die than take his crumby job. My car keys snag on the zipper as I pull them out of my purse. I look down to yank them free and almost miss Kyle furtively dart behind a tree.

"Kyle!"

This is perfect. If there was ever a time I needed my friends, this is it. I can't think of a better way to end my life than with my best friends. That and a big bowl of Foster's Chocolate Decadence ice cream. Heck, the ice cream shop would be a great place to be at 3:12 today. Maybe I'll choke on a maraschino cherry or develop a fatal case of brain freeze. Death by chocolate.

"Kyle!" I jog after him. He takes a left at the end of the block. "Kyle!" I know he can hear me. Everyone in Carroll Falls can hear me. Why won't he answer?

I turn the corner and immediately know something's wrong. Kyle does an about-face and slogs toward me with his hands sunk deep in his pockets and his eyes locked on mine, burning a hole through my skull. He's pissed off, but what really concerns me is his soul.

It still glows way brighter than mine, but the line that I thought was a trick of the light yesterday is now a thick, jagged black fissure that starts in the middle of his forehead and zigzags over the bridge of his nose. It doesn't compare to the hairline crack in Mrs. Lutz's face. Kyle's is much wider and uglier.

Kyle is marked—whatever that means—and what's showing through the inch-wide break in his soul is foul and black and festering.

He scowls as he approaches and pushes by me without a word.

"What's wrong with you?" I say. Does being marked mean you're angry? Somehow, I think there's more to it than that. He's definitely angry, but my mom was angry the night I left Max alone in the house and her soul didn't look like this.

Kyle's back stiffens and he stops walking.

"I don't know, Libbi!" He whirls around and scorches me with his eyes again. "What's *your* problem?"

"You're the one hiding behind trees and avoiding me, not the other way around."

"You could've fooled me." He reaches in his back pocket for his drumsticks. The black sludge inside his mark pulses.

"What the hell are you talking about, Kyle? I'm not avoiding you."

"Oh, yeah? Well, first, you were being all bitchy." He holds up a hand to count off my offenses on his fingers. "Then you refused to talk to me. You kicked me off your front porch yesterday. And last night you were supposed to come to the Battle of the Bands, like you promised, and you didn't. I mean, what the fuck, Libs? What am I supposed to think?"

Oh my God, I forgot his show. I fell asleep on the couch last night and slept right through it. And I've been so wrapped up in Aaron and my impending demise, I didn't remember that I'd forgotten. No wonder he's pissed. I suck as a friend.

"Oh, Kyle, I'm so sorry." I take a tentative step toward him. "Did you win, at least?"

"No." He doesn't back away, but he beats his leg furiously with one stick and his eyes remain as dark as the stuff showing through that jagged mark. "You're my good luck charm, Libs. Of course we didn't win."

"I'm sorry for missing the show. For everything. I wanted to come. I just couldn't."

"What's going on with you?" A spark of warmth and concern flickers in his eyes.

"Nothing," I say, and the spark vanishes. His eyes chill and he starts to turn away. "I mean, something. But it's no big deal."

"Bullshit, Libs. I've known you since the second grade. Something's up, and you need to tell me what it is."

I can't lie to him anymore. He'll know if I lie. But I can't tell him the complete truth, either, so I settle for the safe middle ground and hope it's enough to make the angry split in his soul disappear again.

"I didn't come to the show last night because I fell asleep on the couch. I hadn't slept in two days. Mom and I had a fight about babysitting. It was stupid. But this morning she said Ms. Lena could babysit if I ever needed a break. So it's all okay now." I smile, but it's not okay.

Ms. Lena might babysit Max a lot after today, but not because *I* call her. I fight hard against the lump in my throat. Hot tears shimmer in the corners of my eyes, but I hold the reassuring smile.

"That's it?" His lips press together and form a tight line. "That's why you've been distracted and jumpy and nasty lately?"

"That about sums it up."

He shuffles his feet against the sidewalk and looks over my shoulder down the lane. A frown bunches the skin of his forehead together.

"Then who's this Aaron guy Max told me about?"

I cringe and instantly wish I hadn't. The name coming from

Kyle's mouth sounds like a swear word. The black stuff within his mark boils.

"He's just some new guy at school," I say.

"Max says he's your boyfriend." *Ta-tap, ta-tap, ta-tap* against his thigh. "Is that true?"

"He's not my boyfriend. It's not like that at all." Blood rushes to my face and I hope Kyle doesn't read it the wrong way, like I wish Aaron were my boyfriend. Because I don't wish that. And even if I did, it doesn't matter, since I'm about to die. "Even if he was my boyfriend, which he's not, why do you care who I date?"

"I don't care," Kyle says quickly. "I don't. I just never thought you'd ditch me for a guy you just met. That's all."

"I didn't ditch you. I fell asleep. I swear."

He slips his drumsticks back into his pocket. For a full, uncomfortable minute, his burnt-wood eyes study me. The tar-filled crack weaves an uneven trail down the middle of his face. "I have to go, Libbi."

He turns to leave, but I can't let him go. He doesn't believe me and he hasn't forgiven me, and I need things to be good between us before my completely non-romantic date with Death.

"Wait." My hand darts out and grasps his upper arm. "Will you and Haley be in town this afternoon, around two thirty? I'd really like to go to Foster's for ice cream, like when we were kids. My treat."

He hesitates for a moment. The mark hasn't disappeared, but at least the black sludge inside it has settled down a bit. "Yeah, I guess. But I don't know about Haley. She's really mad at you."

"I know. Winkler's a douche. But you know how to sweet-talk her. Can't you make sure she comes? Say whatever you have to, just get her there. Please? I need to see her today, Kyle. I need both of you."

I give him the most pathetic set of puppy-dog eyes I can muster and pray he isn't too mad for them to work.

He stares at me for a long time and then sighs in defeat.

"All right," he says. "I'll try." He turns and walks away.

"Thanks, Kyle," I call to his back, but he doesn't even lift his hand this time. He strides to the end of the block and is gone.

The treetops sway against the bruised sky as I walk up the sidewalk and back to my car. A gust of wind yanks the car door out of my hand and plasters my shirt against my body. Thunder rumbles in the distance, and the air grows thick with the scent of ozone. It won't be long before fat drops polka-dot the sidewalk.

I check my phone as I duck into the car—11:40—and chuck it onto the passenger's seat.

My keychain jingles as I stuff my key in the ignition, but I don't start it up. I just sit and stare out the windshield.

The tufts of purple flowers on the lilac bushes lining the driveway sway in the wind. Any other day, I'd try to figure out how to replicate that color on a canvas. Today, I don't really see the flowers at all. Instead, I see Kyle. I see the angry set of his jaw and his hard eyes.

Lightning splits the sky, followed by the low growl of thunder, but instead I see the black gash across his face. The first drop of rain plops on the windshield and begins a slow trail down the glass, but instead I see the swirling, boiling sludge bubbling inside Kyle's mark.

Aaron said the crack in Mrs. Lutz's soul means she's broken. Is Kyle broken too?

Did I break him?

I need to talk to Aaron. Jumpers' Bridge is only a few minutes away, and it's practically on the way to Camp Constance. If I stop at the bridge first, I should have plenty of time to drive out to see Max and back before I meet Kyle and Haley for ice cream.

If I hurry.

12

Raindrops pelt my cheeks. My feet slap the hard-packed dirt of the bike trail and splash muddy water over the toes of my tennis shoes. Wet branches whip my face, but I don't care. I don't have time to waste. I'll run as fast as my feet can move, because once I reach the railroad tracks, the uneven ties and gravel will force me to walk.

Aaron might not be there.

The thought scatters my focus. What will I do if he's not there? He said he lives close to the bridge, but I have no idea where. The woods surrounding the falls are too thick to explore, especially if I have no clue where to start. If Aaron's not at the bridge when I get there, I'll have no choice but to wait until he shows up for my death to talk to him about Kyle's mark. I hope I'll have time to ask before I die.

The bike path u-turns around an elm tree, but instead of following it back to the parking lot and my waiting car, I push through the trees and follow a different trail. Kyle called it a deer trail when we first discovered it. That was before we knew it already had a name: the party trail. It ends at a steep, gravel incline.

The railroad cuts through the trees in both directions, stretched like parallel silver snakes, shiny and slick with rain. I climb the incline and follow the tracks, skipping from rail tie to rail tie.

Carroll Falls rumbles ahead. The wet, mineral smell of it surrounds me. I'm close.

Around the bend in the tracks, Jumpers' Bridge waits, a skeletal giant suspended over sheer cliffs. The muscles in my legs twitch, ready to run, to move faster, but I hold back. I don't want to trip and bust my head open or break my neck. Lying unconscious and bleeding beside the railroad tracks is hardly as nice of a way to go as choking on ice cream. And I wouldn't be able to say good-bye to anyone.

The curled back of the bridge comes into view and the rain abruptly stops, like God turned off the faucet and turned on the sun. Glittering sunlight breaks through the clouds as I skip-hop the last curve of track. Without the cooling rain, the air is muggy and oppressive. I peel off my soaked hoodie, tie it around my waist and wring out my ponytail. Attractive.

Dripping wet, I stand at the mouth of the deserted bridge, exactly where Haley and Kyle stood hand in hand at the beginning of my dream. The wooden ties are intact for the entire length of the bridge and no black hooded figure with bloody fingers lurks beneath the metal truss. I turn and scan the forest and the railroad tracks behind me. Nothing. I'm alone.

I could look one more place before I give up and drive to Camp Constance, but I don't think Aaron'll be there. He'd have to jump off the bridge to get down to the river. But, in the interest of being thorough, I'll check.

I lift my foot, and the thought of crossing Jumpers' Bridge, of standing in the same spot where I watched my best friends die in my dream, stops me. I know I'm being superstitious and stupid, but I back away from the bridge entrance and scramble down the gravel, off the tracks.

Fifty feet from the bridge, a scrawny tree clings to a patch of dirt near the edge of the cliff. Maybe, if I use the tree as support, I could see the riverbed from there.

Terrified the dirt will crumble under my weight, I inch up to the tree. When I'm close enough, I throw my arms around the trunk and wait for my heart to stop playing leap-frog with my lungs. I lean out as far as I can without letting go of the trunk, but I can't see the river if I'm hugging the tree. I say a silent prayer, grip the closest branch with both hands and lean over the rim.

Holy crap, I'm high. Wind whips my ponytail back over my shoulder as I watch the sharp boulders slice the foaming, white water far below. The only living thing I can see down there is a blue heron perched on a fallen tree branch, watching for fish at the surface of the water.

Aaron isn't down there. He isn't here at all. I've wasted twenty minutes of the last three hours of my life for nothing.

I tighten my grasp on the tree branch and pull myself back. Gulping air as my heart rate slows, I seize the tree trunk and look back to the bridge. From this angle, I can see between the metal supports of the bridge. And I see Aaron.

He stands in full view, barefoot and bare-chested, feet balanced on top of the safety railing at the mid-point of the bridge. His eyes are closed and he grips the bridge supports on either side of him. It's hard to see from this distance, but his chest and belly look strange, discolored in places. Maybe it's the mist drifting up from the falls.

But what the heck is he doing up there, hanging onto the bridge with nothing but air and four inches of railing between him and the boulder-strewn riverbed? Does he have a death wish, or something?

The breeze ruffles his dark hair as he leans out and dangles his body over the abyss. Tempting the wind to blow him off. Daring Death. His toes curl around the railing, but that won't keep him from falling. Only his firm grip on the steel support bars keeps him from plunging from the bridge now.

"Oh my God, Aaron!" I scream. "What are you doing?"

If he hears me, he doesn't show it. He smiles and turns his peaceful face up to the sky. And he lets go of the bars. His body drops through the misty air in an arch, plummeting below the ridge of the cliff where I can't see him.

"Oh my God!" I let go of my tree and race along the edge of the cliff. "Aaron! Aaron!"

I have to get to him. There must be a way down. I can't swim, but if I could get down there, I could find a branch and fish him out. If he isn't unconscious or already dead, that is. On the other side of the bridge, a steep path littered with empty beer cans and liquor bottles leads down the cliff face to a flat boulder near the bottom.

I can get down to him, if I cross the bridge.

I've always been mildly afraid of heights, but that fear isn't what's holding me back now. It's the stupid dream. I need to suck it up and cross the damned bridge. Aaron could be bleeding to death down there.

"Hey, Libbi."

I yelp and spin around as Aaron steps from the bridge entrance, a huge grin plastered to his face. His shoes are tied together by the laces and slung over one shoulder. His shirt is back on, and he's completely dry.

Add two more to his list of superpowers: death-defying swan dives into boulder-filled rivers and teleportation. He skids down the gravel embankment and saunters toward me.

"What the hell was that all about?" I ball up my fist and whack his arm. "You just scared the shit out of me!"

"What? You were watching me?" His cheeks flush crimson as he rubs the spot where I punched him.

"I thought you were trying to kill yourself, you know. I was about to jump in after you."

His face goes slack for a moment, then he shakes his head and smirks. "So you were going to jump off that cliff and save me then?"

"Maybe I could have...well, no." My cheeks burn. I brush invisible dirt from my pants and shirt until the fiery sensation goes away. "What the hell were you doing, anyway? It almost looked like you wanted to..." I sweep a hand out toward the bridge. "I don't know."

"I was just having a little fun, that's all," he cuts in before I can say any more. But, I don't really buy it. That peaceful smile right before he let go of the bridge told me it was more than "just a little fun."

He nudges my elbow and gives me a playful smile that causes my knees to wobble and makes me forget for a moment that he's Death incarnate.

"So, what are you doing here so early?" he says.

"Early? You knew I was coming here?"

"Of course. Did you make your decision?"

"Don't you know?" I cross my arms over my chest. "Isn't mindreading one of your superpowers?"

"No. Knowing where people will be when they die is my job, Libbi." He doesn't actually roll his eyes, but he sounds like he wants to. "If you continue on this path, you'll be at this bridge when it's your time."

"Really?" I say to him, and then mumble under my breath, "But I wanted to be at Foster's when I die. Death by chocolate."

"Well, Foster's is where you were going to be, until a few minutes ago. Something changed." He raises his eyebrows. "Did you make your decision?"

"Actually." I bite my lower lip. "I have a few questions first."

"Okay," he says. "Shoot."

"At school yesterday, you said Mrs. Lutz's soul is broken. What's wrong with her?"

Aaron doesn't answer. He doesn't move. He just watches me with his hands on his hips, like some closed-lipped pirate.

"Well?"

"That's a lesson for another day," he finally says. "If you take the job."

"Well, I'm not taking the job without an answer."

"Why do you want to know?" He sounds amiable, but he still hasn't moved. If not for his lips, he could be a statue.

I draw in a deep breath. My initial tactic isn't working. I should stop trying to bully the information out of him and tell him the truth. Maybe he'll take pity on me.

"Look, my best friend has a crack in his face like Mrs. Lutz has. Except his is much blacker and thicker and the stuff inside of it looks like it's, I don't know"—I shudder—"alive."

"Oh," Aaron mutters. "I get it." His eyes shift down to my feet.

"He didn't have that thing yesterday. What does it mean, Aaron? How are Kyle and Mrs. Lutz broken?"

Aaron finally moves. He drops his hands from his hips and turns toward the tree I used to peek over the edge of the cliff.

"Margie Lutz is marked because she helped someone she shouldn't have helped. She didn't know what she was doing at the time, which is why I think her mark is faint. Hopefully, it won't affect her too much, in the end." He turns back to me and his eyes shimmer in the sunlight. "As for Kyle, I don't know why he's marked. He hasn't done anything yet."

"Yet? Kyle's mark is showing something that hasn't happened?"

"Yes." Aaron glances at the bridge. "If he'd done it already, we would know."

"What? We would know what?" My nails dig into my palms, but I ignore the painful pinch.

"If he altered the plan."

"Aaron, you're talking in circles and pissing me off."

"All right, I'll explain." He paces in front of me, his jaw set with determination. "There's a Death Plan, sort of like a schedule. The dimming of the soul tells us a person is reaching their scheduled time of death."

"I already know that," I interrupt, and he rolls his eyes.

"Will you just listen?" He gives me a cold glance before he continues. "But people have free will. Free will means you never know for sure what choices a person will make. And sometimes they choose to change the Death Plan."

"Wait, what do you mean? Do you mean murder?"

"Yes." Aaron meets my eyes briefly and continues to walk and talk. "But not accidental deaths. A guy who accidentally runs over a girl with his truck doesn't count as a murderer. That's a scheduled death. A person must willingly cause an unscheduled death to get a mark. The more directly responsible they are for the death, the wider and blacker the mark."

"But you said Kyle's mark shows something that hasn't happened yet. How can he be marked for something he hasn't even done?"

"I don't know how it works, exactly, but sometimes the mark shows up before a person has done anything. Sometimes, I think, before *they* know they're going to do something." Aaron shrugs. "It comes in handy. I can feel when a mark appears, and

I know I need to keep an eye on that person, so I'm there when they do it."

"And by 'do it,' you mean murder someone."

Aaron nods.

I replay the angry conversation I had with Kyle in my mind. I remember the way he beat his drumstick against his thigh and how he smacked the stop sign. But what I mostly remember is that black, boiling sludge that bubbled in the crack in his soul. That stuff looked evil, but was it evil enough to murder someone?

That can't be right. Kyle wouldn't hurt anyone. Sure, he beats and smacks things; he's a drummer. But of the three of us, he's always been the calm one, the cool contrast to Haley's fiery personality. Aaron's wrong. He has to be.

"You think Kyle's going to kill someone?" Even as a question, the words sound wrong. They don't belong together.

But Aaron nods again and my stomach clenches.

"He's either going to kill someone else or himself," he says.

Suicide. Now, that makes more sense. I can see Kyle hurting himself before I can see him hurting someone else, though I can't imagine what would bring him to do that either.

"So what does it mean when someone gets marked?" I say. "What happens to them?"

"I don't know what happens when they leave me, but I can guess it isn't good." Aaron shivers. He shakes his head, and even though the sun streams through the clearing rainclouds, his eyes grow dark. "I know a marked person doesn't see me as a lost relative or friend when I come for them, no matter how hard I try. They see me as the traditional Grim Reaper. Black hood, sickle—you know, the works."

The works. That can't be good at all. The Grim-Reaper-Aaron from my nightmare comes to mind so forcefully I can almost see the terrifying image superimposed over the real Aaron's body. Cold, skeletal fingers dripping with gore. Face hidden by a black, tattered shroud.

A person forced to see that demon couldn't possibly be headed to the Pearly Gates.

"So they go to Hell?" My damp shirt drips rainwater as I

nervously twist the hem.

"I hope not." Aaron's voice is soft and low. "But I don't know. Not for sure."

He may not want to admit it, but that's what it sounds like to me. And someday, that's what's waiting for Kyle? For committing suicide? It doesn't seem right.

"Do you appear as the Grim Reaper for suicides too?" I say a silent prayer that Aaron will say no. He has to say no. That can't happen to Kyle. My best friend shouldn't have to deal with that.

"Yes." Aaron scowls at the ground at my feet and my stomach summersaults. "A suicide is an unscheduled death carried out by free will. I have no choice."

"But that's not fair." I move toward him, my voice rising with every step. "A suicide isn't hurting anyone but themselves. It's an illness, not something that should be punished."

"You don't have to tell me." Aaron backs up a step, his hands up in front of him. "You're right. It's not fair. But that's the way it is. As much as I wish I could, I can't change it any more than you can."

"So that's it then?" My hands fall to my sides. "Kyle might go to Hell, and there's nothing I can do about it."

"I told you, I don't know what happens when they leave me." Aaron sinks his hands into his pockets. "But he could avoid the question all together if he changes his mind."

My heart leaps as I grasp desperately at the line Aaron has just thrown me.

"Does the mark go away if he changes his mind?"

"It has happened. That's the beauty of free will." He grins, and I let my breath out in a puff. Aaron must see the relief on my face, because he shakes his head slowly and says, "Not to bring you down or anything, but it doesn't happen often. In forty years, I've only seen a mark heal twice."

I don't care if he's only seen it heal twice. Twice is better than never. Twice means Kyle has a chance. And he has me. Now, I just need to make sure he changes his mind. But how can I do that if I decide to die in a few hours?

"So, was that it?" Aaron startles me. "Do you have any more

questions?"

"Actually, I do." I walk past him. I don't want him to see my scheming eyes. "You said I would train with you for seven days, right? Learn how to use your powers and stuff."

"Yes."

"What if after the seven days, I decide I don't want the job. Am I forced to take it?"

"No, but there are consequences."

My stomach does a back flip. I might be able do this. If I work the system and train with Aaron, I could buy myself seven days to figure out Kyle's mark and make sure he changes his mind. Then, when my training is over, I'll tell Aaron "thanks, but no, thanks" and be on my way to the Great Beyond. Screw the consequences.

"Okay." I face him. "I choose to tell you my answer after the training."

"I'm sorry, Libbi," he says, though I'm not convinced he truly is sorry. "It doesn't work that way. I need to know your answer today."

"Why? If I'm not forced to take the job, why do you need to know today?"

"Because I can't train you if you don't have the powers."

"But I do. I see souls. I had the headache. Remember?"

"You have some of the powers, but not all of them." He twists the ring on his thumb slowly. "And I can't give them to you without a commitment. You have to be all in or the transfer won't work."

"And if I say I'm in, but don't really mean it?"

"You die. Today. At 3:12, sharp. It's not me you're trying to fool, Libbi. You'd have to fool yourself. And if you change your mind after you've accepted the job—"

"Let me guess." I drag my forefinger across my throat.

"Yeah. The very next time 3:12 p.m. rolls around. It's automatic. There's nothing you or I can do about it. But there's something else." He scratches his cheek. "You'd have to face Abaddon for backing out of your contract."

"Why? What would changing my mind about being a Reaper

do? I was already scheduled to die, and you're already a Reaper. Nothing would change."

"Yeah, but this is a serious job with a long-term commitment that includes a lot of training. That's why I have to tell you what it's like to be a Reaper before you take the job, so you can't say you didn't know. I guess Abaddon wants to make sure only serious people accept it. He doesn't take kindly to his Reapers breaking their obligations." Aaron's face drains of color briefly, then he smiles and shrugs. "But you don't have to accept the job, Libbi. Your friend will stay marked, but you can still die today, if you want. No consequences."

My simple but brilliant plan shrivels.

I don't want Aaron's job. It's horrible. Roaming the streets of this stupid town, year after year, a perpetual teenager, and never able to leave. Watching my family worry when I don't come home then mourn when they decide I must be dead. And me, unable to explain, comfort, or help in anyway. Would they think I was murdered?

Of course, I'd use the seven extra days to make sure Kyle's mark heals, but what if it comes back? What if Haley gets a mark? Or Mom? Or Max? I'd be aware of everything, but invisible. Silent. Always watching but never able to step in.

Then, to make it even more terrible, I'll be there when each of them dies. Who wants that kind of life? Aaron may say it's great, but he's also the one trying to get out of it.

But I don't want to die either. At least with the seven extra days, I can fix Kyle's mark and have time to say good-bye to my friends and family properly.

Aaron says I have a choice, but both of my options suck. Why can't I just live? Why isn't that an option? I want to live. Why can't I grow up, go to college, have a career and a family, and *live*?

Watery sobs shake my body. My knees buckle and I collapse at Aaron's feet. I bury my face in my hands and let it out. All of the fear and worry and sadness that has built up inside of me since Aaron first saved my life pours out in a steady stream.

Aaron sits down in the grass beside me and places his hand

over mine. I imagine a trail of blood trickling over the skin where he touches me, but I don't pull away. Instead, I lean into him and rest my cheek against his shoulder. He wraps his arm around my waist and pulls my head to his chest. The sweet, earthy scent of him fills my nose and I inhale deeply. My shaky breaths match his pounding heart.

"Do you need more time to think?" he whispers into my hair. "You still have two hours, if you need it."

I shake my head. No matter what he says, the decision is an illusion. I don't have a choice. I never had a choice, because I'm dying either way.

Kyle needs me, and I need time. If signing up as the fourth horsewoman of the apocalypse buys me time, then hand me a scythe and call me Grim.

"No, I don't need more time to think." I lift my head and find his face. His eyes are calming now, but I don't think Aaron's using his relaxing power. I think it's because my mind is set. I've made a choice.

"I'll do it," I say. "You have my word, one hundred percent."

"Really?" Aaron squeezes my hand and tries to hide the smile I can still see in his eyes.

"Yeah," I say. "Are you surprised?"

"I don't know. With all the crying, I thought you were going to say you wanted to die."

"Well…" I wipe the tears from my cheeks with my sleeve. "I guess I'm chock full of surprises. Aren't I?"

Aaron chuckles and hugs me closer. It feels nice to have his arms around me, even if he's the one causing me pain.

"I have one more question, Aaron," I say when I'm sure the tears aren't going to overwhelm me again.

"Yes?"

"Is it true? Did you really kill someone?"

A few moments pass and I think he's not going to answer. Then he sighs and his breath tickles my forehead.

"Would my answer change your mind?" His voice is strained, exhausted.

"No. I just want to know." I'm surprised. I actually mean

that.

His arms tighten around me, and he breathes in deep and lets it out slowly.

"It's true," he whispers into my hair. "I killed two people."

I pull back from his chest and search his overly bright soul for the remnants of a black fissure. There is none. He's as clean as Max.

How can that be? He just said murderers get marked. How can Kyle be marked for something he hasn't even done yet, when Aaron admits to murdering two people and he's mark-free?

"But you're not marked," I say.

"I'm a Reaper. My marks are forgiven." He won't look at me. Instead, he watches a black bird sail across the sky. "You've changed your mind now, haven't you?"

Of course, what Aaron did bothers me, but that was forty years ago. And I can tell by the sadness in his eyes and the grim line of his lips that he's sorry. But it doesn't matter anyway. I'm not doing this for Aaron.

I'm doing it for Kyle.

"I haven't changed my mind," I say firmly. "I said I'll do it, and I meant it."

13

"All right." He drops his arm from around my waist. "We should get started then."

"Now?"

He stands and reaches down to me and I take his hand.

"Right now." He hoists me to my feet. I jog to keep up with his long strides as he pulls me toward the railroad tracks. When we reach the gravel hill supporting the tracks, he drops my hand and starts to climb.

"Where are we going?" I say.

"Up on the bridge."

The bridge. Of course.

My shoes slip in the stones as I scramble up the hill after him. I climb onto one of the wooden railroad ties and dust myself off.

Aaron stands at the entrance of the bridge with his back to me. Mist drifts from the falls and wraps tendrils around his ankles as he stares into Jumpers' Bridge. I wish I had my sketchpad. The tense lines of his body contrast against the steel bridge in a beautiful, yet strangely eerie composition.

I walk up behind him and touch his arm. He jolts.

"Are you okay?"

"I'm fine," he says dismissively. "Let's go." His hand brushes my lower back, touching bare skin. I feel the soft warmth of his fingers long after his hand drops away.

We enter the bridge together. The spaces between the ties are too narrow for us to fall through, but I keep my eyes on my feet anyway and ignore the vortex of water swirling far below.

"Why do we need to come up here again?" I swallow.

"This is where I died." He stops walking and a chill rolls over me. We are exactly where we stood in my dream. "Well, it's where I would have died, if Charlotte hadn't saved my life."

"Charlotte?"

"The Reaper before me."

"Oh."

"Anyway, this is a significant place for me, for a lot of reasons." He surveys the bridge around us, his eyes sad and distant. "Since this is where I was supposed to die, I thought it'd be the perfect place for you to officially accept my job." His eyes meet mine. A blush colors his cheeks. "Does that make sense? Or am I being stupid?"

"No. It makes total sense," I say, but it doesn't make me any less afraid of heights.

"All right." He smiles and takes my icy hand in his. The cool metal of his ring feels sharp against my skin. "Are you ready?"

"Yes."

"Okay." His deep blue eyes search mine. "I need you to say you'll take over for me as the next Carroll Falls Reaper."

I close my eyes and bow my head. Tears streak down my cheeks and I let them fall.

"I will take over for you, Aaron. I will be the next Carroll Falls Reaper. I promise."

Warmth spreads where our hands meet. Light penetrates my closed eyelids and I open my eyes. Aaron's thumb ring burns with white light. It throws out sparks and tendrils of smoke seep from the ring and circle our wrists like a pair of handcuffs, binding us together. The smoke dissipates into a glowing ball of light, brighter than the light that surrounds Aaron, encircling our joined hands. It grows to encompass our forearms, our shoulders, our chests, and then our entire bodies. The air inside of the bubble hums with energy.

"It's okay." His voice sounds muffled. "It won't hurt."

The ball of light surrounds us for what feels like an eternity and then collapses back on itself, moving down Aaron's face and chest. It shrinks smaller and smaller, until only a sliver of light twinkles on the surface of the metal ring, and then it disappears.

"That wasn't so bad, was it?" Aaron says.

He looks different. The over-intense aura that has radiated from him since the day I first started seeing souls has dimmed. Now, he glows with the same intensity as Max and Mom and everyone else who still has a life ahead of them. Basically, he's the same as everyone except me.

But that isn't true. My hands are glowing now. Brightly. I follow my arms up to my body, and even in the harsh beam of sunlight streaming through the truss I can see my skin shining. I'm not a tea candle about to blink out anymore; I'm as bright as Aaron. The overabundance of light that was in him has somehow shifted between us and filled what was lacking in me, balancing us. Making us both normal.

We are now the same.

"As long as we're together, you'll be able to use all of my powers." He lets go of my hands. "But when we're apart, you'll only have some of them, like seeing souls, the warning headaches, and the pulling sensation."

"And I won't have to worry about getting struck by lightning or hit by a car anymore, right?"

"Right. You can even throw your asthma inhaler away, if you want. Your naturally ordered death has been postponed." He glances at me through his black bangs and combs the hair back with his fingers. "Well, unless you change your mind, that is."

"Great. I'll try not to do that."

"Come here." He walks to the safety railing and places a foot on the bottom rung. "Since you were concerned enough to jump off a cliff for me," he says, grinning over his shoulder, "I want to show you something."

I follow and stand beside him as he climbs to the top rail, but I keep both of my feet planted firmly on the wood. Reapers may have the power of teleportation, but I'm not about to try jumping off this bridge.

"I'm not climbing up there, Aaron."

"You don't have to." He holds the bridge supports on either side of him and slides his feet along the top bar, spreading his legs apart. The breeze flutters his shirt and yanks it tight against his chest, giving the hint of toned abs under his black tee. I've always been so focused on the depth of his eyes that I never noticed how defined his muscles are.

"Now, watch me the whole way down." He smiles again and lets go of the metal supports. He tips forward. Arms wide and legs spread, he drops from the bridge like a skydiver. The mist from the waterfall swirls around his body, clearing a path. And right before he's about to smack into the jagged rocks at the bottom, he disappears, like a freaking magician. He's just—poof—gone.

I grip the support beams and search the swirling mist for his body, but it's not there.

"Cool, huh?" he says in my right ear, and I scream. He erupts in a fit of laughter, slapping his knee and holding his stomach, as if scaring the shit out of me is the best entertainment he's had in years. It probably is. Asshole.

"Stop doing that!" I struggle to hold my already balled fist at my side.

"Sorry." He manages between fits of laughter. "You should have seen your face."

"Shut up."

"Sorry." He arranges his features into a serious scowl. It's hard for him. His stupid grin keeps peeking through the frown. "I just wanted to show you that once you become a Reaper you can't die. If you ever put yourself in a fatal situation, you'll be removed from it before you get hurt."

"So no matter what, you can't die?"

"No. I can't die." There's a pinch in the corners of his eyes. I'm not sure if he knows it's there, but I see it.

The peaceful smile he had before he let himself drop from the bridge earlier floats to the surface of my memory. There's no doubt in my mind that, to Aaron, jumping off this bridge means something. The thought scares me.

"Why do you want me to take over for you so badly, Aaron?" I ask him, outright. A strand of hair tickles my cheek, and I tuck it behind my ear.

"I already told you." He swallows and leans against the railing. The grin has disappeared. In its place is a hard scowl. "There's something I need to do—"

"Like what?" My fists dig into my hips. "Kill yourself?"

He looks back at me with hard eyes and pursed lips. He doesn't say a word, but he doesn't have to. His face says it all. I just can't understand it.

"Why?" I say. "I thought you said being a Reaper is great."

"It is." He sighs and looks over his shoulder at the falls. "But I've been doing it a long time. Maybe it's my time to go. Maybe dying is the only way I can solve a big problem."

I lean against the railing next to him and give him a sharp look. The only reason I agreed to take his job is because I want to stop Kyle from killing himself. But by agreeing to do it, I've made it possible for Aaron to kill himself. Ironic. If it wasn't for the sadness tugging at his face, I'd think this was a sick joke.

"There are other ways to solve your problems, Aaron."

"No, there isn't." He glares at me, his eyes hard and cold. "Not with this. You wouldn't understand."

"What do you mean, I wouldn't understand? I'm not an idiot. I can handle it."

"I don't think you're an idiot. Jesus, Libbi, you are so stubborn sometimes." He pushes away from the railing and paces back and forth in front of me like a caged animal. "Never mind what I said. I just want it over, okay?"

"But, you said…"

"Forget it. I want to die. That's all there is to it." His eyes hold mine for a moment and I know he's done. He's not telling me anything more.

"Well, how are you supposed to do it, then? You said you can't die. How are you going to kill yourself, if you can't die?"

He stops pacing and stares at me, eyes wide and cheeks pale. "I have a way," he says.

I open my mouth to push him a little further, but a giggle drifts along the curve in the railroad tracks. I smack my lips closed and turn toward the noise. Voices, and they're moving closer. At least two guys and a girl. The girl giggles again and it sounds like a high-pitched machine gun.

I know that laugh. It belongs to Makenna Collins, a senior with a serious party-girl reputation.

The group emerges from behind the trees. I'm right. It's Makenna and two senior boys, Scott Walters and Travis Harton. They stroll around the bend in the tracks and Makenna pushes Travis playfully. He stumbles and catches himself before falling face-first into the gravel. A cackle bursts from Scott, like he's a hyena on speed and watching Makenna push Travis is the funniest thing he's ever seen. Loser.

"Don't worry. They can't see you when you're near me," Aaron says as he sulks down the tracks, toward the end of the bridge and the group of seniors.

"Because when we're together, we share powers, right?" I ask.

"Right."

"Well, how far away from you do I have to be before they can see me?" I don't want to stray too far from Aaron and appear out of thin air, right in front of them. Not that they'd remember. They look hammered.

"Pretty far, actually, but within shouting distance. You'll know you've moved out of range when your soul gets dull again."

The trio skids down the gravel embankment supporting the tracks and onto the grass. Makenna spreads a baby-pink blanket out under the little tree, right where Aaron held me until I bawled myself silent. Before she can let go of the ends, Travis plops down and stretches out on the blanket, legs crossed and hands clasped behind his head.

"Move oudda way, blanket hog!" Scott shoves Travis' hip with the tip of his boot.

"I wouldn't be kickin' the man with the goods, Scotty." Travis continues to lay diagonal across the blanket as he yanks two liquor bottles out of his deep pants pockets. "But there's plenty of room for Makenna..." He pats his lap and waggles his eyebrows at her.

"Ugh!" I say. "If I have to listen to any more of this, I'm

gonna hurl."

Aaron nods, but instead of continuing down the tracks past the drunken picnic, he stands frozen, eyes locked on the trio. Maybe he is a creeper, after all.

"Can we go now?" I say.

"Wait. Can't you feel it? The energy in the air has changed. Someone is about to get marked. Right now."

He points down the hill to the party on the blanket, but I don't see anything out of the ordinary. Just three drunk teens, two of them about to get busy. But I can feel it. The air is charged, electric.

"Now?" I say, but then Travis seizes Makenna's wrist and yanks her down on top of him. Both of his hands reach around her hips, grab a hold of her butt, and squeeze. Makenna pushes herself off of him and rubs her wrist.

"Hey, asshole, that hurt!" She giggles, but it's a nervous laugh, not her usual machine-gun burst.

And then I see it. One moment Travis' soul is bright and intact and the next a four-inch-long, paper-thin fissure snakes over his left eye. It's so fine I can barely see it, for now.

"Oh God!" I say. "Is he gonna kill her?"

"I don't know." Aaron's hands clench and unclench at his sides. "But if he does, it's not going to be today. The mark would be wider and darker if it was today."

"Come on, Makenna." Travis pouts and slides his hand a little too high on her thigh. "You know I'm just playin', right? Tell her I'm just playin', Scotty."

"He's just playin'." Scott squats on the other side of Makenna, boxing her in between them. "But I don't know why you're acting all virginal and shit. Jayce said you like it rough."

"What are you talking about? I never hooked up with Jayce." There's no laugh in her voice now, nervous or otherwise. Travis digs his fingertips into the meat of her inner thigh.

"Ouch!" She pushes his hand away and tries to get up, but Scott seizes her ankles and yanks her back down. "Oh God! Help!" she screams. Her eyes widen and her bottom lip quivers when Travis rips the fly of his jeans down. Scott forces Makenna back on the blanket and grabs her left breast. He pinches it so hard she cries out in pain. He smacks his hand over her mouth.

I jump to my feet. I'm not going to stay up here on this stupid bridge and watch this happen. I can't. I step over the rail, intent on plunging down the gravel incline and slugging Travis in the jaw and then kicking Scott in the balls, but Aaron grabs my hand and yanks me to a halt.

"They're gonna rape her, Aaron." I rip my hand free. "Can't you see that?"

"Yes." His murderous eyes don't move from the scene on the blanket.

"Are you just gonna stand there and let them?"

"Normally, I'd walk away." His lips barely move, his voice hushed with anger. "That's all I can do, usually. I wouldn't be able to stop them no matter how hard I tried, and watching it is…awful. But not today. Today is different."

Makenna screams for help again, and the scream ends in a sob.

"We have to do something," I whisper. Tears roll down my cheeks.

"Today, we can. Together, we can." He meets my eyes and slips his hand into mine. "What I'm about to do is pretty scary. But underneath it all, remember it's just me. Don't be afraid of me."

Aaron squeezes my hand once then lets it go and steps back.

He closes his eyes and his legs start to grow. Taller and taller. Then his arms and body stretch like he's made of taffy and he's being pulled. When the growing stops, he's at least four feet taller. The skin around his head and face hangs loose and wrinkled—something I would think impossible after all of that stretching, but I'm looking right at it. His face collapses inward and disappears and his jet-black hair juts forward, but it isn't hair anymore; it's a black, tattered shroud. It wraps him from head to toe and hangs from his body like cobwebs on a skeleton. Aaron's beautiful face is gone, and what's there instead is hollow, dark, and cold.

The ring on the creature's boney thumb cracks open and he catches it in his fist before it falls to the ground. It unfolds in his hand, again and again, getting longer, adding bulk, until he holds the black wood of a long staff. A four-foot-long, curved blade springs from the wood like a switch-blade and glitters malevolently in the sunlight.

"I want to stop them," he says. "But they can't see me without you. I need your help. Give me your hand." The voice from the hole where his face should be is a deep growl that rumbles the air between us, and I'm afraid. I shouldn't be—he said not to be—but I am.

I take a deep breath. The earthy scent of freshly turned dirt wafts from the dark creature in front of me, and I swallow down the fear I feel creeping up my throat. It's just Aaron. This frightening demon is just a costume. That black shroud is really Aaron's messy hair. And inside of what looks like a dark, endless hole are Aaron's full lips and piercing eyes and day-old stubble.

I close my eyes and hold my hand out. His boney fingers close around mine.

A low popping sound, like the crackle of burning firewood, and my eyes spring open. Something must have changed because Grim-Reaper-Aaron suddenly drops my hand and whips away from me. He swoops down the hill toward Makenna and her attackers. He moves impossibly fast, so fast I look at his feet to see how he's doing it, but they aren't there. He floats two feet above the ground, and in his wake his shadow writhes and bubbles, as if it's alive.

The group on the pink blanket doesn't see him coming. Sweat drips from Scott's brow as he fights to hold Makenna's arms down. Travis struggles with her belt as Makenna twists and kicks under him.

Grim-Reaper-Aaron's skeletal hand extends from the folds of his robe and the crescent-shaped metal of the scythe glints. He hovers behind Travis and lowers the blade in front of the rapist's face, resting the razor's edge against his throat.

"I would stop that, if I were you," Grim-Reaper-Aaron growls, and Travis' flushed cheeks instantly go white. Scott's eyes bulge as he lets go of Makenna's wrists and crab-walks back a few steps.

Aaron points a boney finger at Makenna. "Run."

Makenna screams and jumps up off the blanket, eyes wide and focused on the horror that is Aaron. Then she follows his advice and runs. She barely misses kicking Scott in the face as she races away.

"Get up," Grim-Reaper-Aaron says to Travis, but before he can move, Scott rolls to his hands and knees and jumps to his feet.

Grim-Reaper-Aaron disappears from behind Travis and reappears in front of Scott, the point of his blade held inches from Scott's right eye.

"Don't try to run from me, Scott Dwayne Walters. You will never get away." Aaron's voice has changed from the low growl he used on Travis to a dry, raspy whisper.

A dark spot blossoms at Scott's crotch and drips down his leg.

"I am the Grim Reaper," Aaron continues, seemingly oblivious of Scott's lack of bladder control. "If you touch that girl, or any other girl, ever again, I will come for you. Do you understand that?"

Scott swallows hard and nods. Sweat drips down his pale face and off the tip of his chin.

"Good." Aaron says the word long and slow, holding the *o* in such a way that it becomes threatening, terrifying, a warning. "Now, get out of here."

Scott turns and runs before Aaron finishes his last sentence. He scrambles up the gravel hill, onto the train tracks, and takes off without looking back.

Aaron turns back to Travis with the scythe resting on one boney shoulder. Travis cowers next to the little tree, as far away from Aaron as he can get without falling off the edge of the cliff. His pants are still unzipped but at least they're dry.

"Travis James Harton." Aaron speaks with the growling voice again. He disappears and reappears directly in front of Travis, holding the scythe to his throat. "Did you hear what I said to your friend?" He says the last word with disdain, and Travis nods.

"Do you believe it?"

He nods again, and as he does, the edges of the long crack in his face pull together, shrinking the size of the gaping, black fissure.

"Answer me with words."

"Y-yes." The edges of Travis' mark touch. The hole in his soul seals with a soft sizzle, like a wound being cauterized, leaving his broad features unblemished.

"You have no idea how easy you're getting off right now," Aaron growls. "And how lucky you are you met me today, of all days. But remember this." He drags the sharp end of the sickle in an arch an inch from Travis' throat. "Next time you try something stupid like this, you won't be so lucky. Now go."

Travis bolts across the field. Holding his pants up with one hand, he follows Scott up the hill and down the train tracks as fast as he can manage.

Aaron's black shroud billows around his feet as he settles to the ground and walks back to me. With each step he gets shorter until he's back to his normal height. His face pops forward like it's a deflated balloon that has suddenly filled with air and the hood pulls back, becoming his normal, black, disheveled hair. The scythe in his hand folds in on itself. When it's small enough, it wraps his right thumb—the silver ring it was before.

It takes me a moment to remember I'm not supposed to be afraid of him, but then he smiles at me—a big, beaming smile—and I smile back. I can't help it. I've never seen him look this happy before, this real.

He leans in close and, using his normal voice, he says, "Give me a second to figure out how to make us invisible again."

Aaron grabs both of my hands and closes his eyes. After a few seconds, the popping sound surrounds us and just as quickly as it started, it stops. My mind races with questions, so many I can't decide which one to ask first.

"We did it. You and me," he says before I get a chance to talk. "I knew it would work. I *knew* it!" He's glowing and his wide smile dazzles me. I can't help but grin back.

"What exactly did I do, again?"

"You and I share powers when we're together," he says, like I should know what the hell he's talking about.

"Yeah, but I don't have any powers to share with you."

"Yes, you do. You can interact with the living, Libbi. I can't do that. You just let me use your power to scare those jerks." He barks a laugh. "That was fantastic!"

He throws his arms around my waist and pulls me tight against him. My stomach flutters as he lifts me up and swings me around once. He carefully places my feet back on the ground, but his hands stay at my waist, keeping my body close to his. He pulls back just enough to look into my eyes. His thumbs make soft circles in the small of my back.

"You know," he says. The excited smile is gone from his lips but it remains in his eyes. "I'm so happy, I think I could kiss you." His gaze locks on mine. He leans down and my stomach twists with panic.

Oh God, he wants to kiss me. And those gorgeous eyes are asking if it's okay. And it is okay; it would be more than okay, if I didn't feel like I'm about to puke.

I've never technically kissed a boy—well, I kissed Kyle a few months ago, just to know what it felt like, but that doesn't count. I can't have my first real kiss end with nerve-induced vomit. That would be so unsexy. I clear my throat and gently push him away.

He blushes a deep crimson and lets me go. His hands leave a hot memory on the skin of my back.

"Sorry," he mutters. "You're right. I shouldn't have."

"So," I say before he can continue. I need to say something or we'll both die of embarrassment. "Remember when I said you're creepy? Well, with the two freaky voices and the no face and the floating...Aaron, you're more than creepy. You're terrifying."

"Is that why you wouldn't kiss me?" He fidgets with the hem of his shirt.

"No. That's not it at all," I mumble. My cheeks burn. "I just thought it wasn't a good idea because—"

"You're right. It wasn't a good idea." He cuts me off before

I can admit I was afraid of barfing on him, but he steps closer to me anyway. I hold my breath as he gently tucks a loose strand of hair behind my ear and his fingers linger on my cheek. Then his eyes turn hard and he drops his hand from my face. "It's not a good idea."

I try not to let the disappointment show on my face. I want him to kiss me. Really badly. And now that I'm prepared, I don't think I'll throw up. But it's too late. Thanks to my stupid, overactive stomach, he's decided it's not a good idea.

I have to change the subject.

"So, all we needed to do to heal Travis' mark was scare the crap out of him?"

"Yeah." He smiles. It's not the dazzling grin he gave me before he picked me up and swung me around, but its close. "Wasn't that great? It felt so awesome to actually *do* something, Libbi. You have no idea how many times I've wished I could do something like that and I've had no choice but to walk away. People do a lot of crappy things when they think no one's watching."

"Yeah, but how did that work?" I glance over to where Makenna sat on her blanket. "How did scaring him heal his mark?" If I plan to help Kyle, I need to know everything I can about that stupid mark.

"I don't think he would have killed Makenna today, but this rape might have started a violent streak in him that eventually ended in murder," Aaron says. "Or it could have started a chain reaction of guilt that led to suicide. Who knows? Either way, we stopped the rape, put a bit of the fear of Death in him, and ended it before it got started."

"So all I have to do to stop Kyle from killing himself is stop the chain reaction." I say the words quietly, more to myself than to Aaron, but his head snaps up and he stares at me.

"What makes you so sure Kyle will commit suicide, Libbi? He could be marked for murder. You'd be surprised at all the bad things good people do in the right circumstances."

"Yeah, maybe. But I know, for Kyle, it's suicide," I say and stalk away from him. I don't want to hear anything else Aaron has to say about Kyle. He doesn't know him. He doesn't know anything.

"You don't know that," Aaron says at my shoulder. He's doing that annoying following trick and I stop myself from elbowing him in the gut. "Don't get me wrong. I hope it is suicide. I just don't want you to be disappointed if it isn't. Be realistic."

"It's suicide, Aaron." I whip around and try to convey determination in my dark scowl. "I know it is, because I know Kyle. He's no murderer. Speaking of Kyle..." I pat my pockets for my cell phone, but I don't have it. I must have left it in the car. "What time is it?"

"It's a quarter to three," he says without looking at a watch. As he says it, I know it's true as surely as I know my last name is Piper. And I know if I want to, I can tell the time without a clock too, down to the millisecond. That must be another handy power of a Reaper.

"Crap! I was supposed to meet Haley and Kyle for ice cream at two thirty. They're gonna kill me. I'm sorry, Aaron, I have to go." I walk around him and start the climb up the hill to the tracks.

"Wait."

I stop and look over my shoulder at him, eyebrows raised.

"Your first lesson is tomorrow morning. Meet me here at nine o'clock."

"Okay," I call back as I continue to climb. "Nine o'clock."

14

The ringtone I have programmed for text messages is so loud I can hear it bleeping inside my car as I race along the last stretch of the bike trail to the parking lot. Then it's quiet. I swing open my car door and my phone jumps to life again, chirping and vibrating on the front passenger's seat of my car, right where I left it. I snatch it up and read the message that appears on the screen. It's from Kyle.

Kyle: Where are you? If you don't text back in 5 min we're leaving.

I scramble my thumbs across the screen and type out a reply.

Me: Sorry. Crazy day. Give me 10 min. I'm on my way.

I hit send and say a silent prayer that Kyle and Haley don't leave. I have a full week added to my life now, and I want these last seven days to be the best they can be. I can't have my best friends pissed at me.

I jam my key into the ignition and twist. The engine coughs and then roars to life and I slam my foot on the gas. The back tires spit up a rooster-tail of gravel behind me as I tear out of the lot.

The drive through town is short, but I spend every minute of it worrying about Kyle and Haley. I've messed up pretty badly with both of them lately. I have to make things right, if they'll let me.

Foster's Ice Cream Parlor sits on the corner of Diablo Road and Main Street, in the center of downtown Carroll Falls. Though I can hardly call it a bustling metropolis, the corner of Main and Hell's Highway is about as close to "downtown" as this town gets. The movie theater across the street from Foster's added three screens last year when they bought out the supermarket, giving them a grand total of six screens. Next door to the theater is a McDonald's and an Applebee's next to that. That's about all the excitement this town can handle. If you want something more, like an actual mall or a Best Buy, you have to drive forty minutes.

But in seven days, I won't be able to pick up and drive wherever I want anymore. In seven days, it will be all Carroll Falls, all the time.

My insides churn, and I lift my foot off the gas slightly. Can I do this? Will I really be able to stay in this town, year after year, for eternity, or at least until another teen dies? Looking at the worn, red-brick buildings in the center of town, I think it's impossible. I can sort of understand why Aaron is so ready to hand the hood and scythe over to me. Forty years stuck in this shit-town must've been miserable for him.

I parallel park in front of Foster's and check the clock on the dashboard. It's 3:10. If I really wanted to, I could change my mind. Right now. Aaron said if I change my mind within these seven days of training, even just a little bit, I will die the next time 3:12 p.m. rolls around, and right now it's only two minutes away.

Something flutters in my peripheral vision and I glance up from the clock. Kyle sits at a high-top table at the window inside Foster's by himself. One of his hands grips the glass dish of a half-eaten chocolate sundae, while the other hand gestures for me to come in and join him.

I guess there was a part of me that hoped the mark would be gone when I saw him again. Maybe I thought whatever had caused it would resolve on its own in the hours between our argument and now, but I was wrong. The mark is still there, displaying that mucky blackness across his face like a war wound.

I smile and wave.

"Hurry," he mouths as he jabs his thumb toward the back of the restaurant, "Haley's in the bathroom."

I don't know why I was thinking I could change my mind. I can't. Not now. I have a puzzle to solve and a suicide to prevent. What kind of a friend would I be if I took the easy way out and just died?

I gather my phone and my purse, paste the smile back on my face, and head into the ice cream shop.

"Hey," I say as I pull back a chair and sit next to him.

"Good of you to show up." He glares at me from either side of his bubbling mark.

"I'm sorry, I just…"

"You don't have to tell me, Libs." He holds a hand up to stop me. "I don't care. But before she gets back," he leans over and whispers to me. His wavy, blond locks swing into his eyes, covering part of his mark. "Haley is pissed. I've never seen her this mad before. She doesn't know you're here. I had to lie to get her to come."

"Aw, really?" I slap my hand against my forehead. "She's that mad? I didn't know that stupid history test meant so much to her."

"Well," he says as he picks at a callous on his thumb. "It's not just the test."

"It's not? What else did I do? Is it about missing the Battle of the Bands?" I say, but he doesn't get a chance to answer. Haley barrels across the crowded restaurant and snatches her bag off the table in front of me, like I'm going to steal it or something.

"What is *she* doing here?" Her eyes focus on Kyle, not even glancing in my direction.

"Hi, Haley," I say to the back of her head, and she twists around to look at me, as if she's just noticing me. Her usually pink, bowed lips press together and her eyes bore into mine. She's more than angry, she's hurt, and I can't think of anything I could have done to hurt her this bad.

"I'm not talking to you," she says. "I'm talking to him."

"Look, I'm sorry about the test. I tried to fix it with Winkler, but you know him. He's an asshole."

"Do you really think this is about that stupid test?" She scoffs and rolls her eyes. "I already talked to Mr. Winkler. He gave me an A."

"He gave you an A?" I can't keep the irritation out of my voice. She's always the teacher's pet. "That's not fair. I deserve an A, too. I studied hard for that test."

"Well, he was sure you cheated for your A. And he has a good track record of As with me."

I take a breath in through my nose and let it out slowly. I'm not going to get mad about this. The test doesn't matter. Passing history doesn't matter. Not even placing in the art show matters. I'm a walking dead girl. What matters is Haley. But if she got an A, then why does she look like she could tear my head off with her teeth and feed it to starving puppies?

"If it's not about the test, then what's wrong?"

"If you don't know, then I'm not telling you. You can figure it out." She looks back at Kyle. "I'll see you later, Kyle. I'm not going to stay here with her. I'm walking home." She whips around and her curly ponytail bounces as she stomps away.

"What is her problem?" I say to Kyle. He twirls his spoon in his hand and starts to say something, but Haley spins around and charges back to the table.

"And, one more thing…" Her hands are shaking balled fists at her sides. "I thought we were best friends. I thought we told each other everything. I told you everything…everything." She gives me a look, and I know exactly what she means by "everything." "How could you not tell me, Libbi?"

"Tell you what?" I really don't know what "everything" of mine I should have told her, but if she thinks it's the "everything" she shared with me, I haven't even come close.

"You know what." She takes off again, and this time she storms out the door.

Six months ago, Haley lost her virginity to her boyfriend, Mike. He ended up dumping her two months later, but that night she texted me almost as soon as it happened and then came right over to my house. We ignored Max's incessant knocks at my door and stayed up all night, stuffing our faces with ice cream and chips, while she filled me in on every disgusting, but exciting, detail. She never told Kyle any of it. She said he would find Mike and kill him if he knew. I'd laughed at that then, but now, with that gaping mark across Kyle's face, I sort of wonder if she was right.

I don't know what she heard, but if Haley's pissed because she thinks I lost my virginity without telling her about it, she got some seriously bad info. I couldn't even think about kissing Aaron without feeling like I was going to throw up.

"Do you know what she's talking about?" I ask Kyle. He shakes his head and then stands up. His drumsticks are in his hand before I even notice him reaching for them. "Yes, you do. She's your twin sister. You have to know."

"I know she's mad about something other than the test," he says without meeting my eyes. He taps a quick rhythm on the table. "I should go after her. I don't want her walking home alone. There are crazy people out there."

Travis and Scott pop into my mind and I shake my head to get rid of the terrible image. Kyle's right. Haley shouldn't walk home alone. Not with people like that around.

"Wait, I'll come with you," I say as I throw my purse over my shoulder.

"No, Libbi." He places a hand on my arm and pushes me back in my seat. The black stuff inside of his mark bubbles like it did when he was angry with me. Maybe he still is. "Let me handle it. She needs time to cool down. If you come, you'll just make it worse."

"Okay," I say. What else can I say? Haley doesn't even want to tell me why she's mad. "I'll text you later. Okay?"

"If you remember," he says, and then he pushes through the crowded store. The front door bangs against the wall when he barrels through it. And I'm alone.

What the hell was that? I almost follow him anyway, despite the warning to give Haley some space, but decide not to. It might make him angrier than he already is. The more pissed they are at me, the lower my chances are of fixing Kyle's mark. I only have seven days to figure all of this out. I can't afford to make things more difficult for myself than they already are.

I weave my way through the tables to the counter. I planned on eating a Chocolate Decadence sundae this afternoon when I thought I was going to die. Even though it won't be my last meal, I still want that sundae. Screw the carbs. I order a large Chocolate Decadence sundae with extra hot fudge, to go.

As I turn, bag and change in hand, I glimpse Mrs. Lutz strolling by the front window of the ice cream shop. Her broad shoulders sag with the weight of the bags dangling from her hands. Her round face drips with sweat, but I can still see the thin, black line of the mark cutting through her soul.

Aaron said she was marked when she unknowingly helped someone change the Death Plan. It doesn't seem fair for her to get a mark when she didn't even know what she was doing. It's almost as unfair as marking someone for committing suicide.

Who makes these stupid rules, anyway? Is it that guy Abaddon Aaron keeps talking about? It's obviously not Aaron. He was almost in tears when he talked about Mrs. Lutz and her mark.

Wait. Before her perfume forced me to leave the computer lab, Mrs. Lutz said she knew Aaron before he disappeared. She said he would never do what they say he did. But Aaron admitted to me at Jumpers' Bridge that he's a murderer.

Did Mrs. Lutz help Aaron kill someone without realizing it? Is that why she's marked? If so, no wonder he got all defensive when I asked him about her. He's the reason she's marked. He's the reason Mrs. Lutz may be doomed to Hell.

I have to talk to her.

I sprint across the shop to the front door and slam it open, almost smacking a little boy with the metal handle.

"Mrs. Lutz!" I call as I run down the street after her. She stops. The bags in her hands swing when she spins around to see who's called her name.

"Mrs. Lutz," I say again and wave. "Wait a minute."

She transfers her bags to one hand, shades her eyes with the other, and squints. When I'm close enough for her to see me, she drops her hand from her forehead and smiles. Though I probably shouldn't call it a smile, it's more of a grimace.

"Libbi?" She takes a few steps toward me. The breeze lifts her heavily hair-sprayed bangs in one stiff piece.

"Hi, Mrs. Lutz." I clear my throat. "Are you in a hurry?"

"I was on my way home, actually." Her eyebrows wrinkle together in the middle. "Why? Wasn't one joke enough?"

"What?" I say, but then I remember. When I first asked her about Aaron, she thought I was messing with her. "I wasn't joking the other day. I really do want to know about Aaron. Do you have a minute to talk?"

She studies me for a few seconds and then purses her lips.

"I really need to get home," she says. "Maybe another time."

"Please?" I dangle my Foster's bag in front of her. "I'll buy you ice cream…"

Her dark brown eyes narrow as she considers my offer. "Tempting, but honestly, I don't know what I could tell you." Her gaze slips from me to the sidewalk at her feet. "I don't know much."

"Maybe. But you knew him, right?"

"Yeah." She nods.

"Then that's all I need."

"And this isn't some strange joke?"

"I wouldn't know how to joke about this, Mrs. Lutz. I don't know anything about him."

"Then why did you run out of the computer lab the other day?" She tilts her head knowingly. "Running off to tell your friends how you pulled one over on me, I imagine."

"No. That's not it." How can I explain my reaction to her perfume without hurting her feelings? "It was my asthma. I wasn't running from you. I swear." I hold my hand up in front of me in a pledge. "Please, come back to Foster's with me. I promise, I'm not messing with you."

She scrutinizes me for what feels like forever and I think she's about to refuse again, but she surprises me.

"Oh, all right. I guess I could use a scoop of mint chocolate chip. I've had a rough day." She relaxes her shoulders and her face softens into a real smile, not the grimace she gave me before. For someone about as old as my grandma, she's actually quite pretty when she smiles.

15

"So, why are you so interested in Aaron Shepherd?"
Mrs. Lutz asks as she settles into the same window
seat Kyle had occupied.

I take a bite of my sundae. I have to think fast. If I say
something wrong, she'll probably grab her ice cream—glass
and all—and bolt out the door faster than Max bolts from a dark
room.

"A girl mentioned his name in class," I say after the ice
cream in my mouth melts and I have no choice but to swallow
and answer. "I asked who she was talking about and the teacher
told me to look it up."

"Did you find anything?"

"I found an article in the library about him, but that asthma
attack made it impossible for me to stay in there and read it. Dust
allergy..." Mrs. Lutz doesn't need to know it was her perfume
that set it off. "Um...that's why I came into the computer lab.
I wanted to Google him. But the asthma wouldn't settle down
and I had to get outside. So I still don't know anything about
him. But I thought, since you knew him, you might have more
information than Google or an old newspaper anyway."

That sounds good to me. It must sound good to Mrs. Lutz
too, because she nods and digs her spoon into her ice cream. Her
soul shimmers around her like glowing cellophane, but the thin
black line of her mark still cuts her face in two. What did she do
to deserve that? I wish I could just ask her, but I can't. It will take
finesse to get that info out of her.

"You're right." She talks around the glob of green ice cream in her mouth. "Those newspapers are full of lies. Which article did you find?"

"I only read the headline, but it said something like 'Teen Murderer Disappears'."

Mrs. Lutz drops her spoon, and it clinks against the glass dish. "See? Lies. I know for a fact Aaron didn't kill anyone."

I would disagree with her, given the confession Aaron gave me a few hours ago, but it's probably best if I keep that to myself.

"Really?" I say instead. I lean in and fold my hands on the table in front of me. "What do you know about it?"

"I just know he didn't do it." Fear flashes across her face, and then her lips form a thin, determined line. I can almost see the curtains behind her eyes swinging closed. Stupid. I knew coming at her directly wouldn't work. She's too guarded. I need a different approach. Now. Before I lose her.

"Okay, Aaron didn't do it. But who was he accused of killing?"

Mrs. Lutz props her elbows on the table and leans toward me. I take a bite of my Chocolate Decadence sundae and gooey, hot-fudge goodness coats my mouth.

"He was *accused* of killing his mother and stepfather," she says. "The town gossips say he bludgeoned them to death in front of his little sister. They say that witnessing the murders drove poor Sara insane. More lies, of course."

Now I remember why Aaron's name sounded familiar to me. A few years ago, I went to a sleepover with Haley and a few other girls in our class. True to preteen form, we spent half the night sitting in a tight circle on our sleeping bags telling scary stories.

We all were supposed to tell one. I made mine up as I went—something about a babysitter and a one-eyed killer with hooks for hands—but Salma Byrd (this was before she was too cool to talk to us) told the scariest story of all. It was the scariest because it was true and it happened in Carroll Falls. She knew it was true because her Grandpop told her it was and to our twelve-year-old minds, that was all the proof we needed.

I don't remember the details of Salma's story, but what I do remember seems far-fetched now. She said Aaron killed his parents because they made him eat broccoli and he hated broccoli, and her description of the murders was chock full of unrealistic gore, of course. But I definitely remember that his little sister watched the murders and went crazy. And I remember the song.

After the story was over, Salma sang a song that went along with the story. I remember the last creepy lines as if she were whispering them in my ear now:

Some say he still roams Carroll Falls, even if he has departed.
Looking in windows for his sister, hoping to finish what he started.

For a month after that party, I slept with my closet light on and my shades drawn tight, convinced the boy in the story would look in my window and mistake me for his sister.

It's sort of funny now. Aaron does still roam Carroll Falls, but not for the reasons the song says. Sometimes, I guess, the truth really is stranger than fiction.

"Oh, yeah," I say, nodding. "I've heard that story. Seriously creepy. But if it isn't true, then what happened?"

"I don't know much." Mrs. Lutz shrugs as she pushes a chunk of chocolate around the bottom of her bowl with her spoon. "All I can say is I knew Aaron and his family. And from what I knew of them, Aaron didn't kill anyone. It's a lie."

Ugh. We're back to that again? How can I get her to stop saying "It's all a lie" and "Aaron didn't kill anyone" and start really talking?

"You knew his family? How did you know them?"

"I grew up next door to the Shepherds. Actually, I still own that old house. I couldn't bear to sell it." Mrs. Lutz wipes her mouth with a paper napkin and then stuffs it in her empty dish. "Aaron was my first boyfriend, you know. He was my first kiss."

I almost choke on my ice cream. Aaron dated Mrs. Lutz? And he kissed her? Ew. He's so hot and she's so...old. And well, she may be a little pretty when she smiles, but even without the crack in her soul, she's what my grandma calls a "handsome woman." I swallow my ice cream down and pray Mrs. Lutz didn't notice my instant reaction.

"It's okay," she says and actually chuckles. So much for not noticing. "I imagine it's hard for you to picture me as a young girl, but I was actually a bit of a hottie back then. I had quite the pair of…" She holds her hands out in front of her chest and winks. "Well, you know."

All I can do is nod. I'm afraid that no matter what I say, I'll jam my foot in my mouth the moment the words leave my lips. I clear my throat and take a few sips of soda before I continue.

"So, what do you know about the murders, Mrs. Lutz?" I say. "The real story."

"My father was the sheriff at the time, so I heard bits and pieces from him." She studies her folded hands. "He said some partiers found Mr. Shepherd's body around two that night. On the rocks under Carroll Falls Bridge. Almost every bone in Mr. Shepherd's body was broken. At first, my father thought he was just another Jumpers' Bridge suicide, until he went to their house to break the news to Mrs. Shepherd. That's when he found her, beaten and dead, on their living room floor."

Chill bumps raise on Mrs. Lutz's bear arms and she slides her hands up and down over them. I'm actually a little hot with the sun beating on us through the window, but I have a feeling it's not the temperature that's giving Mrs. Lutz gooseflesh.

"My father found Sara curled up in the hallway closet, muttering to herself. He could hardly understand her, but he was able to make out two things: 'Aaron did it' and 'I'm so scared.'"

"How old was Sara when this happened?" I say as I cross my arms over my middle and rub away my own chill bumps.

"Eight. Maybe nine."

Max's age.

"I have to tell you," I say with a nervous laugh. "You're doing a terrible job of convincing me that story is a lie. Honestly, it sounds like an open and shut case to me."

Mrs. Lutz flinches before she says, "I know it sounds bad, but you didn't know them. You didn't know *him*."

"That may be true." I stir the remaining ice cream in the bottom of the dish and hope Mrs. Lutz didn't hear the lie in my voice. "But what's there to know that would make that sound any better?"

"Well, first of all, Aaron could never have done something like that. Ever. I am so tired of the gossips in this town painting him as a monster. He wasn't a monster. He was kind and thoughtful and always did what he thought was right." Her voice trails off as she gazes at her hands. She clears her throat. "And second, Sara didn't go crazy. She may be a touch eccentric, but not crazy. She was always a quiet girl, so when she lost both her parents and her half-brother, she withdrew into herself and shut out the rest of the world for a while." Mrs. Lutz meets my eyes for the first time since she started telling this story. "You know, you'd probably like her, Libbi. She's an incredibly talented artist, just like you. One of her paintings hangs above the librarian's desk in the school library."

"The one with the apples?" I ask, flabbergasted. "Aaron's sister did that? I love that painting. It's so raw. So emotional."

Mrs. Lutz nods and watches me closely. "Sara may be a little socially awkward, but she can certainly communicate with a paintbrush."

"Ms. Weese said that was painted by a local artist. Does that mean Sara's still in town?" I ask, more shocked than I probably should be.

"Yeah. Well, sort of. She lives about a mile outside of town with a menagerie of animals." Mrs. Lutz smiles fondly. "I visit her sometimes."

"Is she married? Does she have kids?" My forgotten sundae has melted into ice cream soup in front of me, but I don't care. I've turned into a fangirl.

"No, she lives alone. Well, except for the zoo. Like I said, Sara has always been a bit on the odd side. It just got worse after—well, you know." She twists the rings on her left hand around and around her finger. "But it didn't matter to Aaron if she was strange. He adored her. Even if he *had* killed his mother and stepfather, which he didn't, I know he wouldn't have left Sara alone like that. He loved her too much."

Mrs. Lutz folds her arms over her chest like she's presented an airtight alibi for Aaron.

"I get that he loved his sister." I pause and study her, unsure of how she'll take what I'm about to say. "But I don't understand why you're so convinced Aaron didn't kill them. It seems obvious to me he did it. What makes you so positive he's innocent?"

"I just know." She smiles like that's all she's willing to give me and all I need to know. "So, enough of my story, tell me what gossip you've heard about him. I'm curious to see how the story has changed over the years." She sips her soda and raises her drawn-on eyebrows expectantly.

I'd rather not regurgitate the horrible story Salma told us. Given how adamant Mrs. Lutz is that Aaron's innocent, she probably won't take it well. But her direct stare says she's done talking, and the only way to keep this conversation going is if I spill what I know. So I do.

I tell her the bits of Salma's story that I remember, including the over-the-top gore and the dumb reason she said Aaron did it. The more I say, the more horrified Mrs. Lutz's face becomes. Halfway through my sucky rendition of the eerie song, she raises her hands and tells me to stop.

"That is ridiculous! They have a song about it now? Really?" Mrs. Lutz shakes her head in disgust. "I can't believe it. People who didn't even know him." Her cheeks flush crimson. "And they say he killed his mother and stepfather over broccoli, of all things. Come on! He didn't kill anyone. He wasn't even there—"

Mrs. Lutz stops talking. Her face goes white, making the dark line of her mark stand out in contrast—a jagged, black scar.

"How do you know he wasn't there?" I say, when she doesn't continue.

She bites her lower lip and her fingers spin her rings so fast I'm afraid the friction might start a fire. Then she stops. She stops spinning her rings and biting her lip and she leans close to me. Her face a mere inches from mine. I can smell the sweet mint and chocolate on her breath.

"I can't believe I'm about to do this." She sneaks a peek over her shoulder. "If I tell you something, can you promise to keep it quiet? Because you can't talk about this to anyone, Libbi." She grabs my hand and crushes it in her grip. "No one. Promise me you'll keep this between us. No matter what."

"Yeah, sure," I say, forcing myself not to yank my hand out of her sweaty grasp.

"I need to hear you promise me," she whispers, her eyes glued on mine.

"Okay. I promise. Cross my heart." I draw an X across my chest for good measure.

"Because if you talk, I'll deny everything."

"I won't tell anyone."

She closes her eyes and bows her head, her forehead less than an inch from mine. She stays like that for a while, and I'm about to say something to get her talking again when she finally speaks.

"I know Aaron didn't kill his parents," she says so quietly I struggle to hear her above the noise in the busy ice cream shop. "I was with him the night they were murdered."

"What?" I say so loudly an old woman at the table next to us shoots me a dirty look. I lower my voice. "Why haven't you told anybody?"

"I would have, but Aaron disappeared the next day and I was scared." A tear gathers in the corner of her eye. "I was afraid everyone would think I had something to do with it. I'm still afraid of that."

"But everyone thinks Aaron's a psychopathic killer."

"I know." She glares at me. "Don't you think I know that? I've been listening to that crap for forty years. Not being able to say anything has tortured me. I told myself when he came back I'd back him up. I'd be his alibi, but he never came home. And then I started thinking about Sara and how he'd never leave her alone, and that's when I knew. I knew he was dead, too." The tears spill onto her cheeks and make two tracks in her heavy makeup. "And the thing that scares me the most? I think if I had said something, if I had told my father that Aaron was with me that whole night, he would still be alive today. But Aaron is dead, and it's all my fault."

The tears flow down her face in miniature streams, and she

hiccups a sob. It crosses my mind to pat her shoulder and tell her not to cry, that Aaron is alive and well and waiting at Jumpers' Bridge, but I think better of it.

"You don't know he's dead. And if he *is*, I'm sure it's not your fault," I say. "Why would you think it's your fault?"

"Because my father killed him," she says to her empty ice cream dish. "After he found poor Sara rocking back and forth in the closet next to her mother's body, he did his policeman duties and then he came home. The sun was just starting to peek through the trees when he brought me downstairs and sat me at the kitchen table. He told me about Mr. and Mrs. Shepherd and asked me if I saw or knew anything about it. I said no. My father would have been furious if he knew I'd snuck out of the house to be with Aaron. It never crossed my mind that he'd think Aaron was a killer. How could he think that? Aaron wouldn't have hurt anyone."

I nod in agreement, which is odd since I know what she just said isn't true. Aaron admitted it to me himself at Jumpers' Bridge. But even with his confession fresh in my mind, it's hard for me to see him as a cold-blooded killer.

"After I told him I didn't know anything," Mrs. Lutz continues, "my father stood up, took off his badge, and set it on the table in front of me, and then he left the house. I don't know for sure—Daddy never talked about it again—but I think he went after him. I think he hunted Aaron down, killed him, and hid the body somewhere no one would ever find it. That's why Aaron never came home. He wouldn't leave Sara. It's the only thing that makes any sense." The last few words she speaks are so hushed I have to strain to hear them.

"There could be another reason he didn't come back," I say, and she shoots me a doubtful glance. "Maybe he was afraid, like you were, and ran."

"If there's one thing I know about Aaron Shepherd, it's that he was no coward."

That may be true, but since Aaron is alive and well, I know Mrs. Lutz's father did not kill him. But I can see in the hard set of her eyes that Mrs. Lutz truly believes the opposite. I can understand why she thinks her father killed him. What I don't understand is how he managed to kill his mother and stepfather if Mrs. Lutz was with him the entire night. Something doesn't add up. Either Aaron lied to me about the murders, or I'm missing something crucial.

"You said you were with Aaron all night. What were you guys doing?" I try not to cringe as I say it. I don't want to hear about a make-out session involving Aaron and any other girl, much less Mrs. Lutz.

I expect her to blush, but she doesn't. Instead her eyes widen and her cheeks pale. Her hands shake as she spins her rings a few times, then she straightens her back, laces her fingers together in front of her, and meets my eyes directly.

"That was forty years ago, Libbi. I don't remember." She glares at me. "We weren't killing his parents, if that's what you're thinking."

"I wasn't thinking that at all," I say, glad she can't read minds. "I'm just trying to understand what happened that night." And why she has a mark on her soul with no memory of how it got there.

"It was a long time ago. You can't expect me to remember every detail."

"I don't expect you to remember everything. But how can you be so sure Aaron was innocent when you can't even remember what you did that night?"

She doesn't answer. Her hands curl into meaty, white fists and then relax as her brown eyes narrow down to slits.

"I knew this was a mistake." She bends down and hooks her arms through the handles of her bags. "Forget it. Forget I told you anything. I really need to get home now." She stands, hoisting the bags off the floor. "Thanks for the ice cream."

"Wait." I grab the handle of one of her bags.

"I'm sorry, but I can't help you." She takes a step back. I have to let go of her bag or risk falling flat on my face.

She weaves her way through the crowded tables to the door. A bell tinkles as the door swings open and Mrs. Lutz rushes out, leaving me alone in the ice cream shop.

16

I push the front door closed with my foot. I drop my purse on the table inside the door, the same place I've kept it since I was old enough to carry a purse that didn't have rainbows and princesses on it.

It's strange coming home. I thought I'd never see this place again. This morning, I left knowing I was going to die today. But now, as the door clicks into place behind me, I feel like I'm in a bittersweet dream, buffeted by the soapy scent of lavender.

"Libbi? Is that you?" Mom calls from upstairs.

"Yeah," I say, trying to hold my emotions in check. This morning I thought I'd never hear her voice again, and here she is calling to me from the bathroom.

"I'm in the tub," she says, but the smell of her lavender bubble bath already told me that. "Are you going to be here for dinner tonight? I was thinking of making spaghetti."

"Yeah. Sounds good." I hope she can't hear the tears in my voice. She saw enough crying from me this morning.

I trudge into the living room, plop down on my favorite fluffy chair in the corner, and sigh. It's not even five o'clock and I'm exhausted. My muscles ache and it takes a lot more effort than it should to keep my eyes open. My mother's soft singing drifts down the stairs, soothing and familiar, even if it is a touch off key. I could take a nap while I wait for dinner. I could pull my legs up under me, wrap myself in the quilt hanging over the back of the chair, and sleep.

But I can't. Accepting Aaron's job may have bought me a

seven-day extension of my life, but that doesn't mean I have tons of time. If anything, I feel more short on time than I did when I only had a few hours.

I sit up straight and rub my eyes vigorously with the palms of my hands. I can't sleep now. There's too much to do. In seven days I have to figure out why Haley's pissed at me and make up with her; I need to stop the chain reaction that will eventually lead to Kyle's suicide and heal his mark; and I have to train to be a Reaper and work out the mystery that is Aaron Shepherd. Well, learning Aaron's secrets is something I *want* to do more than I have to do, but still.

Time slips away fast. I can't doze on my favorite chair, listening to my mother's throaty rendition of "Bad Romance." I need to do something.

I reach into my jeans pocket for my cell phone. Kyle said I could text him later, if I remembered. Well, it's later, and there is no way I'm forgetting him this time. My thumbs fly over the screen.

Me: See, I didn't forget. Did u talk to Haley yet? Any idea why she's mad?

I drum my hands on my thighs as I wait for his response. My phone lights up and skitters across the coffee table as it vibrates.

Kyle: She won't talk 2 me about it.

Great. That confirms my suspicion that she thinks I lost my virginity without telling her. Haley tells Kyle everything. The only thing she's ever kept from him was that night with Mike. I back out of my conversation with Kyle and find Haley's number. She may not respond, but I know she'll at least read it if I text her.

Me: I don't know why ur mad, but if u think I hooked up with someone, I haven't. I would tell u. U know that.

Expecting to wait a few minutes while Haley decides if she wants to respond, I sit my phone on my knee. It vibrates within seconds and I jump.

Haley: SRSLY?

A few seconds later, my phone vibrates again.

Haley: Leave me alone, Libbi.
Me: Y? What did I do?

A full five minutes passes before I decide she's not going to respond. Fine. If she wants me to leave her alone, I will. For a little while, anyway. I can't waste my valuable time trying to convince Haley to talk to me when there are other, more important, things to worry about. Like Kyle and his mark.

I exit out of my conversation with Haley and go back to Kyle. My mind goes blank as I stare at the blinking curser. How should I approach this? I'll sound insane if I say, "Hey, Kyle! I noticed you have a black, oozing hole in your face that you can't see. Wanna talk about it?" But I have to do something or my promise to take over for Aaron will be for nothing.

After a few false starts, I type out my message and hit send. It takes a moment, but when it appears on the conversation screen I know it's the best thing—the only thing—I can say.

Me: Can you come to my house later tonight?
We need to talk.

There's no way I can figure out why Kyle wants to commit suicide via text. I need to be with him and talk to him. I need to look in his eyes and hold his hand or hug him, if he needs it. I can't do any of those things with a cellphone and a pair of thumbs.

Buzz, buzz. My phone dances across my thigh.

Kyle: Can't 2nite. Have plans.

"Bullshit!" I say to my phone. I know a cop-out when I read one. He doesn't want to see me. Not that I blame him, I've been pretty awful to him lately, but still.

Me: O rly? What r u doin 2nite?

I'll play along. Sure, I've done a few things to tick him off, but I didn't think it was so bad he'd lie so he didn't have to see me. Maybe if I go along with it I'll get some clue why my best friends are both acting like I'm recruiting child soldiers for the Antichrist and it's Armageddon time.

Kyle: Going out.
Me: Can I come?
Kyle: Can't. Family thing.

"That's complete crap," I tell the empty living room. "The Dennises would invite me."

Me: What about 2mar nite? R u busy?

Kyle: Can't. Have plans. Battery is about to die. Turning off my phone.

My hands fall to my sides. The cell phone slips from my loose fingers and thumps to the floor, but I don't pick it up. What's the point? My friends don't want to talk to me.

What the hell did I do? In all the time I've known the Dennis twins they have never acted like this. Sure, we've had disagreements, arguments, and a few all-out fights, but they usually pass quickly. I can't remember a time when a fight lasted longer than forty-eight hours, and I've always had at least a hint of why we were pissed at each other.

Not so much now. With Kyle, I sort of understand why he's mad, but it's not like him to hold a grudge like this. As for Haley, I'm completely clueless.

I expect stubbornness from Haley. It's actually one of the things I admire about her, when she's not using it against me. But Kyle?

Kyle's the referee. He's usually the one standing between us girls, trying to get us to see the other's point of view. Sure, he gets mad, but when he does, he usually goes off and bangs his drums for a couple of hours and then he's better.

What happened?

17

s I approach the last curve in the tracks, I realize I'm exactly two minutes and thirty-three seconds late. The time-telling power. Aaron must be close if I can tell time this accurately without a watch. I glance down at my hands to see if my skin has the same bright glow it had yesterday when we were together. As if on cue, my arms, hands, and fingers surge with eye-burning light.

Shared light, shared abilities. I can use his powers now, and he can use mine.

The crisscrossed supports of Jumpers' Bridge slowly appear from behind the trees. Aaron leans against a pile of half-rotted railroad ties at the edge of the forest, watching me.

I smile and wave as I step off the tracks and skid down the gravel hill to the grass, but he scowls. What did I do now? Is everyone in my life pissed at me?

"You're late," he says when I'm close enough to hear him.

"Only by a couple of minutes," I say. I tug at the front of my T-shirt and hot air billows my face. I should have worn a tank top. It's only nine o'clock in the morning and sweat already drips down the middle of my back and wets the waistband of my jean shorts.

"Only a couple of minutes?" His frown deepens and he crosses his arms over his chest. "As a Reaper, it's your job to be on time, Libbi."

His icy eyes bore into me and I know I'm supposed to apologize and grovel at his feet or something, but I won't. I'm only a few minutes late. He needs to get over himself.

"Give me a break, Aaron. It's my first day," I say. "And I don't have that handy-dandy time-telling thingy when you're not around."

"I suggest you get a better watch then." He fixes me with a disapproving stare.

"All right, all right." I pull my hair away from my face and off of my neck and twist it into a loose bun. "I'll be on time next time."

"Not just the next time. Every time."

"Fine. Every time," I say. "I'll even be early."

"Good."

He gives me one last glare, pushes away from the wood pile, and marches along the base of the gravel incline, heading toward the bridge. I jog to catch up.

This morning, as I followed the rails to Jumpers' Bridge, I had decided to confront Aaron about Mrs. Lutz and his sister and the murders. Even now, as I watch him angrily swipe the dirt from the seat of his jeans, his brow wrinkled by a deep frown, I repeat the words I plan to use in my head.

I talked to Mrs. Lutz and I know about Sara and the murders. I talked to Mrs. Lutz and I know about Sara and the murders.

My lips part, the words ready to spurt from my mouth.

"So, I guess being on time is really important to the job," I say instead, and I don't know why. Maybe it's the tense, angry curve of his lips. Or maybe it's the sadness that pulls at the corners of his eyes. I don't know the reason, but I know I'm not going to bring Mrs. Lutz up today. I've already upset him enough.

"We wouldn't have the power to tell time if being on time wasn't important." He glowers over his shoulder at me and I offer him my sweetest smile in apology. He doesn't smile back, but his frown relaxes, returning his brow to its natural smooth texture. "We need it to keep track of scheduled deaths so we know when to show up."

"Isn't that what that headache is for?" I say.

The railroad cuts a clear passageway through the thick forest and widens into a meadow just before the bridge. The tumbling white water of the falls spills over the lip of the cliff above us, blanketing the field in mist.

"Think of it like this." Aaron moves away from the tracks and follows the line of trees at the edge of the woods. Despite the heat, I shiver when we pass the little tree where Makenna spread out her blanket and Aaron literally scared the Hell out of a rapist. "The headache is the alarm on an alarm clock. It's annoying and will wake you up when you're sleeping. But our ability to tell time is the clock itself. An alarm can be helpful, but you need a clock to plan ahead."

"Okay," I say. "But why? What does it matter if I plan ahead? The headache will warn me when someone's about to die, right? Why can't I wait for the headache and then just show up?"

Aaron stops at a trio of ten-foot-tall boulders at the edge of the woods. They jut out of the ground at all different angles, like gigantic snaggleteeth.

"You could do that, but it's awfully risky. And potentially cruel. A soul can only stay inside of its dead body for a few minutes before it becomes torturous for them. If a Reaper isn't there in time to remove the soul from the body, they won't be able to stand the pain and will try to get out on their own."

"So, they can't get out of their bodies without us?" I say as soft mist swirls between us and wraps a thick band around Aaron's waist.

"No, they can't," he says. "As the pain becomes unbearable, the soul literally rips itself apart trying to escape. Then, all that's left is scraps. The shreds stay close to where the body lands, memories that replay over and over. The smell of the person's perfume or cigars. The sound of their footsteps. But the soul itself is gone, destroyed."

"That's so sad," I whisper, and Aaron nods. "So it's kind of like a ghost?"

"It's exactly like a ghost," he gives me an approving nod. "That's why so many hauntings occur at the scenes of murders and suicides. A murder is an unexpected change in the Death Plan. There is no warning before it happens, no alarm-clock headache. A Reaper might not realize someone is about to commit suicide or murder until it's too late to collect the soul. The victims destroy themselves, trying to escape their bodies and leave nothing but scraps of memories behind. Ghosts." He smiles arrogantly and swings his hair out of his eyes. "But since I took over as Reaper, I haven't missed one."

"Really?" I swipe sweat from my brow. "How do you know when to be there?"

"The mark." He leans against the closest of the three boulders and slips his hands into his pockets. "I can feel when someone gets marked. I follow them, watch them closely, and so far I've always been there to collect the souls when they do whatever it is they're going to do."

"But what about Mrs. Lutz?" I say without thinking. So much for not bringing her name up today. "She doesn't even know she was involved in a murder. Why is she marked?"

I think Aaron cringes, but it's so quick I can't tell for sure. I know he won't look at me, though. He runs his fingers through his hair, keeping his eyes locked on a point over my shoulder. His voice softens and I lean in to hear him over the roar of the waterfall.

"She didn't know what she was doing, but if Margie hadn't helped the killer, the victim wouldn't have died, therefore she was indirectly involved in a murder. And now she's marked."

"That's so unfair." I shake my head to dispel the memory of Mrs. Lutz's mark—the mark Aaron's responsible for—from my mind.

"You're right. It isn't fair. It's the most unfair thing I can think of," Aaron says to his shoes, "but it is what it is and I can't change it. It's already done."

Before I can say anything else about Mrs. Lutz or the murders, Aaron pushes away from the boulder he's been leaning against and closes his eyes. In one swift motion he spins around and steps into the massive rock, like it's some elaborate hologram he can walk through, and disappears.

"Aaron?" I rest my hand on the surface of the boulder where he vanished. It's cool, rough, and definitely solid. A few minutes pass and I'm starting to wonder if he's going to come back when his face, complete with goofball grin, pokes out of the middle of the dark gray stone, inches from my hand. My heart leaps in my chest, but I don't let him see my surprise. I'm getting used to his showing off.

"You know, I'm getting a little sick of these stupid games of yours."

"I'm not playing a game." His knee juts out of the rock followed by the rest of his body, as if he's walking through a wall of smoke instead of solid stone. He stands in the grass next to me and grins. He may say it's not a game, but he sure seems to be enjoying himself.

"If it's not a game, then what do you call it?" I glare at him. "Being an asshole?"

"It's a lesson."

"What?" I gawp at him. "I can't...Do you really expect me to do that? Today?"

"You'll have to learn how first, but yes. You'll need it for your first case."

I gulp. "When's my first case?"

"Tonight."

"Tonight?" My mouth suddenly goes dry and the moisture relocates to my palms.

"Don't worry, Libbi. I'll do most of the hard work this time." He pats my arm reassuringly, but I don't feel any better. I remember how out of place and helpless I felt at Rosie's death, and all I did was stand there and watch.

"Close your eyes," he says.

I give him a little frown and keep my eyes open.

"Stop being hard-headed and just do it," he says. "Before we start walking through boulders, I need to do something. Close your eyes."

"Fine." I close my eyes.

"Now, concentrate on your body." A warm hand presses my shirt against my chest. His fingertips graze bare skin. I hope he can't feel my heart hammering under his palm. "Do you feel anything different?" His voice breaks a little on the last word. I restrain the urge to peek at him.

"Like what?" I frown.

"It kind of feels like a tugging ache. Right here." He pats my chest softly, and my heart decides it would rather live in my throat.

"Like the headache?" My voice sounds almost as squeaky as his did, but he doesn't seem to notice.

"Not really. That comes right before a scheduled death and is much stronger. This is present all the time and it's deeper than the headache. Here, let me try something." He lifts his hand from my chest. "Um, don't punch me, Libbi, but I think I have to touch your skin."

His hand slips under the neck of my T-shirt, and he presses his whole palm against my chest. My eyes pop open and I forget I'm supposed to breathe. Aaron watches me with a strange, almost pained, expression on his face. He swallows and closes his eyes, and I follow his lead.

The skin tingles where he touches me, and the feeling travels to the pit of my stomach. A pinpoint of warmth spreads across my chest and I know it has nothing to do with how nervous I am that he's touching me this way. The burning sensation is coming from his ring. If I open my eyes, I'm sure the thing will be blazing against my skin.

"When you wear the Scythe, you'll be able to use these powers without me. But until then, this will probably be hard for you. You still need to know how to do it, though. So don't get discouraged." The hand he doesn't have pressed a little too close to my boobs slides over mine. "Now, I want you to concentrate on the clock in your head. What time is it? Exactly."

I don't even have to think about it. The answer is in my mind before he finishes the question.

"It's 9:23 and forty-four seconds. Do you want milliseconds too?"

"No, that's good." He squeezes my hand. "Now take that a step further. Imagine you are spinning the hands of the clock forward, but suddenly they stick and no matter how hard you try to move the hands, you can't."

This is much harder to do. I focus on the image of the clock in my head, but it doesn't have hands. My clock is digital. So instead of rotating the hands, I pretend I'm pushing the buttons. On the illuminated face, the seconds become a blur and the minutes flicker. Then the hours change, faster and faster until the glowing red numbers finally stop. I press the buttons of my imaginary clock several times, but the numbers won't change. They're stuck.

"Did it stop?" he asks.

I nod.

"What time did it stop on?"

"On 6:27 and thirty-eight seconds," I say.

"Perfect. You're a natural at this." Another squeeze of the hand. "Now, I want you to look very closely at that clock, Libbi. Do you see anything in the glass?"

The red numbers of the clock in my imagination blur as I focus on the glass surface, searching for some kind of an image. And I see it. The reflection is so clear I don't know how I didn't see it before.

A pale, middle-aged man rocks back and forth on a pink couch with his hand over his heart. Sweat collects on his upper lip and drips from his chin. His lips pull back in a grimace.

"I can see him, Aaron. I think he's having a heart attack."

"Well, not yet. But tonight he will. And he'll die from it at 6:27 and thirty-eight seconds."

"And there's nothing we can do to help him?"

"Yeah. We can be there for him. On time," Aaron says. I can hear the scold in his tone, but I ignore it. "Now, I want you to try this on your own, Libbi. Hold on to that image. Keep it in your mind, no matter what. I'm not going to help you anymore."

He squeezes one last time and lets go of my hand, but keeps his palm and the ring pressed close to my heart. The clock in my imagination fades in brightness and the image of the man in the glass moves in and out of focus. I grind my teeth together and concentrate on the man, willing the picture to come back as clear as it was when Aaron touched me. My fingers ache from squeezing my hands in tight fists and I hear someone grunting. I only vaguely realize the noise is coming from me.

"Can you still see him?" Aaron asks after a few seconds have passed.

"Yeah. Kind of." The picture becomes fuzzy again, and I curse under my breath at Aaron for distracting me.

"Now, tell me his name."

How the hell am I supposed to get his name? I can hardly keep the guy's picture in my head. My fingernails dig into my palms and the image of the man sharpens—bulging eyes, pale skin, shaking hands. I will him to tell me his name. Nothing happens.

I try again, but this time I ask out loud.

"What's your name?" My gritty, strained voice startles me. I sound like I'm hurt or sick with some kind of monkey flu. The image of the man flickers and then fades away to the red numbers on the digital clock. I try to refocus and bring the man back, but I can't. He's gone.

My legs feel like I ran five miles, and I can't catch my breath. I lower myself to the ground and wrap my arms around my knees, huffing and puffing like I'm having an asthma attack. Aaron squats next to me and places his hand on my shoulder.

"His name is Jon Hilkrest." His fingers massage slow, reassuring circles at the base of my neck. A wave of tiny shivers race down my spine. "Don't worry. It gets easier. And with enough practice, when you wear the Scythe, you'll be able to connect to them without even thinking about it."

"Yeah?" I chuckle, but my laugh sounds weak. "I doubt it."

"I don't. Close your eyes again," he says, and this time I do it without hesitating. "Do you feel that tug now?"

Something stirs deep in my chest, but it's not my heart. It's more than that. It throbs and pulls like something living inside of me, struggling to break free. And it hurts, but the pain isn't sharp. It's an ache. A dull, tugging ache. Just like Aaron said.

"What the hell is that?" My eyelids snap open.

"That's the connection to Abaddon." He tilts his head and smiles. I'm glad he's having fun. "That's what the Scythe does. It connects you to him so you have access to the Death Plan. It also gives you the power to connect to souls and remove them from bodies. And when you're good at using it, you'll be able to connect to anyone in town, at any time, and see their scheduled date and time of death. And when the light of a soul starts to fade, you'll know when, how, and where they're going to die." Aaron twists the ring around his thumb. "It's a shame I can't let you wear it. It's stronger when you're wearing it and it would make training a lot easier."

"Why can't I wear it?"

"It won't come off until I know you're ready."

I touch the silver ring. The Scythe. My finger glides over the ice-cold metal, though I can feel Aaron's warm skin on either side of it.

"So how long have you known about me?" I say.

"About you?" His eyes widen. "It's a small town, Libbi. I've known about you for a long time."

"I mean, how long did you know about my death?"

He looks down as he rolls his shoelace between his fingertips. His hair falls forward, partially covering his face. All I see are the soft curves of his lips. I take a mental picture and file it away for later, when I have my sketch pad.

"I knew the details of your death for a month."

"If you knew all about me, why didn't you talk to me sooner?" I say. "Because you really freaked me out."

"I did?" He looks up at me, catching me off guard with the concern in his eyes. "I'm sorry. I can't talk to anyone until twenty-four hours before their scheduled death. I tried to talk to you the night of the art show, but your mom interrupted. And then I got cold feet." He shrugs and looks back down at his laces. "I was going to let you die in the accident on Thursday. I didn't decide to ask you to take the job again until I came to collect your soul. And by then, there wasn't enough time to explain myself. I tried not to seem like a nut job."

"And you thought popping up out of nowhere and following me like a creeper would make you seem like less of a nut job?" I nudge his knee with my elbow and he laughs, a real laugh, no underlying sadness. It's nice.

"I said I tried." He chuckles and his cheeks indent with the hint of dimples. "I guess it didn't work."

"Oh, it worked, all right," I say, holding back a giggle. "I didn't think you were a nut job, I thought you were a crazy stalker."

"I thought I told you—" He leans into me playfully and I sway to the side. "I'm not crazy."

"Says you!" I shove his shoulder as hard as I can with both hands. He tilts over and falls to his side in the grass with a melodramatic huff and groan.

"Why do you always have to hit me?" He rolls onto his back. Grinning, he places his hands behind his head and his T-shirt rides up a few inches, revealing a stripe of his belly. Dark-pink, puckered lines crisscross the skin there, punctuated by small, circular marks.

Scars.

"What happened to you?" I reach over to lift his shirt up, but before I can, he seizes my wrist in a hard grip and pushes it away.

"Nothing." He yanks his shirt down over his belly and quickly sits up.

"That is not nothing." I move to lift his shirt again, but he backs away.

"Look, I'd rather not talk about it, okay?" Aaron folds his arms protectively over his middle. "It's not a big deal."

"It is a big deal. Someone hurt you, Aaron." I scoot closer and tenderly slide my hand around his wrist. "Please, just let me see."

When he doesn't say anything, I gently move his arm away from his middle. Then I move the other one. He watches as I hook the hem of his shirt in my fingertips. His expression is unreadable, a mix between panic and acceptance, as I pull the fabric up.

The scars cover his entire chest and abdomen. Every inch of skin I can see under his shirt is gouged with tough, wrinkled lines. Some of them wrap around his back and some of the small, circular ones form patterns, like bite marks. From something really freaking big.

"Oh God, what happened to you?" I repeat in a hushed voice. "It looks like a dinosaur used you as a chew toy."

My fingers tremble as I trace one long and ugly scar that slices across his ribs, down, down, down to end somewhere below his waistband. When my fingertips reach the portion of the scar just below his bellybutton, Aaron seizes my wrist. I look up into his pain-filled eyes. We're face to face and so close I can feel the heat radiating off of his skin.

Suddenly, I'm more aware of my body than I've ever been in my life. Every nerve ending, every pore and hair follicle. Our faces inch closer and I breathe the same air he exhales. The fear and pain fades and his eyes deepen with intensity and longing.

A tingling wave ripples over my skin as he releases my wrist and glides his fingertips up my arm. He dances them over my collarbone and then cups my chin in his hand and tilts my face up. His thumb gently sweeps my hair away from my lips.

I close my eyes and concentrate. I will not get sick this time. I am ready for this. I want this. My stomach lurches, but it's not the unpleasant, vomit-inducing heave it did before. It's excitement. And anxiety. But mostly excitement.

This is not like the time I kissed Kyle. Kissing Kyle had felt weird and I ended it before it went any further than touching lips. But waiting for Aaron to kiss me is different. I feel a little awkward—mostly because I'm afraid to screw it up—but I don't feel weird. And I know when it happens, when our lips finally touch, I won't stop it.

But they don't touch. Instead, his forehead rests against mine for a moment, and then he sighs and pulls away. I open one eye, and then the other.

Aaron watches me with the same intensity as before, but the longing is gone. In its place is a subtle frown.

"I'm sorry, Aaron. Whatever happened to you, it doesn't...I mean, I don't need to know. Are you okay?"

He blinks a few times and shakes his head.

"Yeah." He gently pushes me away and sits up. "You shouldn't be sorry. You didn't do anything. If anyone is sorry, it should be me. I don't know what came over me just then. That was way out of line."

"No. It's okay. Really." I touch his arm, afraid he might pull away, but he doesn't. "I know you thought I didn't want to last time, but I'm okay with it."

"Well, I'm not." He jumps up from the ground and backs away a few steps, as if I'm the beast that tore him up.

"Why not?" I say. "Did I do something wrong?"

"No. It's not you." He paces in front of me, his hand pressed to his forehead. "There's nothing wrong with you. You're smart and funny and beautiful and so talented. It's Abaddon and the rules and this whole stupid situation that sucks," he says, but all I hear is the word beautiful. He thinks I'm beautiful.

Snap out of it, Libbi. I tell myself. *The guy's a murderer.* But, even as I think it, I'm not so sure. Mrs. Lutz is convinced he's innocent. Maybe those scars came from trying to fight off the real murderer. Maybe Aaron feels responsible because he wasn't able to stop it.

Aaron stops walking and faces me. "I want to kiss you. So much. But I've chosen you as my replacement. That means in less than one week, I have to die. It doesn't matter if I don't really want to. I have no choice in the matter anymore. I made my choice when I saved your life." His intense gaze lowers to the ground. "Even if you really did want to kiss me, Abaddon would not be happy."

My breath catches in my throat. I thought he wanted to die. I thought the whole reason he saved my life was because he wanted to leap off Jumpers' Bridge. He said it was his time.

"But why? Why do you have to die? Why can't we both be Reapers?"

"Forget it. There can only be one Reaper in a territory. Those are the rules." His arm covers his middle for a moment, guarding his scars; then he drops it with a look of defiance. "I don't know what I was thinking when I thought I could kiss you. It was stupid and it won't happen again." He shoves his fists into his pockets and turns to the closest boulder. "We have a lot to cover today. So forget that ever happened and let's get to work walking through this effing rock."

"You can't be serious." He's kidding. He has to be. He just admitted he wants to kiss me, but he can't, and that he doesn't want to die. How can he expect me to learn how to walk through a boulder after that? Not to mention walking through a boulder seems like a lesson for my third or fourth day of training, when I'm more advanced.

"I'm serious. You have to learn this." He pats the rock and raises his eyebrows. So he's not kidding. He's lost his mind.

"Are you insane? Didn't you see what happened to me when I tried to figure out that guy's name? I was a mess."

"Come on, Libbi." He flashes a soft smile that dimples the curve of his cheek, but the sadness has returned to his eyes. "This is a lot easier to do than that was. This power has nothing to do with the Scythe. I'll show you how to do it."

And he does, but it's not easy. I try over and over again, and after smacking my face into that boulder about a hundred times, I know: it's freaking hard.

He keeps saying stuff like "mind over matter" and "you have to believe you can do it." Every time he goes all Yoda on me, I roll my eyes. But eventually, I get it. It turns out that walking through things is the only power out of the dozen Aaron shows me that I'm able to do on my own. I don't know if that makes it easy, but I guess it's easier than the rest.

Aaron's a patient teacher, despite his lecture on being late and the almost f-bomb he dropped right after he almost kissed me. He's willing to repeat something over and over until I get it, without getting frustrated. That's a true gift. My chest swells with pride as he explains the principles of invisibility for the tenth time. I have to repeat it back to him twice before I finally get it. And then Aaron says something about a mirror and I'm completely lost again. I've always been a bit hard-headed.

He figures that little tidbit out when we practice speed.

"This can be dangerous, so don't let go of my hand," Aaron says, and then he takes off running, dragging me with him.

We pick up speed and follow the gentle curves of the cliff, keeping far from the edge. My feet pound the dirt and my ponytail whips wildly as the surrounding scenery blurs into brown, green, and gray stripes.

A half hour of racing up and down the river passes. It seems pretty easy. Easier than walking through that rock did. All I have to do is run. Really, really fast. I don't need him to do that.

I drop his hand.

Big mistake.

I swerve and smash into Aaron's side with so much force he catapults into the air. Dirt and grass kicks up from my feet as I slide to a halt and whip around. He slams to the ground and skids toward the edge of the cliff, feet first, leaving a long drag mark in the dirt. When he finally stops moving, his butt is halfway over the ledge and his legs dangle over the river.

Trembling, Aaron scrambles back from the edge and sits up, breathless.

"Uh, sorry..." I walk up to him slowly. "I thought I could handle it."

He stares between his knees at the rolling white water below. Pale and breathing fast, he rubs the arm I crashed into absentmindedly until the color returns to his cheeks, and he finally speaks.

"When I tell you not to do something, Libbi," he says in a low, controlled voice, "for the love of all that is good and holy, don't do it!" Then he jumps up, dusts the mud and grass off, and we continue training.

The rest of the day goes well, for a stubborn idiot like me. Aaron never mentions my slip up again, thankfully. He doesn't mention his scars or the almost-kiss, either. But just before he closes my car door behind me in the bike trail parking lot, he reminds me how important it is to be punctual.

18

Muse blasts from my car stereo and my seat rumbles with the beat. It's a good song with a killer bass line, but I really shouldn't be listening to music right now. The someone's-about-to-die headache hasn't started yet, but it will soon. And it's probably a little too tongue-in-cheek for a Grim-Reaper-in-training to arrive at a death scene accompanied by a song with the lyrics "give me your heart and your soul" in it. I twist the volume knob all the way down as I turn onto Jon Hilkrest's street.

Aaron told me to meet him outside Jon's apartment at six o'clock. He wants to go over a few things before we go in for Jon's heart attack. That works for me. The more we go over, the better. Aaron may have worked with me all morning and well into the afternoon, but I still feel like I know nothing.

There is so much to know. Too much.

I pull to the curb in front of the apartment building and check the dashboard clock. 5:55. No lecture from Aaron tonight. I'm five minutes early.

The tugging feeling in my head returns, urging me out of the car and into the apartment building. The headache isn't as bad as it was that first night with Rosie. It's more annoying than painful. For now.

I shift into park. Aaron's face appears in the passenger's side window and I scream. He smirks as he melts through the car door and settles his long body in the seat next to me.

"Did I scare you?" He grins like an idiot.

"You can be such a jerk sometimes."

"Sorry," he says through his prankster smile. "Drive around the block."

"Why?" I shift back into drive.

"In a small town like Carroll Falls, you don't want to be seen parked close to every death scene for a week before you disappear yourself. No matter how natural the deaths may be, people will talk." He points to the street he wants me to turn down. Rumor Avenue. Fitting. "Believe me, you don't want gossip like that floating around about you when you can't defend yourself or your family."

"Speaking of families and rumors..." I bite my lower lip. The steering wheel glides under my palms as it returns to center. "I ran into Mrs. Lutz yesterday. We had ice cream together and talked." I glance over at him. "About you."

His lips press together and the muscle in his temple bulges.

"And...?" His lips barely move.

"She says she knows for a fact you didn't kill your mom and stepdad. Which is sort of funny, since you say you did."

His fingertips dig into his jeaned thighs as he glowers out the window. "Margie's always been a sweet person. She doesn't like to think the worst of people." He cocks his head to the right. "Park here, in the grocery store parking lot."

My tires bump over the fluorescent-yellow speed humps. Aaron points to a spot near the back corner of the lot, and I head in that direction.

"Maybe. But she says she was with you all night that night." I pull my car into the parking space nose-first and cut off the engine. "I don't think she's lying. I mean, what would she have to gain from that? But why would you lie and say you did something so awful if you didn't do it? None of it makes sense."

"I thought I told you in the library to drop this stuff, Libbi."

"I thought I told you 'fat chance,' Aaron."

Aaron snorts and shakes his head. "You really are stubborn, aren't you?"

"The stubborn-est."

He stares at me and I stare right back. If I look away now, I'll lose this battle of wills, but if I hold my ground, I might actually get somewhere with him.

"Fine," he says, after what feels like an eternity of staring into his determined eyes. "It's really none of your business, but if it will help you focus on what's important here, I'll tell you why Margie thinks I'm innocent."

"Really?" I'm not sure if I heard him correctly.

"Yeah." He runs a palm over his face. His hand stops on his chin and he tilts his head, studying me through his bangs. "Under one condition."

"Okay," I say, before he can change his mind and take it back.

"You have to help me with something tomorrow. No questions asked."

"Okay." I suppress the smile that threatens to lift the corners of my mouth. I can't believe I actually won the staring contest. I never win those things. Max holds the undisputed title in our family. "What can I help you with?"

"I'll tell you tomorrow." He runs his fingers through his hair and stares out the window. I wait for him to start talking, but when a full minute passes and he stays silent, I nudge his elbow.

"Aaron, are you going to tell me why Mrs. Lutz thinks you're innocent?"

"Yeah." Aaron massages his temple. "She didn't see me do it. She thinks someone else did it before we got there that night, but..." He swallows. "She's wrong." Aaron sits up straight and turns toward me. His thigh knocks into the gearshift, hard enough to sink into his flesh, but he doesn't seem to notice. "Now, can we drop the subject and concentrate on Jon and the job we have to do? Please?"

"Who does she think killed them?" I ask, and Aaron sighs.

"I only agreed to tell you why she thinks I'm innocent. That's it."

"But you didn't tell me anything," I say.

"No more. We have a job to do and it's getting late." His eyes bore into me and I can almost see the door slam shut behind them. If I couldn't sense how hard it was for him to say what he already said, I'd feel cheated, because he's done talking.

"Are you nervous?" he says. It's an obvious change of subject, but I'll play along. I'll let him win the battle, this time.

"A little," I say with a shrug. What I feel like saying is: Hells-to-the-yes, I'm nervous. Are you freaking kidding? But I don't want Aaron to lose confidence in me.

"Good. You should be nervous, but not too nervous." He winks and pats my knee. I must not look as stoic as I think I do because he says, "It'll be okay, Libbi. I'm sure you'll do fine."

"Yeah, of course I will." I swallow the bucket of sand in my mouth and give him my bravest smile.

"There are a few things we need to go over before we go in. You know, rules and stuff," he says. "First, there are a few powers that can't be used without an actual soul to practice on, so some of this stuff will be brand new to you. And since this is your first time, I'm not going to let you try anything—not even what we practiced today—unless I'm touching you and walking you through it, step by step. Second, when I touch you, Jon will not be able to hear the conversation between the two of us. He will only hear what is said to him directly. That way I can instruct you without him hearing. Just remember, if you have anything to say that you don't want Jon to hear, you have to touch me. Okay?"

"Okay."

The dull, pulling headache suddenly leaps from annoying to crushing in less than ten seconds, and I squeeze my eyes closed and massage my temples.

"I think we're running out of time, Aaron," I say, keeping my eyes shut. "We need to get moving." I swing my door open, jump out, and look back in the window at Aaron. He hasn't opened his door yet. "What are you waiting for? Let's go."

***

I step on the jack-o'-lantern doormat in front of Jon's apartment door, and it lets out a howl of terror. A little early for Halloween, isn't it? Or maybe Mr. Hilkrest is a lot late bringing the mat back in. Who knows?

"Jon isn't ready to go, like Rosie was," Aaron whispers. "So I don't think it would comfort him to see us, no matter who we look like."

"How do you know he isn't ready to go? I thought you said we can't read minds?"

"We can't, technically. But for about an hour before they die, we get a sense of their emotional state, if we don't let our own emotions get in the way. It gives us a better idea of what we're walking into. Oh, and if they think something directly at us, we can hear it as if they're talking out loud."

"Oh," I say. That explains why I heard Rosie's voice in my head that first night. "Are you going to teach me how to do that? How to sense emotions?"

"Yeah, of course. But one thing at a time." He grabs my hand and holds it in both of his. "First, we need to become invisible to Jon. If he sees us now, he'll panic. We don't want him to panic."

Aaron reviews how to become invisible to the almost-dead, and with him holding my hand, I'm able to do it. It's a lot easier for me than it was this morning, and so is walking through the door. I don't even hesitate when we step through the closed apartment door together. And I meet no resistance, like walking through a cool curtain of smoke.

The reek of spilled beer and stale cigarettes smacks me on the other side. Aaron leads me down a narrow hall and we pass a tiny kitchenette with dirty dishes stacked on every inch of counter space. One look around the cluttered living room—piles and piles of dirty laundry, old newspapers, all manner of holiday decorations, and empty boxes of take-out—and I can guess Jon wasn't trying to get a head-start on Halloween this year with his doormat. That rug has probably been there for years.

Mr. Hilkrest sits in the center of the mess, rocking back and forth on the same pink couch I saw in my clock vision. The same hand clutches his chest and the same grimace distorts his face. The light of his soul is almost as dim as mine when I'm not sharing Aaron's brightness.

Hand in hand, Aaron and I enter the room like Hansel and

Gretel entering the dark, scary forest. We stop in front of Jon and block the TV, but he doesn't care. We're invisible to him.

A framed photo of a woman with her arms around a laughing toddler sits on the table next to him. Their eyes are identical to Jon's, close-set and dark brown. On the table in front of the picture is a cream-colored telephone with a long, curly cord.

Jon hisses air between his teeth and rubs his chest with his closed fist. His other hand reaches for the phone, but then he stops. He eyes the phone like it's untrustworthy and then pulls his hand back into his lap.

"Why won't he call someone?" I ask Aaron.

"Who knows?" Aaron shrugs. "Maybe he thinks he has indigestion and it will go away."

I want to grab the phone and dial 911 for Jon. My hand darts forward and Aaron smacks it back.

"We can't, Libbi. Even if you could call, they wouldn't get here in time. This death is impossible to change," he says. "It's scheduled. It's his time. We have to let him go. It's our job."

"Ugh!" My hand flaps down to my side. "I hate this!"

"Tell me about it."

I remember the time I called Aaron supernatural and all-powerful. He scoffed at me then, but now as we stand in front of Jon—watching him struggle, watching him die—I know why. I've never felt more powerless in my entire life.

"And we can't do anything to help him?" I say.

"Well, we can do this."

Aaron places his free hand on Jon's arm and the man stops rubbing his chest with his fist and smiles. His shoulders sag and his eyelids droop to half-mast as he slumps in his seat like a drunken wino.

"What did you do to him?" I ask.

"I just relaxed him. You should remember. I did it to you that day in the library." He grins over his shoulder at me. "You told me never to do it again."

My eyes dart back and forth between Aaron and Jon. Drool stretches from Jon's bottom lip and pools on his food-stained sweatshirt. "Oh God. I didn't look like that, did I?"

"No. I gave him a much stronger dose than I gave you."

Aaron takes a step away from Jon and pushes me forward. He positions me directly in front of the half-conscious man. My knees graze his knees and my heart races.

I can't help but shiver when Aaron places my shaky hand on Jon's shoulder. I'm touching a dying man. My stomach lurches, and I can't tell if it's from nerves or because I'm a little freaked out. If Aaron hadn't have saved my life, I would have been on the receiving end of this process. Aaron would have done this to me to calm me before I died.

Aaron spends the next couple of minutes teaching me how to relax someone with my touch. Not an easy task for someone as far from relaxed as I am. That power may come in handy for Aaron, but I don't think I'll ever use it. It seems wrong to mess with someone like that, whether they're about to die or not.

I know the moment Jon dies. The dim light of his soul surges for a brief moment and then it collapses in, toward the center of his body. His chest stops heaving and his head hangs limp. His soul goes dark.

The clock in my head says it's 6:27 p.m. Right on schedule.

"It's over," Aaron says, rubbing his hands together. "And now it's time for us to step in."

"What do we do now?" I ask.

"First, we put a mirror up before we let him see us," Aaron says. Great. There goes that mirror stuff again. I give him a "WTF?" look, and he smirks and continues. "When Jon looks at us through the mirror, he won't see you and me. He'll see the reflection of whomever he wants to see on the other side. We won't know who he sees until he calls us by name, so I'd try to stay neutral."

"More tricks?" I frown. "Why not just be honest with him?"

Aaron heaves a big sigh and returns my frown.

"When you're a Reaper, you can do whatever you want. But I think people respond better to the shock of being dead when they're greeted by someone they know and expect to see. The mirror does that for them. It makes it easier." He glances at Jon's limp body on the couch. "And there are fewer runners that way."

"Runners?"

"A soul that tries to run away once I get them out of their body. The runners are usually people who are surprised they're dead and aren't ready to go, like Mr. Jon Hilkrest here." Aaron tilts his head toward Jon. "I always catch them, but why waste time chasing after a soul when you could use something as simple as a mirror to keep them calm?"

He has a point. I had wondered why Rosie kept calling Aaron "Bruce" and me "Kate" that night. Now I know why. Aaron must have put a mirror in front of us.

"I'll let you try to place your own mirror," Aaron continues. "But if you take too long, I'll have to step in. Now that Jon's body is dead, we don't have much time to mess around with this. We still need to remove his soul, before it gets painful for him."

Aaron explains how to place the mirror, and after a few attempts I think I get it, but there's no way to tell for sure. The only person the mirror will work on is the person it's set to reflect. The real test will be when I allow Jon to see me.

But first, we need to get him out of his body. My heart and my throat switch places. This morning, Aaron said removing the soul is the most dangerous part of the job. If it's not done right, the soul could be destroyed. Aaron made it look so simple with Rosie, but he's been doing this forever. I doubt I can do it with even half of his grace.

"This part is so important and dangerous, I think I'll do it myself this time," Aaron says. My taut neck and shoulder muscles instantly loosen. "I'll talk you through everything I do, step by step, and you can do it the next time. Okay?"

"Good! Okay," I say with a little too much enthusiasm. I smooth my shirt down and clear my throat. "I mean, that'll be fine."

Aaron slides his hands around Jon's hands without moving them and the Scythe instantly blasts to life. It throws off sparks and tendrils of smoke that wrap around Jon's wrist.

Aaron talks me through every detail of removing a soul, from how to us the Scythe to connect to the soul, to how to separate it from the body. And as the youthful soul of Jon Hilkrest stands up out of his aged, dead body, Aaron tells me to remove my invisibility so Jon can see me.

"Mom?" Jon's eyes fix on me. My mirror works. Okay. I can do this.

I nod slowly, fighting an inappropriate grin.

"What are you doing here?" Jon asks me. "You're dead. Am I dreaming? What's happening?"

I twist the hem of my shirt and bite my lower lip. I have no idea what to say to him. Anything I say could send him running.

"You've had a heart attack, Jon." Aaron answers and I shoot him a grateful glance. "You're dead now too. Just like your mother."

"Uncle Marty? Is that you?"

Aaron doesn't confirm or deny anything. He just stands there, all creepy, staring at Jon with his hands in his pockets. No wonder Aaron has runners. He seriously needs to work on his people skills.

"That's right, Jon," I say. "You're dead, but that's not a bad thing. It just means you get to spend time with us now." I pat Jon's ice-cold, glowing arm like my mom would do. He smiles and then I add, "We've missed you."

Jon's ghostly eyes shimmer with tears. He opens his arms to me, expecting a hug.

"I've missed you so much, Momma," he says and I take a step back. This is getting a little too weird for me. Maybe Aaron was onto something with his standoffish approach.

"Okay, Jon." Aaron steps between us, breaking the bizarre, fake mother/son moment. "We have to go now. We have somewhere important to be."

I touch Aaron's wrist so Jon can't hear me when I ask, "Am I going with you this time?"

"Of course." Aaron gives me a little smile. "How else will you know where the Gateway is?"

19

The early summer heat tackles us like a sweaty sumo wrestler as we step through the front door of the air-conditioned foyer to the steaming concrete sidewalk. Sweat instantly springs to my upper lip and armpits. It's even hotter now than it was at Jumpers' Bridge this morning.

Aaron hooks his arm around Jon's elbow and his grip on my hand tightens.

"Keep up with me, Libbi," Aaron says. "And, for the love of Pete, don't let go this time. And don't stop running."

"I wo—" But before I can finish my sentence, Aaron launches us across the lawn and down the street. The houses, trees, and cars smudge into a background of unidentifiable colors and shapes as I run as fast as I can to keep up with him. Jon can't be doing well with this. I've had practice and I can hardly keep up.

I lean forward to peek around Aaron and check on Jon, but he's gone. A long sheet of rippling, brilliant fabric hangs from Aaron's crooked elbow, billowing behind him in the wind.

"Where's Jon?" I yell over the roar of air in my ears. "And what the heck is that thing?"

"Oh," Aaron glances at me and then at the glowing sheet hooked around his other arm. "That's Jon. He doesn't have our speed," Aaron shouts. "Whenever we move too fast for a soul to keep up, it turns into that fabric-looking thing. I don't know why, but it sure makes things a lot easier when they decide to run or fight."

"Do a lot of them fight?" I say, hopeful the wind drowns

out the note of fear in my voice. The closest I've ever come to a physical fight was when Haley slapped me after I called her a bitch once. I can't imagine actually brawling with anyone, much less the disgruntled soul of a dead man.

"Not too many. But if they are going to fight, it's usually at the Gateway."

"Why? What's wrong with the Gateway?"

"You'll see. We're almost there."

Aaron slows our pace and the surrounding streaks and blurs of color take on recognizable shapes again. I see the school and Haley and Kyle's house and then my own house as we zoom by it. And I see cars...below us.

We're flying. We are freaking flying twenty feet off the ground, directly down the center of Hell's Highway. My feet connect with nothing, but Aaron told me to keep running, so I continue to pump my legs. I will not repeat what happened this morning.

Somehow we flew from one side of town to the opposite side in ten minutes. Probably less. I knew we could run super-fast and I saw Aaron floating when he was in his scary Grim-Reaper form, but I didn't realize we could fly like this. It's exhilarating.

I extend my arm out like a wing. The wind catches the cup of my palm and lifts my arm up. When I turn my hand slightly downward, my arm dips and I giggle like Max does when he does the same thing out the car window on long trips.

The wind slows to a light breeze as our feet touch the ground. We stand a few miles outside of town on the graveled shoulder of a sharp curve Mom calls Dead Man's Bend. The dense forest casts the road in soft, green-tinted shadows. A mile north, the forest gives way to rolling hills and farmland. A mile south, the houses on the outskirts of town start to appear. But this curve of Hell's Highway is isolated, encased in thick foliage on all sides.

"This is the northern limit of our territory." Aaron scans the trees and road surrounding us. "This is as far out of town as we can go. And over there"—he points to a small, perfectly round clearing in the underbrush on the other side of the guardrail—"is the Gateway."

"What's going on?" Jon steps out from behind Aaron. Now that he can keep up with us, Jon has graduated from sheet status back to humanoid. His eyes snap back and forth between us. "What are we doing all the way out here?"

"Let's go." Aaron leads Jon and me to the guardrail. He swings one leg over and then the other and jumps down. Jon scrambles after him, but I decide to walk through the barrier. I could use the practice. When all three of us are on the other side, Aaron hooks Jon's elbow, takes my hand again, and heads directly for the circular clearing. The Gateway.

We break through the thick brambles of underbrush and enter the circle. I expect Aaron to stop, or at least slow down, but he doesn't. He barrels straight into the center of the clearing, dragging Jon and me with him. And then the forest disappears. The grass, the trees, the guardrail, the road. All gone.

Blackness surrounds us. But it's not just dark. This blackness is tangible, like a solid wall of oil all around us, like I could scoop up a handful of it and put it in my pocket. I glance over my shoulder. A rectangular doorway floats in the blackness behind us, framing the woods and Diablo Road.

"What's going on? Is this...H-Hell?" Jon breaks the silence. Then he points to something in the distance. "What. Is. That?" The level of awe in his voice rises with each word.

A speck of white light sparkles on the horizon far ahead of us, like a distant star. The tiny light could be hundreds of miles away, but in the almost complete darkness it's like a beacon, guiding us forward. And I really want to go to it, run to it, but I know I can't. Not yet.

Aaron squares his shoulders and faces Jon. He seems taller, broader, and darker, somehow, as if the darkness around us has sucked some of the light from Aaron's soul.

"Jon Robert Hilkrest." Aaron's voice is as deep and official as his scrutinizing stare. "This is your judgment. If your good choices in this life outweigh your bad choices, there's nothing to fear. But if not..."

The dark around us stirs. It bubbles and boils like the goop inside Kyle's mark and emits the foulest odor I've ever smelled in my life: thick and pungent, like blood mixed with burnt bacon and the smell Lulu, my hamster, had when we found her dead under the kitchen sink.

Screaming faces with clawed hands stretch against the surface of the oily blackness, reaching. Muttering voices, all around, grow louder and louder. I struggle to understand what they're saying, but I can't.

Then it all stops.

The three of us stand in the perfect silence, in the dark, with the door to the real world on one side and the distant pinpoint of light on the other. Jon squeezes his eyes closed and whips his head back and forth.

"Everybody makes mistakes." His voice echoes around us. "Nobody's perfect. You can't blame me for that. You can't. You can't blame me."

"It's time." Aaron grasps Jon's upper arm.

Jon snaps his eyes open and gawps at Aaron, his lower lip quivering. Then his eyes narrow and he rips his arm out of Aaron's hand and stumbles back. His head ticks back and forth a few times between Aaron and me before he spins on his heel and sprints for the open doorway back to Carroll Falls.

Aaron reacts instantly. He transforms into Grim-Reaper-Aaron before Jon has a chance to take two steps toward the door. One moment my Aaron stands next to me, and the next he's the tall, faceless figure in the black hood.

He darts after Jon. His tattered robe swells and flaps behind him like black fire. Jon glances back and whimpers, but he doesn't stop. He runs faster. As his silhouette darkens the doorway, Aaron lunges. A swooshing sound slices the air and the business end of the Scythe pierces Jon's back.

Jon's eyes bulge and he cries out in pain as his chest tents forward and his head and feet collapse back. His body bends backward, covering Aaron's blade as if he were made of a thin sheet of silk. The Scythe finishes its long swipe and Aaron swings it up to rest on his bony shoulder. Jon's glowing, sheet-like soul dangles from the tip of the blade like a coat on a particularly lethal coat rack.

"D-did you kill him?" I whisper.

"He's already dead," Grim-Reaper-Aaron growls from the black hole where his face belongs. "I just stopped him from running."

He plucks Jon's soul from the end of the Scythe and holds it at arm's length like it's a dirty rag. Aaron's legs shorten and his body shrinks as he returns to normal. The Scythe folds in on itself, smaller and smaller, and wraps Aaron's thumb with a soft metal-on-metal clang.

Free from the blade, Jon's sheet-like soul ripples and then plumps out. His arms and legs and body reform, and his face becomes recognizable. Aaron holds Jon's arm in a tight grip.

"I guess you ran because you think you won't get to that light in the distance," Aaron says as he spins Jon around and marches him away from the doorway back to Carroll Falls and toward the pinpoint of light. "Well, I can't tell you where you're going, my friend. But I will tell you this: You can't outrun me. I'm not your uncle. I'm Death. And I'm inescapable." Aaron steps in front of him and grips his shoulders. His fingers dig into Jon's ghostly flesh. "Are we clear on that?"

Jon nods.

"Now, you have to do the rest on your own. I can't go with you, and neither can she." Aaron tilts his head in my direction and Jon glances my way, but quickly looks back at Aaron. "But if you decide to run again, I will catch you. And believe me, I won't be nearly as nice the second time. Do you understand?"

Jon nods again and Aaron steps aside. He nudges Jon in the middle of his back and the guy lurches a step or two toward the white light. The blackness stretches out in front of him like a spiraling funhouse tunnel. A very long funhouse tunnel.

"Now walk. Your life choices will be measured as you go. If you can make it to that light"—Aaron points to the distant star—"your life has been mostly good. But...well, I think you can guess what happens if you don't make it to the light."

Jon stares over his shoulder at Aaron with innocent saucer-eyes, as if Aaron has any say in the matter. After a few seconds, Aaron nudges him again.

"Go," he says.

Jon takes one step and then looks back at me.

I don't know Jon. For all I know, he could be a sex-crazed Nazi who enjoys kicking babies and tripping old ladies in his spare time, but when he looks back at me with that petrified-out-of-his-mind look on his face, I feel sorry for him.

"You were awfully rough on him," I say when Aaron rejoins me and I can touch him, ensuring our conversation is private.

"I had to be rough or he would've run again. Or worse, he would've tried to fight."

We watch Jon take a step toward the light and then another. After a few dozen steps without him looking back at us, Aaron's warm hand curls around mine and he gently tugs me away.

"Let's go, Libbi."

"Don't we need to wait until…?" Until what? I have no idea how to finish that sentence.

"We could, but I wouldn't." Aaron's thumb makes small, warm circles over the back of my hand. "There's probably a good reason Jon ran away, and I don't like sticking around for that." He shivers. "It gives me nightmares."

Aaron lets go of my hand and steps through the doorway, out of the darkness and into the clearing on the outskirts of town. Before I follow, I sneak one more peek over my shoulder at Jon. He seems so small, so alone back there. His glowing soul is the only source of light, other than the star in the distance, but that could be hundreds of miles away.

Something huge and black shifts in the darkness between us.

I snap my head forward and leap though the doorway. Before the Gateway slams closed and my feet hit the grass of the clearing, something behind me growls. I hear a nauseating crunch and a squish.

And Jon screams.

20

My legs buckle on impact and I crumple to the ground in the middle of the clearing. Aaron walks over to me as I push myself up off the dirt and scramble backward on all fours. Away from the Gateway. Away from the monster hidden inside. When I'm as far from the center of the clearing as I can get without sitting in the underbrush, I draw my knees to my chest and wrap my arms around my legs, hugging myself.

"I'm so sorry, Libbi." Aaron offers his hand, but I look away from him. "I was hoping your first would be one of the nice ones. Most of them aren't like Jon."

"What the hell was that?" I glare up at him. "I thought you said only marked people get 'the works.' Jon wasn't marked, Aaron. He wasn't marked."

"No, you're right. He wasn't marked," he says with a shake of the head. "But I think you misunderstood me. When I said marked people get 'the works,' I only meant I have to show up as the traditional Grim Reaper for marked people. I don't know why. But I can't predict what the Blackness will do with any of them."

Aaron settles in the grass next to me, pulls his own legs up to his chest, and rests his chin on his knees.

"The Blackness? Is that what you call that…that thing?" I restrain the intense desire to look over my shoulder. It's not behind me. I know it's not. "What did Jon do that was so bad he deserved that?"

Aaron runs a hand over his face and then looks at me with bloodshot eyes. "I don't know. And I don't think I want to know."

I lean my forehead against my knees and watch the patterns of light on my legs change as the trees behind me sway in the breeze.

"I lied to him, you know," I say.

"I know."

"I told him he'd be able to spend time with his mother and uncle now."

"You didn't know it was a lie when you said it. I should have warned you not to say stuff like that."

"And I thought you were being a jerk to him." A humorless laugh escapes me. "Shows how much I know."

"Don't be so hard on yourself, Libbi." Aaron's warm hand rests on my shoulder. "So you made a mistake. It's no big deal. You're still learning. You're bound to make more."

"Yeah, I guess." I hug my legs closer. "It just sucks. I wish all of this was different."

"Me too." Aaron's voice is sad and small. "I can't tell you how much I wish things were different."

I meet his eyes, blue jewels above sleepy, dark smudges. Forty years. He's been doing this crappy job for forty years. And it is crappy, no matter what Aaron said. As I sit at the edge of this clearing with the Gateway and the thing Aaron calls the Blackness twenty feet in front of me, I can't imagine doing this job for forty seconds, much less forty years. I don't blame him for wanting out of it.

"Why have you done it for so long?" I say. "I'm sure there have been plenty of teen deaths over the years. I'm not the first."

Aaron sighs and picks at the grass between us. "Part of it has to do with my commitment and the rules of being a Reaper. Once I committed, I really didn't have a choice anymore. Same as you." Aaron glances up at me. "And I didn't want to die. I wasn't ready."

"But you're ready now?"

"I have to be." He stares straight ahead into the heart of the clearing. I cover Aaron's busy hand and curl my fingers around his. He turns his over so we are palm to palm, weaving our fingers together.

"You shouldn't have to die," I say. "There has to be a way out of this."

"There isn't." His thumb traces a soft line over my skin. "I've spent most of my free time researching every Grim Reaper story and myth I could find. It's mostly useless garbage. But I know that everything Charlotte said during my training has been true, and she said when I choose a replacement I have to die. It's one of Abaddon's rules."

"Did you ever think of running?" I whisper to the dandelion between my feet. "Just crossing the border of your territory and never looking back?"

"Yeah. Once." Aaron shakes his head. "Right after my mother and stepfather died, Sara went to live with our aunt in Harrisburg. I had to see her, you know? To make sure she was okay. To make sure all that had happened wasn't too much for her." The breeze lifts his hair out of his eyes and one tear sneaks down his cheek. Aaron quickly wipes it away.

"Charlotte told me about the invisible force field holding us in town. She said it's impossible to get through and when you get too close it throws you back and stings like hell. But I had to see for myself. For Sara. She needed me. Even if she couldn't see or hear me, I knew if I could get to her I'd be able to help her, somehow." His voice quivers and he clears his throat.

"On a day I knew I didn't have any scheduled deaths, I tried to go see her. But Charlotte never told me Abaddon monitors the force field. And she didn't tell me how furious he'd be if I tried to cross it."

"Who is this Abaddon guy? He sounds like a jerk."

Aaron laughs humorlessly. "Basically, he's my—our—boss. If everything runs smoothly and goes as planned, he doesn't come around. And that's a good thing." Aaron shivers, and his hand slides to his abdomen. "Because, when things don't go as planned...well, he makes the Blackness look like a puppy rolling over for a treat."

I shiver along with Aaron. Anything that makes that monster seem like a huggable pet is something I want to avoid.

"Did Abaddon do that to you, Aaron?" I touch the hand he holds over his middle. "Did he attack you the day you tried to see your sister?"

Aaron grimaces and glances up at the Gateway. Then he turns to me with clenched jaw and hard eyes and nods.

For once, I don't know what to say. Aaron sits with his knees drawn up to his chest and one arm curled around his scarred belly, and I have no words for him. None at all. So I go to him.

I move close to him and wrap my arms around him and hold him as tight as I can, pressing my cheek against his firm shoulder.

"You didn't deserve that," I finally say, but the words seem cheap.

"What I don't understand," Aaron says, "is why. Why did he do it? He kept saying I broke the rules just by *trying* to leave. He said the border's off limits." He meets my eyes and frustration and confusion dances across his face. "But I couldn't get through. No matter how hard I tried, I was stuck in Carroll Falls. Why would he take the time to come here and do that to me if I couldn't even get through? It doesn't make sense."

We sit hand in hand for a while. Neither of us speaks as the sun dips below the canopy of trees. The shadows get darker and longer and creep toward us as the sun sets. A car takes the hairpin curve on Hell's Highway and the headlights skim over the trees above us. I think I hear a hiss and I'm sure something big and black moves in the shadows to my right, but when I look, there's nothing there.

"I'm sorry," Aaron whispers so quietly I would think it was the wind if I didn't know better.

"For what?" I match his hushed tone.

"For tricking you into this."

"It's okay, Aaron." I squeeze his hand. "I would have taken the job anyway."

And that's true. I didn't take the job because of the lies Aaron told to make it sound appealing. I took it to help Kyle.

Aaron in his Grim Reaper get-up is nothing compared to

those screaming faces and that growling, hulking monster in the dark. That's what could be awaiting Kyle. And soon. For what? Suicide? Murder? I don't know, not for sure, but neither of those choices makes any sense to me.

It shouldn't be that way. Kyle shouldn't have to meet Grim-Reaper-Libbi or the creatures in the Gateway. Not Kyle. It's not right. I have to stop it.

"Aaron?" I say, and he startles. He blinks his puffy eyes a few times before focusing on me. "Were you asleep?"

"Um...sorry." He gives me a sheepish grin. "I haven't been sleeping well lately."

"I have to go." I stand and brush the dirt from the seat of my pants. My legs feel numb and tingly so I shake them out.

"I can take you home." Aaron jumps up faster than I do, though he looks exhausted.

"I'd like that." I smile up at him. "But I'm not going home. I'm going to Kyle's."

***

The wind whips through my hair and plasters my clothes against my body. My legs pump and pump, but my feet hit nothing but air. The scenery is too blurry to tell, but I'm sure we're flying again. Aaron has got to teach me that.

The world comes back into focus a block from my house. Aaron slows our pace to a sprint and my feet smack the earth. A moment later, we stop on the sidewalk in front of Haley and Kyle's tiny, white house.

I take a step toward the front door and Aaron grabs me by the arm. He leads me to the far corner of the property and squeezes into a tight space between a tall bush and the neighbor's picket fence, pulling me in behind him.

"What are you doing?" I say. A branch digs into my spine and I wince.

"Hiding you," he says. "If you hadn't noticed, you've been invisible all day. I don't want you to just appear out of thin air in the middle of the street."

"Oh, right."

The crackling sound that accompanies a change in visibility surrounds me, filling my head with thoughts of fire. Of scorched flesh and screaming faces. Of rotting meat and hungry monsters. Of teeth. Of claws. Of the Blackness.

Of Abaddon.

"Libbi?" Aaron caresses my cheek with the back of his hand. "Are you okay?"

"Yeah, I'm fine," I say, but I can't stop the shiver that runs through my body.

"You don't look fine. You're trembling." His hand slides around my shoulder and he pulls me close. I wrap my arms around his middle and run my hand up his back. I can feel the raised lines of his scars through his shirt, but I ignore them. If I think about those scars, or Abaddon's rules and his screwed up idea of punishment, I'll change my mind and have to meet the asshole personally.

I press my cheek to Aaron's chest and breathe in his earthy-floral aroma. How can such a dark scent smell so good, so comforting?

"Are you going to be all right?" He softly strokes my hair.

"I'll be okay…eventually," I whisper.

I take Aaron's hand and lead him out from behind the bush and onto the sidewalk.

"I guess." I turn to face him, but he places a finger against my lips.

"Don't talk to me anymore. I'm still invisible and you have an audience." His eyes dart to the right and I turn to see Ms. Wellings at her front door with one of her many cats making figure eights between her legs. She squints to see me in the low light.

"Hi, Ms. Wellings," I call and raise my hand in greeting. "It's just me, Libbi Piper."

She doesn't smile or wave back. She nods once, nudges her white fluff-ball back with her foot and shuts the front door.

"Crotchety old bitch," I mumble. "That woman has never liked me."

"I should go." Aaron yawns wide. I guess his nap in the clearing next to the Gateway wasn't enough for him. "I'll see you tomorrow, Libbi."

He shakes his head no when I open my mouth to ask him what time.

"She's still watching," he says, and I snap my lips closed and glance over at Ms. Wellings' house. She's peeking through her window blinds. "We can talk tomorrow."

He strolls across the street with his head high and his hands in his pockets. I wait until he reaches the corner before I spin around and head for Kyle's front door. I don't care if he doesn't want to see me. I'm not giving him a choice.

The door swings open a moment after I knock. Dark brown eyes scorch me from under a mop of tight blond curls.

"Hi, Haley," I say.

She looks me up and down and then pushes the door closed in my face. I catch it with my foot and push it back open.

"I know you're mad at me for some reason, and I wish I knew why, but I can't worry about that right now. I need to talk to Kyle. It's really important. I mean life-or-death important."

"He's not here." She tries to close the door again, but my foot is in the way. "Move your foot, Libbi."

"Not until you talk to me." I cross my arms over my chest.

Haley glances over her shoulder. The scent of peppers and onions wafts through the open door and my stomach grumbles. I haven't eaten since breakfast. Dishes clink together as Ms. Lisa hums in the kitchen. The blue glow of the television flickers from the living room. Mr. Andy barks a laugh.

"Fine." Haley stomps past me onto the porch, yanking the front door closed behind her. She stands with her head cocked and her hands on her hips. "What do you want?"

"Where's Kyle?"

"I already told you. He's not here."

"Yeah, but where is he? He won't talk to me or answer my texts or anything."

"Join the club." Her frown deepens into a scowl. "He left with Matt and Tyler a couple of hours ago. I don't know where they went, but ever since Red Motive lost the Battle of the Bands, Kyle's gone out with them every night and he hasn't come home until way after Mom and Dad is asleep." Her lips purse as she scrutinizes me, accuses me. "And he reeks of alcohol and weed."

"What? You think that's my fault?" The pang of hunger in my stomach disappears.

"Yeah, it's your fault."

"I didn't even know he was drinking. How is that my fault?"

"If you don't know, you're a moron."

She shoves me aside and yanks the front door open, but I step in front of her, blocking her way. I have at least fifteen pounds on her, probably twenty. If I have to, I'm not afraid to tackle her.

"Then I'm a moron, Haley, because I don't know." My cheeks flush with heat. "I have no effing clue what you're talking about, actually."

"Oh, yeah? Well, who's this guy Aaron then?"

"What?" My brain does a back flip inside my skull. "What the hell does Aaron have to do with any of this?"

"Is he your boyfriend?" She smirks like she has it all figured out, but she obviously has it all wrong.

"No." I shake my head. "It's not like that."

"Well, Kyle thinks it *is* like that." Haley leans against the porch railing and gazes off in the same direction Aaron went a few minutes ago.

"Even if Aaron was my boyfriend, what does it matter to Kyle? He's supposed to be my friend. Shouldn't he be happy for me?"

Haley swings around and stares at me, eyes wide and mouth gaping.

"Really? Are you that blind?" She shakes her head like I'm the simplest idiot she has ever met. "Do you remember a few months ago, after me and Mike...you know?"

"Yeah?"

"You were complaining that you hadn't even kissed a guy and I suggested you ask Kyle if he'd kiss you—"

"So I would at least know how it felt," I finish for her.

"Yeah, well..." She gazes across the street again. "Kyle put me up to that."

"He did what?" My heart pounds in my ears.

"He asked me to set you up with him." Haley touches her temple. "Honestly, Libbi, I can't believe you had no clue about this. The boy's been drooling over you since the third grade."

"Why?" I sink into the lawn chair next to the door. "I mean, why didn't you tell me?"

"When we were kids, I thought it was gross. You're like a sister and he's my brother, you know?" She shrugs. "But when we got older, Kyle begged me not to say anything. He used the Twin Oath of Secrecy on me. And as he fell deeper and deeper, I thought it was so painfully obvious, I didn't *have* to say anything." Haley meets my eyes. The anger has melted away, and all that's left is sadness. "He would do anything for you, Libbi. Can't you see that? When I was mad about the test, he didn't leave with me, his twin sister. He stayed with you. He walks with you to school. He practically lives at your house, on your front porch, sun or snow. Do you think he does all of that for Max?"

Now that Haley has pointed it out, I can't believe I didn't see it before. I really am blind and a complete and utter idiot. That mark showed up on Kyle's face right after I caught him and Max talking on the porch about Aaron. Jealousy was the beginning of Kyle's suicide chain reaction. How did I not see that?

"I've never thought of him that way." I rest my head in my hands. "And I'm sorry, but I don't think I ever will. He's like a brother to me."

"I know. But I think he hoped one day you'd come around." Haley settles in the lawn chair next to me. "And I always hoped you'd have the decency to break his heart gently."

"I swear I wasn't trying to hurt him, Haley. I didn't know he felt that way." I glance over at her, and she meets my eyes and nods. A huge weight lifts. She believes me. "But it doesn't matter anyway. Aaron's not my boyfriend. So, technically, I haven't broken Kyle's heart."

"Yeah, but you have to tell him how you feel, Libs. Now that you know, you can't string him along anymore. It's cruel."

"I know," I say, though I wonder if stringing him along would mend his heart enough to mend his mark. It would only be for a couple of days, then I'll be a Reaper and disappear and he'll never know the difference. "Just let me handle it. Okay, Haley?"

My phone buzzes in my purse, and I dig it out. It's a call from a number I don't recognize.

"Hello?"

"Libbi? It's Max. Did you forget you're supposed to pick me up tonight?"

"Oh, crap!" I slap my hand to my forehead. "I'm sorry, Max. Are you still at camp?"

"Yeah."

"Okay, I'm on my way. I'll be there in twenty minutes."

As I snap my phone shut, I realize that it will take me a lot longer than twenty minutes to get to the camp. I left my car in the supermarket parking lot, around the corner from Jon's house.

"I'm sorry, Haley. I have to go." I slip my phone back in my purse. "I have to pick Max up from camp."

"It's fine." She smiles. It's a tired smile, but it's still a smile. And it's much more than she would have given me even five minutes ago. "Tell Max I said hi."

"I will," I say as I hop down the front steps.

It's not that far of a walk to the parking lot where my car awaits, but after a day of running around Carroll Falls at supersonic speeds, it feels like forever.

Finally behind the wheel of my jalopy, I relax.

Hell's Highway rolls under my tires. As much as I'd like to avoid that road and what waits at the edge of town, it's the only way to get to Camp Constance. I'm not superstitious enough to drive all the way around town to avoid driving past the Gateway.

I slow my car as I come to the hairpin turn in the road and glance over the guardrail at the clearing in the underbrush. The sun has disappeared and the full moon has just poked its head above the trees. The grass in the clearing shimmers in the silvery light like knives. Like little, metal teeth.

I shake my head and laugh. I've become very good at scaring myself lately.

It's only after I finish the curve and continue down the road another two miles that I realize I wasn't knocked back by the invisible force field holding Aaron in town. It must not work on Reapers-in-training.

21

"This is so disgusting." Max stirs his soggy cereal and then pokes at it with his spoon.

"You know," I say as I shove his Avengers lunchbox into his backpack. "I've heard if you eat that stuff right away, it doesn't get all mushy."

Max gives me a skeptical glance. He swirls the cereal one last time and drops his spoon into the bowl. Gray milk splashes onto the tabletop.

"Can I be done now?"

I peek at the clock on the microwave. We're both ready for school with fifteen minutes to spare. That never happens. I suppose I'm a little eager to get to school and talk to Kyle. Aaron didn't say what time he'd meet me today, but I'm sure he'll pop up at some point and take me away. I need to see Kyle before he does.

"I guess you can be done," I say.

"Yes!" Max scoots his chair out and heads for the living room and the Xbox.

"Hey, wait a second." I tug his sleeve and Max freezes midstride, like he's been zapped by an ice-ray gun. "You fell asleep as soon as I picked you up last night and I haven't seen you all weekend. How was camp?"

"It was awesome!" He unfreezes and beams at me. "There was a bonfire and a lake and Dominick said a sea monster lives at the bottom." The smile drops from his face as he leans toward me and whispers, "I think I saw it."

"Oh, yeah?" I rumple his hair. "Lucky you!"

"I know, right?"

I sit down in the kitchen chair, grab both of his hands and pull him in front of me. He tilts his head with curiosity and my breath hitches in my throat. I'm not going to fall apart like I did with Mom. Big, blubbery sobs would make this worse and scare the kid, so I gulp back the tears and try again.

"Max, I want to apologize for being a jerk and leaving you alone the other night."

"It's okay." Max shrugs and tries to pull his hands out of mine, but I hold them tight.

"It's not okay. I shouldn't have done it and I shouldn't have gotten mad at you for calling Mom. You did the right thing. I was being stupid. And I'm sorry. Do you forgive me?"

"Yeah, of course I forgive you. You're my big sister." He grins and his green eyes sparkle under his flaming-red mop. I kiss his forehead and pull him into a humongous bear hug, rocking him back and forth. I won't get many more of these hugs and I intend to make every one of them count.

"Ugh! Libs! Stop! I can't breathe," he says, but his arms wrap around me nonetheless.

"What can I do to make this up to you?" I say, once I reluctantly let him go.

"Hmm..." He touches a finger to his chin. "Can I take your Alaskan meteorite to school today? I want to show it to Shane."

"You know what?" I slap my knees. "You can take it to school with you every day, if you want. It's yours. I'm giving it to you."

"Really? Your Alaskan meteorite?" His face lifts with joy. "I thought you loved that thing."

"I do, but I want you to have it," I say. It's not like I'll need an Alaskan meteorite once I'm a Reaper. "You can have anything of mine that you want, Max. Anything. Take it all."

"I don't want *all* of your stuff. You have girly things like a Hello Kitty alarm clock and makeup." He frowns. "And bras."

I laugh, but the laughter loosens the tight grip I have on my tears and warmth spreads over my cheeks. My throat becomes thick and my vision clouds. It takes me a minute to choke it all back enough to continue.

"Then don't take that stuff," I say, once I have myself under control again. "But anything else is yours. Okay?"

Max's smile slips away as he studies me. "You're being even weirder than you were last week," he says. The ridge between his eyes deepens.

"No, I'm not." I smooth down my shirt and meet his stare.

"Yes, you are. You're never this nice to me."

I open my mouth to protest then snap it closed. He's right. Even if I've never been outright mean to him, I would never have handed over my prized possessions. Until now. But I'm not about to tell him why.

"Well, it's about time I started. Don't you think?" I grin.

Max doesn't return my smile.

***

The clock over the blackboard must be broken. It feels like only one minute has passed since it said Kyle had ten minutes to get to homeroom, but now the bell is about to ring. Time is cruel like that. It goes faster when you want it to slow down and creeps when you need it to speed up.

Kyle didn't knock on my door this morning to walk me to school. Not a big deal. It is the second to last day of the school year, and Haley told me he was out all night. Whenever Kyle's late for school, his dad drives him, but he usually texts me if that happens. This morning he didn't.

I glance at the door and then at Haley.

"Where is he?" I whisper. The morning announcements end and the PA system gives one final squeal before clicking off.

"He was still in bed when Mom and I left this morning." Haley checks the clock on the wall again and shrugs.

Haley gets to school an hour earlier than us. To me, it wouldn't be worth the early wake-up call to be the vice president of the student council and on the debate team, but Haley doesn't mind. She loves it.

"Did you physically see him in bed?" I say, a note of panic in my voice.

"Well, no," she says, and my stomach lurches. What if I missed it? What if Kyle killed himself without me getting a chance to change his mind? "But I heard him. The boy snores like a pig. Especially when he's drunk." She yanks her history book out of her bag, peels off the cloth book cover, and stacks it on her desk with the rest of her naked textbooks. "Don't worry, Libbi. He has his chem final today. He'll be here."

As if on cue, the door swings open and Kyle stumbles over the threshold. The stuff inside his mark seems blacker than ever as his bloodshot eyes scan the classroom. They lock on me briefly, but he doesn't acknowledge me or Haley. He slogs up to Mr. Winkler's desk, deposits his late note, and slips into his seat at the front of the classroom.

Since we already took our history final, Mr. Winkler uses his last class of the year to regale us with every detail of his trip to Rome last summer. When he starts talking—or should I say spraying—about the fountains, I glance over at Kyle. I expect him to snicker or make a joke about sprinklers, but he doesn't. He keeps his head down on his desk, using the crook of his elbow as a pillow, his back rising and falling rhythmically.

The bell rings and I rush up to his desk. He sits up slowly, wiping the drool from his lower lip with his sleeve. Haley comes up from behind us and parks herself in front of Kyle's desk.

"So good of you to join us, sleepyhead," she says. "Late night?"

"Shut up, Haley." He rolls his eyes and grabs his bag from the floor.

"Good luck, Libs." Haley pats my shoulder before turning to leave. "See you at lunch."

"Hey, Kyle," I say. "Can we talk?"

He mumbles something I can't understand, but it probably has the word no in it because he stands up and pushes by me.

"Wait up!" I jog out the door after him. "I need to talk to you about something."

Kyle tucks his hands in his pockets and turns down the hall.

"Something important."

He picks up his pace and files in with the steady flow of students in the hallway.

"About Aaron."

He stops. The girl following him quickly jumps to the side and barely avoids smacking into his back.

"Jesus Christ! Watch it," she says, but Kyle doesn't pay her any mind. He slowly turns around and looks at me, his brown eyes colder than Aaron's blue-ice-colored eyes have ever been.

"Oh, so you're finally ready to tell me about Aaron, huh?"

"It's not what you think it is, Kyle," I call as I push my way down the hallway to meet him. "He's not my boyfriend."

"Oooohhh…he's not her boyfriend," some kid with a stupid red mohawk says as he walks by us.

"Mind your own business, asshole!" I call after the kid and he raises his middle finger over his shoulder. Classy.

This is not going to work. I can't talk to Kyle here. I grab his arm and yank him out of the middle of the walkway. He lets me lead him down the hall to the janitor's closet. The door eases closed behind us, blocking us from eavesdroppers and the noisy hallway.

The scent of harsh detergents mixed with mold and mildew fills my sinuses. My mind instantly turns to asthma and the location of my inhaler. Then I remember I threw my inhaler away. I don't have asthma anymore.

Kyle studies me, his arms crossed over his chest. He taps his drumsticks impatiently against his shoulder. In the dingy overhead light, his skin appears yellow, sickly. Except for the mark. That's blacker than anything I've ever seen, other than the Blackness itself. I shiver and force that thought out of my mind.

"So," he says. "You wanted to talk? Then talk."

"Haley says you've been out partying every night this weekend," I say.

"Yeah? And?"

"That's not like you."

"How do you know?" He leans against a metal shelf loaded down with bottles of different cleansers. "Maybe it's exactly like me."

"Are you kidding? In fifth grade, you wouldn't drink grape juice because you thought it would make you drunk."

"That was fifth grade." He scowls at the floor. "I'm not a kid anymore, if you haven't noticed."

"Yeah, but Haley also said she thinks she knows why you're partying so much," I say, and his eyes dart up and meet mine. Pink splotches bloom on his cheeks. "But you have it all wrong, Kyle. I'm not dating Aaron."

"Oh, yeah? Then why did you blush like a ripe tomato when I asked you about him?" The ooze inside Kyle's mark bubbles and churns. "And why do you keep blowing me off or forgetting about me? And what about that letter? Max told me you got a love letter. He said you left him alone at the house to go on a date with this guy. Then he said you came back, but left again, and you were gone all night. All night!"

"I know." I shake my head. I didn't realize Max knew I left twice that night. "I've done all of those things. Except it wasn't a love letter, Kyle. And I didn't do any of this because I'm dating Aaron. I can't date him. It's impossible."

"But you want to, don't you? You want to date him." His voice is harsh, but underneath I hear the broken voice of the boy I painted a few months ago. "Maybe I'm trying to forget you. Maybe I'm trying to make you happy by staying out of your life."

His eyes search my face, asking me to tell him he's wrong about me wanting to date Aaron. Begging me to say I want to date him instead. It would be so easy to tell him what he wants to hear. But I can't. He's my friend and I can't lie to him anymore.

"I'm sorry, Kyle," I say. "It's—"

The black stuff pulses inside Kyle's face and I hear a small pop like static. Pencil-thin cracks extend from the ends of the fissure in his soul, like a broken eggshell, and the edges of the mark pull apart, exposing two more inches of black, bubbling sludge.

I'm making it worse. Shit. Telling him the truth isn't healing it; it's making it grow.

"What I mean to say is, it's impossible to date Aaron, when…" I look down at my trembling hands. "I'm in love with you."

Kyle's elbow slips and knocks over one of the bottles on the shelf; it hits a few others, causing a domino effect. He scrambles to grab them before they fall to the floor, and then he sets them all right again. Once everything is back where it belongs, he steps away from the shelf and closer to me. The janitor's closet is too small to back away without causing another avalanche, so I hold my ground.

"Is that true?" Kyle's wide eyes search my face, pausing at my lips far too often. "You're in love with me?"

"Um…yeah," I say and watch his mark closely. The edges haven't started to mend yet, but they haven't grown any farther apart. And the black stuff has stopped boiling. The surface of it settles and becomes as smooth as black glass.

"Do you have any idea how long I've waited for you to say that to me?" He brushes my cheek with the back of his hand and traces my bottom lip with his thumb. I harness my inner actress and stop myself from slapping his hand away.

"I guess as long as I've waited to hear it from you." I curl my hands into fists to stop them from fidgeting.

I can do this. I can pretend I love him for a few days, if it will heal his mark and save him from the Blackness. And I do love him, in a sisterly way, so it's not a complete lie. Still, everything about this feels wrong.

"I love you, Libbi. I love you so much." He steps closer. Joy and pure shock transform his tired features. His chest touches mine and his hand slides around to the small of my back. "I've loved you since the third grade when Todd Lance tripped me and you chased after him with a stick."

Kyle chuckles at the memory then tilts my chin up and leans in. His morning-after breath reeks of stale beer.

I was wrong. I can't do this. I can't kiss Kyle. If the first time I kissed him felt awkward, this will feel a hundred times worse. But if I want to save him, I have to. I have to somehow get through it.

I close my eyes and Aaron's face appears behind my lids. His piercing eyes under disheveled black hair. His stubbly chin punctuated by the bruise I gave him the day we met. I imagine his soft, full lips pressed against mine, dancing in perfect harmony, and the firm warmth of his body as I grip the back of his shirt and pull him against me.

"Wow!" Kyle says when he finally pulls away and I open my eyes.

"Yeah, well." I run a hand through my hair.

"God, Libbi! I can't believe that just happened. I wish I could stay in here and do that all day." Kyle bends down and I stop his lips with my hand. One kiss is enough.

"Aren't you late for your chem final?" I grab his book bag off the floor and push it into his chest, at the same time pushing him away. He takes it and swings it over his shoulder.

"Yeah, I guess." He gives me a little pout and the acid in my stomach churns. "I'll see you after school, though. Right?"

"Well, I'm not sure. I have plans with...my dad...He's picking me up early from school and I don't know when I'll be home." That sounds good. I hope he buys it.

"Your dad? You haven't seen him in months."

"He called me last night and said he wants to talk." I shrug and try to look as surprised by this out-of-character behavior as Kyle. My father hasn't bothered to come see us since he hooked up with his girlfriend months ago. "But I promise to text you as soon as I get home. Okay?"

"Yeah, sure." His eyes dance over my face and a huge grin turns up the corners of his mouth. He bends down and kisses me again. It's quick and spitty, and I've never seen him look so happy in my life. Why do I feel so terrible?

"Oh and one more thing," I say as he turns the doorknob to leave. "Don't tell Haley about us yet. I want to tell her together. You know? I want it to be special."

"Yeah, you're right. She is going to flip a shit when we tell her." He laughs. "She's been saying you don't like me like that for years. She has a humongous I-told-you-so coming her way. When do you want to tell her?"

"How about Saturday night?" I say. "At Foster's."

"Great! Saturday night," he says. "I can't wait."

I leave out that I'll be an invisible Grim Reaper by Saturday afternoon.

22

I wait all day for the familiar, I'm-being-watched feeling that accompanied Aaron's previous visits to school, but it never comes. As the second to last class of the day ends, I decide I have to leave, with or without him. If I show up in last period, Kyle will know I lied to him about seeing my dad today, and I can't risk that.

When no one is looking, I push open one of the side doors and slip out of the building. It's a short dash across the lawn to a strip of woods behind the school. I duck under a tree limb and into the cool shade.

My walk is short, but it's not easy to sneak home without getting caught when your house is directly across the street from the school. After a few detours, I finally sneak in the back door of the house and make my way up to my bedroom to change and wait for Max. Or Aaron. Whoever shows up first.

Ten minutes go by, and I realize I'm aware of exactly how much time has passed, down to the millisecond. We're sharing powers again, which means Aaron's close. The brightness of my soul intensifies and a quiet knock sounds at the door.

I shove my dirty clothes into the hamper and quickly throw my teddy bear under the bed before I say, "You can come in, Aaron."

Aaron melts through the door and his face lifts in a smile when he sees me.

"Thanks for knocking," I say with a matching smile.

"It'd be rude to barge into your bedroom." He moves across

the room toward me, but stops halfway, at my desk. His eyes drift over the drawings I have strewn over the desktop.

Oh God.

Sure, I got rid of my dirty laundry and childish stuffed animal, but I forgot to hide the stack of sketches on my desk.

Aaron touches the one on top, a colored-pencil drawing where I tried and failed to duplicate the unique color of his eyes. His hand drifts to the charcoal sketch of him standing at Jumpers' Bridge, mist wrapping his legs. He lifts one drawing to reveal yet another sketch of him in profile.

There are more sketches of him, but thankfully he stops looking. He turns with the colored-pencil drawing in his hand, his eyes unreadable.

"We should probably go downstairs." I snatch the picture out of his hand and throw it behind my back. "Max will be home soon."

He doesn't say a word as I shuffle him out of my room and down the stairs to the kitchen. I sit at the kitchen table and pretend to tie my shoes. Anything to avoid his eyes for a few seconds. He places his hands on the back of the chair next to me. The muscles in his forearms bulge as he grips the wood, and I resist the urge to run my fingers over the ripples.

He clears his throat and says, "Are you ready to go?"

"It depends." I tug on my laces and sit up straight. "Where are we going?"

"Yesterday, you promised to help me with something. Remember?"

The front door crashes against the table inside the door. Max shuffles over the threshold, his eyes glued to his handheld video game. He drops his book bag on the floor, looks up at me, and yelps in surprise.

"Libbi! What are you doing home?"

"Kraus let us out early."

"You suck! I wish my teachers were that cool." Max plods down the hallway and slumps into the chair Aaron's leaning on. Aaron lets go and steps back against the wall.

"He can't come with us, Libbi," Aaron whispers, though I'm

sure Max can't hear him.

"Look Max, I have to go out for a little bit and you can't come." I grab my purse from the floor at my feet. "I'm going to call Miss Lena and see if she can come babysit for a couple of hours."

"Why? Where are you going?" Max says, then his eyes narrow and he gives me a mischievous little smile. "Are you meeting your dream boyfriend? What's his name again? Aaron?"

"Max!" My whole head feels like it's on fire. "Stop saying he's my boyfriend! Do you have any idea how much trouble your big mouth has caused?" I kick his chair and it scoots back a good foot, but Max giggles.

He wraps his arms around his middle, rubs his back sensually, and makes kissy noises. "Ooooo, Aaron...I wish you would kiss me..."

"Shut up!" I glance at Aaron. His red face and humongous grin is not making this any better.

"What?" Max feigns innocence. "That's what you said last night in your sleep. You were like, 'Oh, Aaron, I don't care about the stupid rules. Kiss me. I really want you to!' It was so gross!"

Aaron's mouth drops open. His eyes dance back and forth between us and then he pushes away from the wall and walks out of the kitchen. At this moment, I would be perfectly happy to melt into the floor and disappear.

"That's not true!" I say, more to Aaron than to Max. "Oh God, Max! Please stop!" But Max continues to make out with himself at the kitchen table. I grab one of his groping hands and pry it from his own back. "You're embarrassing me!"

"Why? It's not like he's here." He stops rubbing his back and frowns. "He's not even real."

"What?" I gawk at him. "What makes you think he's not real?"

Max gives me the same I'm-really-worried-about-you look he gave me this morning when I told him he could have all of my things.

"Today, my friend Sam said his brother saw you talking to yourself last week, right before the accident. Then you fainted.

When you woke up, you told him you were talking to some guy named Aaron. He said you looked like a crazy freak. And when I got my Alaskan meteorite from your room this morning, I saw that letter you said was from Aaron on your dresser. The one that's folded like a flower. It's blank."

"Why were you snooping in my room?" I glare at him.

"Why do you want to kiss an imaginary guy?" He glares back.

"Um, I'm not imaginary." Aaron steps back into the kitchen. His eyes sparkle, even as he glowers at Max. "Libbi was talking to me on the Bluetooth I let her borrow, and I wrote that letter in disappearing ink."

Max's hands fall to his lap. I must have been so distracted by my brother that I missed the crackle of Aaron becoming visible. Since when could he do that without me? I thought he needed to be touching me to use my visibility.

"Aaron...how did you—?" I press my lips together and start again. "What are you doing?"

"You wanted him to stop, right?" Aaron gestures to Max with one hand. "And now he's stopped."

"Oooo...you're not supposed to have boys in the house." Max points at Aaron. "You are so grounded."

"Not if you don't tell Mom." I lean across the table to him. "Aaron was only in the house for a few minutes, anyway. And we're leaving now, so no harm done."

Max narrows his eyes and watches Aaron. The freckles between his eyebrows bunch together.

"Where are you taking her?" He puffs out his chest, my little protector.

"Nowhere. Libbi's driving." Aaron smiles at Max, but I can tell by Max's stern face that he's not impressed. "But I promise to have her back in one piece. I'll even let you punch me in the gut if she's not home before dark. Okay?"

"But you can't tell Mom he was in here, Max," I say. "I'll take my Alaskan meteorite back if you tell her."

"No!" Max says. "You said I could have it."

"And you can, if you promise to keep your mouth shut."

"And I get to punch him if he hurts you," Max says.

"Absolutely," Aaron says.

"Fine." Max slumps in his chair. "I won't tell."

"Good." I retrieve my cell from my purse and find Miss Lena's number.

"But, what if—"

"Not one more word, Max, or that meteorite is mine."

***

The front door bangs as Miss Lena closes it behind me. I look over my shoulder and catch Max releasing the lace curtain of the window in the living room and ducking under the windowsill. Spy.

Aaron chuckles from the bottom of the stairs. He waits with his hands in his pockets and one foot resting on the bottom step. The sunlight streaks his hair with blue highlights.

"What's so funny?" I plod down the stairs, digging in my purse for my car keys. With Max watching us, we can't disappear and run. I'll have to drive the car somewhere else before we do that.

"Your brother." His eyes flit up to the porch and he shakes his head. "He's a riot."

"Is he still at the window?"

Aaron nods. "He reminds me of my sister. She could be just as embarrassing when she was his age." His eyes bulge and a surprised laugh spurts from his mouth. "Now he's smacking his fist into his hand, like a tough guy! He really wants to punch me, doesn't he?"

"Oh God!" I whip around, expecting to see Max's pseudo-threatening scowl at the window, but instead I catch the curtain swinging closed again. My cheeks burn. He was making that face, I know it. Aaron's toothy grin is enough to tell me my hunch is right.

"You know, I had him under control in there," I mumble. "I know how to handle Max."

"Clearly." Aaron touches his chin in a contemplative pose.

"I do!" I find my keys at the bottom of my bag entangled with an empty gum wrapper and a movie ticket stub. Both flutter away when I yank the keys out. "You didn't have to show yourself to him."

"I know I didn't have to," Aaron says. "I wanted to."

I stop trying to unlock my car door and face him.

"Why would you want to do a stupid thing like that?"

"Why is it such a stupid thing?"

"You could have gotten me into a heap-load of trouble, Aaron." I gesture toward the house in frustration. "I don't want to spend my last couple of days fighting with my mom or grounded because I had a boy in the house."

"I'm sorry." Aaron's face drops. "I didn't think about it like that. I just figured it would look better, less crazy, if Max knew I'm real and not a figment of your imagination. I was trying to keep you out of the nuthouse."

"I would have been fine." I fit the key into the lock on the car door. "How did you do it, anyway? I thought you needed to touch me to be seen by the living."

"I did at first, but now I don't. Same as when you walked through the guardrail at the Gateway. I didn't hold your hand for that. I just needed to be close to you and you did it on your own. Speaking of being close to you, I have a question." He leans against the car door next to me and looks into my eyes. "Those drawings in your room are of me."

"That's not a question, Aaron." I fidget with my keys, but I can't look away. He has me locked in his gaze.

"I guess the question is about something Max said in the kitchen," he says softly, and I lose my breath with the intensity in his eyes. The memory of the kiss where I imagined it was Aaron spirals in my mind. "Is it true?"

"Is what true?" I say, though I know exactly what he's talking about.

"Do you really want to kiss me, Libbi?" He touches my elbow and drags his fingertips down my arm, leaving a trail of prickling heat. His fingers hook my hand and he gently pulls me closer.

CALL ME GRIM

"You already know the answer to that. I told you at the bridge." I would look away, if his faded blue eyes and the light dancing in his hair didn't completely captivate me.

"At the bridge? I thought you were just being nice after I embarrassed myself...and since you saw my scars." He traces the lines of my palm with his thumb. "I thought you didn't want to hurt my feelings."

"Well, you were wrong about that." I drop my gaze to our joined hands. "I wanted to kiss you before I saw your scars. But you said you didn't want to break Abaddon's rules and complicate a crappy situation."

He sweeps a stray piece of hair out of my eyes and traces the line of my jaw with his fingertips. Tingles race over my skin where he touches me.

"Screw Abaddon's rules," he says.

Before I can respond, Aaron's arms circle my waist. He pulls me close, bends down, and touches his lips to mine.

At first, his smooth lips only brush against mine, tenderly searching, as if he's waiting for me to pull away. When I don't, he leans in and molds his lips to mine. The fine stubble of his chin scratches my cheek, but I don't care. I wrap my arms around him and grip the back of his shirt, pulling him closer, inhaling his earthy scent, memorizing the feel of his arms around me. I don't think it's possible for him to be as close as I want him to be, but I try anyway. His lips part and I follow his lead as his tongue dances in and touches mine.

This is definitely not like kissing Kyle. Even when I pretended it was Aaron I was kissing, it doesn't compare. Aaron's lips and tongue move against mine like he's been kissing me for years, not just this once, but at the same time it feels new and exciting and a little dangerous. He ends the kiss way before I'm ready to stop, and I restrain a discontented moan.

He keeps his eyes closed and rests his forehead against mine as my rapid breathing and heartbeat slow.

"That will have to be enough," he says, eyes still shut. Somehow I know he's talking to himself and not me. Then he pulls away and opens his eyes, and I can feel the distance

183

opening between us, pushing us apart.

"It doesn't have to be," I say, once I trust my voice enough to speak. "I don't care about the rules, either."

Aaron lets go of my hand, sighs, and steps back. "I know," he says without meeting my eyes. "But you should." He walks around my car, opens the door, and slips into the passenger seat without another word. I get in the driver's seat.

"So, after I move the car, where are we going?" I turn the key and the engine sputters to life.

"We're going to visit my sister." His eyes fix on something straight ahead and he scowls. "And, if you don't mind, I'd like you to drive. I want to stay visible today."

23

aron directs me through town. Nobody really notices us, except a hairy guy who pulls up next to us on a motorcycle and glances our way. Aaron smiles and waves at the man.

"Sorry," he says when I glare at him. "It's just nice to be seen."

Downtown Carroll Falls disappears behind us as the woods close in and we climb into the foothills. I've lived here all of my life, but I've never been on this side of town. The roads are twisty and confusing, and by the time Aaron finally tells me to pull over, I'm hopelessly lost. I pull in beside an ornate wrought iron gate in the middle of the dense forest.

Tall stone walls surround the place, decorated with colorful Beware of Dogs and Keep Out signs and topped with long loops of barbed wire. It reminds me of the walls of a prison, but rather than functioning to hold inmates in, the wall seems designed to keep people out.

"What if she's not here?" I ask as I take in the fortress-like front gate.

"She is." Aaron walks around the car to stand beside me. "I've been waiting all day for her to come home." He swings his hand in a wide, welcoming sweep. "Ladies first."

I easily melt through the gate ahead of him. His hand rests on the small of my back as he steps over the threshold behind me.

The long driveway winds through the trees and we pass three squat buildings as we walk—white-painted concrete blocks with tar roofs. Whinnies and snorts greet us as we walk by.

"Horses," Aaron says. "Sara used to have five. Now she has two. She sold one last week and she just got back from taking two of them to new homes in Kentucky." He points to another building I hadn't seen. "The goats are over there. The chickens are behind the garden with the rabbits. The cats and dogs used to get the run of the house, but they're all gone now."

"Wow!" I say. "When Mrs. Lutz said Sara had a zoo, she wasn't kidding."

"Yeah." Aaron tucks his hands in his pockets. "Sara always got along better with animals than with people."

I take a step to continue along the driveway, but Aaron grabs my arm and yanks me to a stop.

"You know, I'm not so sure this will work." He rubs his hand up and down on his forearm as if he's freezing, even though sweat collects on his upper lip and drips from his brow.

"What? You changed your mind?"

"No." He shakes his head. "I need to do this. But I'm not sure if walking right up to the house will work. She'll probably freak."

"Okay." I grip his damp hand and squeeze. "What's your plan?"

"Well, first..." The popping sound envelops him. He's made himself invisible again. "I thought you could knock on the door and sort of ease her into all of this. I don't know how she'll react if I just show up after all of these years, looking exactly the same as I did back then. I don't want to make it harder for her."

The flagstone ranch house sits off the driveway, surrounded by trees. There's no denying it's the house of an artist. Dark purple and blue swirls punctuated by orbs of lemon yellow decorate the front door. Fire-engine red shutters adorn the windows and each step leading up to the *Starry Night*-esque door is a different color of the rainbow. Abstract sculptures that vaguely resemble human figures line the last thirty feet of the driveway.

Suddenly, I can't wait to see inside.

Aaron and I climb the rainbow stairs and I lift my closed fist to the door, but Aaron stops my hand.

"I have to warn you," he says. The corners of his mouth dip down. "Sara's marked for suicide."

"And how do you know that?" I park my hands on my hips and glare at him. "You said you can't tell the difference between a suicide mark and a murder mark. You said Kyle's mark could go either way."

"And that's true. You can't tell the difference by looking at them, but Sara's got it all planned. I've read her suicide letter." Aaron gulps and wipes his sweaty hands on his pants. "She's donating most of her artwork to a charity for victims of violence. She's sold half of her animals already, and she has plans to relocate the rest this week. And once they're gone…"

"She'll do it." I twist the end of my ponytail between my fingers. "At the end of this week?"

"Yeah." Aaron nods and rubs the back of his neck.

"But how can I help? I can't even get my best friend's mark to heal, much less a complete stranger's."

"You've already helped by accepting my job and agreeing to train with me," Aaron says. "All you have to do now is stay close enough that I can share your ability to talk to her." He turns back to the blue and yellow swirled door. "If you can convince her to hear me out, that is."

I nod, lift my balled fist to the door, and pause. What am I supposed to say to this woman? I've never met her in my life. She's going to think I'm insane, or worse, that I'm playing a really cruel prank on her. My fist loosens and drops to my side, and I turn away to think.

"Libbi, please." Aaron grabs my arm. "You asked me last night why I did this job for so many years. Why I didn't just get out of it the first time a teen was scheduled to die. Well, it's because of her. I stayed to watch over my little sister. It's the least I could do, after all I've done."

Aaron releases his grip on my arm, but the urgency in his voice keeps me captive. "Sara is the reason I saved your life. She's why I offered you my job and why I have to die. It's the only way I can talk to her, Libbi, to talk her out of it. She's a suicide, an unscheduled death. I don't have twenty-four hours before her death to talk to her, like I do with scheduled deaths. I have to wait until she's dead. Then it's too late."

He takes my hand again, his eyes pleading with me. "Help me talk to her. Please? I can't do it without you."

I know what he says is true. I can see it in the concerned wrinkle of his brow and the way he fidgets with the last button on his shirt. Everything Aaron did this week led to this moment. He saved my life, not because he wants to die, but because he wants to talk to his suicidal sister. To save her from the Blackness.

Like I want to save Kyle from the Blackness.

"I promised to help you yesterday, Aaron." I rap my knuckles against the door and the sound echoes through the house. "When will you learn that I do what I say I'll do?"

The wrinkle disappears from Aaron's brow and he smiles.

"Thank you," he says.

24

The front door inches open revealing a vertical stripe of the darkened interior. A silver security chain pulls taut across the divide and, below that, the cold steel of a double-barreled shotgun aimed at my chest.

"Who are you and how did you get onto my property?" The voice of an older woman drifts through the opening. The owner of the voice remains hidden. All I can see of her are her hands gripping the gun and the glow of her soul radiating from behind the door.

"Um, my name is—" I begin, but I have to stop to clear my throat. I can feel her staring at me through the peephole in the door. "My name is Libbi Piper. I'm from town. It's really important I talk to you, Miss Shepherd."

"How did you get in here?" The gun jabs forward. I take a step back and bump into Aaron's chest.

"She can't kill you," Aaron whispers in my ear. "Your death is postponed, remember?"

"Is there a break in my barbed wire or something?" Sara continues from behind the door. "You're too clean to have tunneled under the wall."

"And, knowing Sara, the gun's probably not even loaded," Aaron says.

"Probably?" I ask him.

"Probably, what?" Sara pokes the gun at me again. "The barbed wire's broken?"

"No, the barbed wire's fine," I say. "I'll explain how I got in

189

and why I'm here, if you put the gun away. Okay?"

"What? Do you think I'm stupid?" The glow of her soul shifts and the gun slides toward me a few more inches.

"No, but I bet you're curious about what happened to your brother, Aaron."

The barrel drops, but only a fractional amount, then it snaps back up and she aims it between my eyes.

"You go away now," she seethes. "I'm not interested in your silly tricks and games."

I lean back and Aaron grasps my shoulders, his fingers dig into my skin. "She won't hurt you, Libbi. Be confident. Tell her you know where I went after her parents died."

I straighten my posture and smooth down my shirt. He's right; she can't hurt me if I'm prepared. I may have left a bruise or two on Aaron when I punched him without warning, but he was able to jump off a bridge without a bungee cord and survived. His death is postponed and, as the future Carroll Falls Grim Reaper, my death is too. She can't hurt me.

"It's not a trick or a game, Sara." I step closer to her and the gun, which is now only inches from my forehead. "I can tell you anything you need to know. I even know where Aaron went after your parents died."

"Stop talking about Aaron like you knew him! You're all of what? Seventeen? He died forty years ago."

She thrusts the barrel of the gun forward with enough force to at least leave a lump on my forehead, but I'm ready for it. I let the barrel slide through the center of my forehead, just as I let Sara's gate and the guardrail slide through my body when I walked through them.

"Holy God!" Sara gasps and the shotgun clatters to the ground at her feet. I reach down, yank it the rest of the way through the door and throw it into the bushes next to the rainbow steps. I know my death is postponed, but it just makes me feel better to know the gun is far from Sara's reach.

"Oh, great!" Aaron throws up his hands. "Way to ease her into the idea. Why not just walk through the door then?"

"What was I supposed to do? Let her brain me?"

"How did you do that?" Sara whispers from the other side of the door. "Who are you?"

"I'm a friend," I say, trying to regain my composure. "And you're right. I didn't know your brother forty years ago. I know him now. He's here with me."

"That's impossible," she says, but the top of her head and one blue eye peeks from the dark space between the door and the doorjamb and searches the porch. "Are you some cruel magician here to torture me or something?"

"No," I say. "I'm just a normal girl."

"I doubt that." She narrows her visible eye and scans me from head to toe. "My gun just went through your head."

"Well, I may be able to do a few things, but deep down I'm the same as you." I hold my hands out, palms toward her in a nothing-to-hide gesture, hoping she understands I'm harmless. "Please, let us in. Aaron has to talk to you."

"He has to talk to me, huh? Well, if Aaron's here with you, where is he? I don't see him."

"I'm right here, Sara," Aaron says as the invisible-to-visible crackling sound fills the air beside me.

"Oh!" Sara stumbles back. A thump and then something glass crashes to the floor. She leaps away from the scattered shards of whatever she knocked over and into my direct line of view. I catch my first glimpse of Sara's face.

Her graying, black braid swings forward as her wide eyes, the same faded blue as Aaron's, lock on him. But I can't assess any other similarities because other than her hair and eyes, her features are hidden. From the bridge of her nose to the tip of her chin, her glowing soul has broken away and exposed a black, pulsing river of sludge that makes Kyle's mark look like a beauty mark in comparison.

"This can't be happening," she says. "You're dead." The goop moves with the motion of her mouth, but I can't see her lips. It's like she's wearing an evil, oily veil.

"Maybe you should sit down, Sara. You look like you might pass out." Aaron, no longer concerned with an invite, walks through the door and the fastened security chain and rushes to his sister's side.

I enter the house behind him, and even though it's not the best time, my eyes scan the paintings that completely cover the walls. Aaron said he thinks I'm talented, but compared to his sister I'm an amateur. Amazing. Sara's work is amazing.

Sara scoots away before Aaron can touch her and her eyes dart between us. She backs down the hallway, her hand on the wall for support. When the backs of her legs hit the sofa in the middle of her sun-drenched living room, she stops.

"I must be dreaming." She sits on the arm of the couch and rubs her eyes. "This has to be some screwed up trick of my overactive psyche."

"It's not a dream." Aaron glides to her side. "Do you want to know how you can tell?"

She turns to him but doesn't answer. At least she's not trying to run away.

"Libbi threw your shotgun into the bushes. Also, you broke the vase Aunt Millie gave you for Christmas last year. If this is a dream, when you wake up, the gun will be back in the corner next to the door, where it always is, and the vase won't be broken. Right? So there's your proof."

Sara searches Aaron's face. She wants to believe him, but I see doubt in the deep wrinkles of her forehead and the sharp scrutiny of her eyes.

"All I ask is that you listen and believe me for now," Aaron says. "You can decide if it's all a dream later. Will you do that for me?"

Sara watches him for a moment, then she nods. Tears glisten in her dark eyelashes.

"Libbi? Could you step outside? I'd like to talk to my sister in private." Aaron takes my hand and leads me to the massive sliding glass door that takes up most of the living room wall. He unlocks the door and yanks it open.

"Good luck." I squeeze his fingers once, reassuringly, and step onto the large, wooden deck. He leans out and gives me a soft peck on the cheek.

"Thank you," he says in my ear, "for everything." He slides

the door closed and pulls the slated blinds over the windows, cutting off my view of the living room.

I turn from the house, close my eyes, and lean my back against the glass. The soft tones of Sara's voice seep through the window, but I can't quite make out what she's saying. Not that I'm trying to listen or anything. Then I hear Aaron and my eyes pop open. His voice is too clear to be coming through the glass of the sliding door. There must be a window open somewhere.

I spin around and search the back of the house. The hushed sound of their voices drifts from the open kitchen window set into the weathered flagstone. The deck's floorboards creak as I inch my way to the window. I get up on tiptoe and peek over the windowsill.

It's a clear shot. Thanks to Sara's open floor plan, I can see the whole house.

Sara sits on the arm of the sofa looking up at Aaron in disbelief. He stands next to her, his hands loose at his sides.

I shouldn't watch this. Aaron wanted privacy and I'm violating that. I push back from the window.

But if I return to my spot by the sliding glass door, I might never know what happened to the Shepherds and how Aaron is involved. I might never know why Mrs. Lutz is marked and why Aaron feels responsible. He'll never tell me and Mrs. Lutz doesn't know.

It may be awful of me, but there is no way I'm moving from this window. I have to hear what Aaron has to say.

"You're so young." Sara lifts her hand and touches Aaron's stubbly cheek with her fingertips. "Where have you been?"

"Ever since you moved back to Carroll Falls, I've lived here, in this house, with you." Aaron covers her hand on his cheek with his. She gasps and pulls away, like he burned her.

Aaron lives here? He said he lives close to Jumpers' Bridge. I turn away from the window and scan the view from the deck. The green-painted back of Jumpers' Bridge curves over the top of the tree line like a monster breaking the surface of a lake. I can't see the river or the waterfall through the foliage, but I can imagine in the winter, when the leaves have fallen, the view is spectacular.

"You've been haunting me?" Sara says.

"No." Aaron chuckles softly. "I've been watching over you."

But Sara continues on as if she didn't hear him. "I guess a haunting makes sense. You must be angry for what I did to you." Tears shimmer and spill over her eyelids, but I can't follow the trails they make because they slip under the black mark and disappear. "I didn't know he would kill you, Aaron. I would have told him the truth. I would have told him I did it."

"I'm not dead," Aaron says, but Sara shakes her head.

"You may not realize it, but you are. Only ghosts could stay seventeen for forty years. Only ghosts can walk through solid doors." Her voice trembles as she studies her folded hands. "A few weeks ago, Margie told me what her father did to you. Before then, I always figured you ran away. I'd have fantasies of you lounging on a beach somewhere with a drink with one of those tiny umbrellas in it." She laughs hollowly then looks up at him.

"I don't know if you'll remember this, since you think you're still alive," Sara continues, "but you told me to tell the police you did it if they ever got suspicious. I didn't want to tell Margie's father that, but he was so frightening. He asked all of these questions and I had the murder weapon hidden in the back of the closet, right behind me, and I panicked. At that moment, with that man—that *police*man—looming over me, I didn't know what to say or do, so I said what you told me to say. I said you did it."

Sara buries her face in her hands and sobs, her back heaving with each soggy breath. "Oh God, Aaron, I'm so, so, sorry. It's my fault you're dead. I killed my father and told Margie's father you did it. He thought you killed them both, and he went after you and he killed you too."

"And that's why you want to kill yourself, isn't it? Because of what Margie told you about her father?" Aaron places his hand on her quivering shoulder. Her head snaps up and she gawps at him. "I know what you have planned. I've been here all along, watching you prepare. I read your suicide note. But you have no reason to kill yourself, Sara. You did nothing wrong and I'm not dead. If I were dead, would you feel this?" Aaron grabs Sara's hand and squeezes. "Would you have been able to touch my cheek earlier? I'm not dead. I know what Margie thinks happened, but she's wrong. Margie's father didn't kill me. And you didn't kill your father." He closes his eyes and bows his head. "I did."

Sara stares at him. I can't see her mouth through the sludge of her mark, but I wouldn't be surprised if it's hanging open in astonishment. I know my mouth is. I was convinced she had killed them both, nine-year-old kid or not, and Aaron had felt responsible for not stopping it.

"No, Aaron." She shakes her head slowly. "Don't you remember? By the time you and Margie showed up, Mom was barely hanging on and Dad was already dead. I hit him over the head with my snow globe to get him to stop hitting her."

"I do remember. I remember everything about that night, but you don't know the whole story. And neither does Margie." Aaron kneels in front of his younger sister and takes her hands, like a boy about to propose to a much older woman. "Do you remember when I went to Jumpers' Bridge with a bunch of my friends, about a week before the night they died?"

Sara narrows her eyes. "Maybe...vaguely," she says.

"That was the night I was supposed to die. I was supposed to fall off the bridge when a train came, but instead the Grim Reaper in charge of my soul offered me an opportunity."

"The Grim Reaper offered you an opportunity?" Sara tilts her head and I almost laugh. It was easy for her to believe in ghosts, but one mention of the Grim Reaper and she becomes an instant skeptic.

"Yes. She told me she could give me an extra week of life to try and prevent a family tragedy, if I agreed to take over for her as the next Grim Reaper. And I agreed." Aaron glances toward the sliding glass door where I imagine he thinks I'm waiting. "It wasn't long after I accepted the job that I learned what our family tragedy would be: your dad was marked to either commit suicide or murder. I wasn't sure which, but after years of him drinking himself into a stupor and beating the spit out of Mom,

I figured he'd kill her. He hadn't touched you since he hit you that one time and I threatened to cut off his balls in his sleep if he did it again. But after I died or became a Reaper, I wouldn't be there to protect either of you anymore. There'd be nothing I could do."

Aaron pushes up from the floor and moves to the sofa. It squeaks softly as he settles in.

"The only thing I could think to do was to help him quit drinking. He was better when he wasn't drinking. The next day was one of his more sober days and, by some miracle, I talked him into going cold turkey. He didn't even get angry. He cried and apologized and promised to get help and get better." Aaron chuckles humorlessly. "I thought I did it. I thought I'd fixed him. His mark looked better. It still covered most of his face, but it was smooth, like glass, and less angry."

Sara gives him a confused look. Aaron doesn't realize what he said makes no sense to her. He's studying his clenched hands. It makes total sense to me, though. I shift my weight and look over my shoulder at the birds soaring over Jumpers' Bridge. This story is becoming a little too familiar, and I suddenly don't want to hear any more. But like a morbid spectator at a car wreck, I can't walk away from the window.

"Then I made my biggest mistake," Aaron continues. "I relaxed. The rest of that week I wasted time doing stupid stuff. I even took you to the carnival. Remember?"

Sara nods as tears drip from her chin and splash to her lap.

"Your dad stayed dry for six days. He took up drinking again that last night—right before my time was up and I had to take over as Grim Reaper." Aaron's hands curl into fists so tight his knuckles turn white. "When me and Margie walked in that night, the house smelled like a liquor store after an earthquake and it looked about the same. Mom was curled up on the floor, moaning and holding her stomach. Your dad was beside her, face down in a puddle of blood, with your snow globe still spinning next to his head. And you stood over him, shaking so hard I thought you might bite your tongue."

Sara sniffs back a sob. "You see? I did it, Aaron. I killed him."

"No. Be quiet, now. I'm not finished yet," Aaron says and then he continues. "You told me you killed him and for the moment, I believed you. He certainly looked dead." He shakes his head slowly. "I should have noticed his soul was still glowing and I didn't have a headache, but I guess I was too shocked to realize that, at first."

"Why was his soul glowing?" Sara asks. "And why would you have a headache?"

"Sorry." He blinks. "I forgot you don't know this stuff. The headache and glowing souls are part of being a Reaper." Aaron goes on to briefly explain some of his powers. When Sara nods understanding, he continues with his story.

"Margie took you into the kitchen; I think to get you away from it all. That's when Mom called me over. I thought she was whispering because she didn't want you to hear, but now I know she was too weak to talk any louder. She made me swear to take his body to the bridge. She wanted it to look like a suicide. She didn't want his death to come back on you.

"I promised her I would. But I couldn't figure out how to move a man twice my size to Jumpers' Bridge by myself. It took all of my strength just to heave him onto his back. And then I saw his face. The mark was still there, blacking out everything but his left eye."

Aaron runs a hand down his face and sighs.

"It didn't make any sense. He shouldn't have been marked. He was dead and Mom was alive. Then my stupid brain caught on and I finally realized he was still glowing. And you weren't marked. If you had killed your father, you would have been marked. Your dad was alive. I don't know if he had passed out or was knocked out from the blow to his head, but he was alive.

"Now it was in my hands. I only had a few more hours before I would disappear forever. Mom was beaten up pretty badly, but she was alive. And I knew if he had a chance to recover, it wouldn't be long before he killed her or you for hitting him with the snow globe. And I wouldn't be there to stop him next time. So I threw a blanket over him, hoping it would hide his shallow breathing, and called Margie into the living room.

"I told her what Mom wanted me to do and she agreed to help me move him, for your sake. I mean, you were only nine years old—too young to be a murderer. I didn't tell her he was alive. He was too heavy to move by myself and I was afraid she wouldn't help me if she knew. I didn't realize helping me would give her a mark too. I figured she'd have to know what she was doing, but I was wrong. I was wrong about a lot of things."

Aaron chokes on the last sentence. He swallows hard and swipes at his eyes with the back of his hand.

"And I do remember telling you to tell the police it was me who killed him. It's the truth, and they could never catch me. As a Reaper, I'm invisible. I just thought I'd try the suicide angle first, since it was what Mom wanted. Don't feel guilty for doing what I told you to do, Sara. It's what I wanted."

"Margie's father didn't kill you because of me?" Sara's voice shakes with uncertainty. "And you killed Dad?"

I glance over at Sara's small form, perched on the armrest of the couch. I've been so focused on Aaron and his story, I almost forgot Sara. Her chin trembles and above her mark, her cheeks glisten with tears. I look back at Aaron to hear his answer, but my gaze snaps back to Sara.

I can see her chin and the tops of her cheeks. I couldn't see anything but her eyes before. It's working. Her mark is shrinking.

"Like I said, I'm not dead. And I didn't want to kill anyone." Aaron's eyes scan over her face and a small smile turns the corners of his mouth. It's a subtle smile, but it's there. He sees the change in her mark too. "Actually, I almost didn't do it. Margie helped me get him down the tracks to the bridge in a wheelbarrow. She helped me lift him up and position him over the safety railing, bent at his waist with his hands dangling over the river. Then I told her to go home. I could hoist him the rest of the way over without her help. I knew Charlotte would be there soon to collect his soul and after that, she'd make me a Reaper. I didn't want Margie there for that.

"But after she was gone, I stood there and stared at his lifeless body. I couldn't do it. He was still alive and I wasn't a murderer. I thought that maybe there was still time to change his mark. Maybe I could go home and make Mom promise to leave him. Make her swear to it, like I swore to make his death look like a suicide.

"I even started to pull him back off the railing. But then my head exploded with the intense pain of an unscheduled death and I knew. Mom was dead. It took a few hours for her to die, but that bastard still killed her. I twisted my fists into the back of his shirt and, instead of yanking him back into the waiting wheelbarrow, I hoisted him up and shoved him over the railing."

The room falls silent. The only sounds I hear are the tick of the clock on the wall and the hushed roar of Carroll Falls behind me.

"Why, Aaron?" Sara glares at him. I think it's pretty obvious why Aaron killed his stepfather, and if I was in the room with them, I would say so. But when Sara continues talking, I'm glad I couldn't say anything. "Why haven't you told me any of this before now? You've let me believe I killed my father for forty years. Did it ever occur to you that I might want to know the truth?"

"I tried to tell you." Aaron stands and walks over to her. "I left you letters, but they just looked like blank pages to you. I made origami and left them all around, but you thought you had made them. I moved things, took things that belonged to me and put them in conspicuous places. I tried to leave you clues, but nothing got through to you. If I took something, you'd forget you ever had it. If I moved something, you'd think you moved it yourself, even if you saw it flying through the air right in front of you. I even tried talking to you in your sleep. We had a long conversation that you promptly forgot as soon as you woke up. It's the curse of a Reaper, Sara. I can't communicate with you unless you're a scheduled death and you're about to die."

"But you're talking to me now," Sara says, then her eyes widen and the mouth I couldn't see moments ago goes slack. "Am I about to die?"

"Not anymore, I hope." Aaron smiles. "I'm able to talk to you today because of that beautiful girl standing outside on the deck." He nods in the direction of the sliding glass door. I can't help but smile. He called me beautiful again. "Libbi is about to replace me as Carroll Falls' newest Grim Reaper, and part of her training allows us to share powers, for learning purposes. But it goes both ways. I can also use her ability to communicate with the living."

Aaron takes Sara's face in his hands, like she's still his nine-year-old baby sister, and plants a gentle kiss in the middle of her forehead.

"I love you, little sis. And I'm so proud of you. I'd hate to see your love, your talent, your life wasted for something you didn't do." He smoothes the hair from her eyes. "I decided to give up this job because it's the only way I could tell you any of this. Please, Sara. I need to know it was worth it. I need to know you won't kill yourself."

"I won't, Aaron. I promise." Sara's lips quiver, but her eyes are sincere. "What if I forget all of this as soon as you leave?"

"You won't. Not if Libbi's here," Aaron takes her hand. "And if you're afraid you'll think it's all a dream, I can write you a letter. Libbi's ability covers all forms of communication. Plus, you'll have the broken vase and the gun in the bush to remind you."

A few minutes later, Aaron pulls back the blinds and lets me back in the house. I pretend I didn't hear anything. The guilt I feel for betraying his trust and eavesdropping on such a personal conversation is enough of a punishment. There's no way I'm admitting to it.

He spends a half-hour writing a letter for Sara. He doesn't tell me what it says, but I know it's the entire story, from his first encounter with Charlotte to me knocking on Sara's door. When he's done, he hands the pages over to her. She carefully tucks them in the front pocket of her flannel shirt and looks up.

"Thank you for doing this." She snakes her arms around me and pulls me into a hug. "It means more than you will ever know."

All that remains of her mark is a thin, black line across her top lip, like someone drew a mustache on her soul with a felt pen, but I have a feeling even that will be gone soon.

Sara grabs Aaron next, trapping him in the biggest bear hug I've seen a woman of her short stature accomplish. He holds her just as tightly and when he tells her good-bye he also assures her that, even though she won't be able to see or hear him, he'll be back later. She watches from her swirly front door as we silently walk down her long driveway.

"If you wanted to, you could have just stayed with her," I say as I settle into my car seat, readjusting my butt to avoid the pinching split in the pleather. "I can get home by myself."

"I know you can, but I couldn't do that." He slams the car door behind him. "I promised Max he could punch me in the gut if I didn't bring you home, unharmed and before dark. What kind of a promise would it be if I wasn't there for his inspection?"

I don't say anything. I just press down on the gas pedal and head home.

25

We drive in silence.

I don't know what Aaron's thinking, but my mind has his story on repeat. As soon as I come to the grisly conclusion, my brain hits the back-track button and I go to the beginning: When Aaron met Charlotte.

When I met Aaron.

I can't help but compare our stories. Aaron's only reason for taking Charlotte's job was for the chance to fix his stepfather's mark. The only reason I agreed to take Aaron's job was for the chance to heal Kyle's mark. Aaron thought he had succeeded when he convinced his stepfather to quit drinking. I thought I had succeeded when I told Kyle I loved him. But Aaron failed. Does that mean I've failed too?

The streetlights flick on as I pull into the driveway next to Miss Lena's car. There's enough light to say it's not dark, so Aaron's safe from a Max-sized slug to the belly, but the sky above us is bruised purple.

"I guess we better get up there." I nod to the house. "Max is probably lacing up his boxing gloves as we speak. Not that he'd be able to hurt you. If you know it's coming, you can make his fist slide right through you."

Aaron doesn't respond. I turn the key and he gets out before the car shudders and dies. He meets me as I open my door.

"I'm surprised," he says as we climb the brick steps to the porch.

"About what?" I turn and face him at the front door.

Aaron shrugs. Over his shoulder the horizon glows pink and orange. The light dances around his head, giving him a fiery halo.

"After we left Sara, I thought you'd start bugging me about my past again."

"Oh, I-I understand," I stammer. "I mean, if it's too private, I don't need to know."

"Thanks," he says, and the weight of guilt grows in my gut. He looks down and his bangs fall across his forehead. He swipes them to the side. "You must think I'm a terrible person now."

"Why would I think that?" I say.

Aaron meets my eyes. "Because of what I did—"

"What you did is sacrifice your life for a chance to save your sister's. You're not a terrible person. You're a hero."

"No. I'm not." He shakes his head slowly. "But I wasn't talking about my sister, Libbi. I was talking about you. What I did to you. I should have let you die when you were supposed to, but instead I dragged you into all of this. I made you choose for my own selfish reasons. I used you."

"Is that what you think?" I step closer to him and he doesn't back away. "I would have done the same thing, if I was in your position and Max was marked." Our chests touch and I trace the remnants of the bruise on his chin with my fingertips. "But since you're so concerned, I'll show you exactly what you did to me, Aaron."

My fingers lace behind his neck as I get up on tiptoe and pull him down to me.

Our lips touch and I don't waste time with tenderness. I kiss him hard, furiously, my fingers twine in his hair and twist into his shirt. He needs to know I'm serious.

It doesn't matter what he thinks he did to me. I understand why he did it. And I still want him. I don't care if I have to take over for him in a few days and he has to die. It's a sacrifice I understand. I want him now. I'll want him tomorrow and I will always want him, even when we're apart.

But why does it have to be this way? Why does he have to die? Sadness settles over me, squeezing my lungs and wrenching my heart. I've waited my whole life to feel this for someone, and now that I do, it'll be ripped away. I understand why he has to do it, but the rules still suck.

Our lips part as Aaron pulls away. He touches my cheek and tears wet his fingertips.

"Don't cry, Libbi."

"I can't help it." I choke back a sob. "I don't want you to—"

Aaron stops me with a kiss. Slow and deep. His hands settle on my hips, pulling our bodies closer, igniting a fire I never knew existed. One hand slips under my shirt and glides up my back as he leans in and kisses me deeper still.

Some kid yells in the distance, but I don't care. All I hear is Aaron's breathing. All I taste are Aaron's lips. All I see, smell, and feel is Aaron.

"Hey, asshole!" The kid yells again. But it's not a kid. I recognize that voice.

I pull back and look up at Aaron. His face registers surprise, but not the surprise of a guy being called an asshole by a stranger. It's the surprise of a guy who's just kissed a girl he didn't realize he cared about as much as he does. I know the feeling.

I peek around Aaron and he glances over his shoulder. The porch becomes unsteady and my knees wobble as I focus on the guy calling Aaron an asshole. A guy I told a great big lie to today.

Kyle stands at the bottom of the stairs. His eyes burn a hole in me. He holds both of his drumsticks in one hand and beats them furiously against his thigh. His face twists into a grimace of anger and hurt. But mostly hurt.

"You must be Aaron." Kyle sneers. "Nice to meet you."

"Kyle, I can explain," I say when Aaron doesn't say anything.

"Oh, I bet you can, Libbi." His free hand curls into a fist at his side. "But can you explain it to Aaron here?" His brown eyes look black in this light as they settle on Aaron. "Did you know your girlfriend has been playing you, Aaron? Actually, she's been playing both of us. She kissed me today too. Did you know that? She told me she loves me."

Aaron locks eyes on me. A different kind of surprise registers on his face now, the kind that makes me wish I could shrivel up and disappear.

"Is that true?" he says.

"Yes. I kissed Kyle today and"—I twist the hem of my shirt—"I told him I love him."

Aaron staggers back. I've seen pain in his eyes before, but not this kind of pain. This is the pain of a broken heart, and it's devastating because I caused it. I caused two broken hearts today.

"I guess it makes sense." Aaron's voice sounds detached, empty. "Your winning painting, it's of him. And you've been so worried. You obviously care about him."

"I do. But not how you think." I touch his elbow. "I only said I love him because I thought it would heal his mark. I didn't really mean it. Not like that."

Kyle yells, "Screw you, Libbi!" and grunts. I hear a whoosh. One of his drumsticks sails through the air, end over end, as Kyle storms off down the street. The drumstick punches through the back of Aaron's skull like he's a ghost and whizzes over my shoulder. It strikes the porch light behind me.

The antique globe covering the light shatters with the impact. Broken glass rains over my back and I lurch forward in surprise. The toe of my shoe catches on a loose floorboard and I trip as glass tinkles to the porch. Aaron tries to catch me, but his hand reaches out a nanosecond too late. Pain sears through my shoulder as I hit the ground and one of the larger shards of glass slices into me. I cry out. Tears spring to my eyes.

"Are you all right?" Aaron grabs my hand and pulls me up. His face turns gray as he touches my shoulder. "Shit! You're bleeding." He shows me my blood on his fingers.

The front door creaks.

"What happened?" Max says as he pushes the screen door open. His shoes crunch in the shattered glass.

Aaron crouches down and his fingers wrap around Kyle's drumstick. "Did he throw this?"

"Libbi!" Miss Lena pushes by Max and grabs my arm. "What happened to you? You're bleeding!"

"It's nothing." I flick my hand dismissively. "I have to go after Kyle."

"He's gone," Aaron says. "And it's probably better if you let him cool off a bit."

"Come in here and let me clean you up." Miss Lena leads me into the kitchen and sits me on one of the chairs. Aaron waits at the front door and Miss Lena waves him in. "You can come too," she says.

It feels weird for Miss Lena to invite Aaron into our house, but at least I know Mom can't get mad at me. But what's even weirder is when she says, "Max, it's time for your bath," and he actually listens to her. He moans and stomps up the stairs like he's trying to crack the wood with each step, but he goes.

"It's pretty deep." Miss Lena presses a wet paper towel to my shoulder. "Do you have a first aid kit?" I tell her where the kit is. She hands the wet, bloody towel to Aaron and says, "Hold this. I'll be right back."

"Are you okay?" Aaron kneels next to me and gingerly swipes the blood from my arm, like he could make it worse by dabbing too hard.

"Yeah. What about you?" I take the towel from him. The wound is so close to my armpit I worry Aaron's feather-light cleansing technique will cause me to break into fits of ticklish laughter.

"I'm fine. Nothing hit me," he says.

"Really? Nothing at all?" I say, pressing the paper towel into my shoulder. "He aimed that drumstick right at your head."

"I let it go through me." Aaron shrugs.

"But you couldn't have. You weren't prepared for it. Your back was to him. You didn't even know what happened until you saw the drumstick on the floor." I glance over my shoulder at the cut and wince. "I thought you could get hurt if you were surprised, like when I punched you."

"Well, you were wrong about that." Aaron stands and walks over to the sink. He rips another paper towel off the roll and wets it. "I can't get hurt."

"Yes, you can." A nervous chuckle passes my lips. "What

about all of those scars? And you still have the bruise I gave you on your chin. And when you taught me to run, you totally flipped out when I bumped into you and almost sent you over the edge of the cliff. If you can't die and you can't get hurt, why did you even care if you fell off the cliff?"

"Because you can hurt me. All right? Only you and Abaddon." He spins around, red-faced and wide-eyed. "Nobody else can hurt me. Not Kyle, not Max. Nobody. I can't even hurt myself. Only you. I chose you to take my job."

"What?" I say; the paper towel slips from my fingers. "What are you saying, Aaron?"

He sinks into the chair next to me and stares at the half-wet towel in his hand. "You asked me once how I was going to commit suicide and I wouldn't tell you. Remember?"

It takes all of my strength to nod. I remember.

"I can't commit suicide, Libbi." He runs a hand down his tired face. "I need to be murdered, and only you can do it. I killed Charlotte when I took over for her and you'll have to kill me."

I shake my head and pain shoots through my shoulder but I ignore it. "No. I can't do that. I can't kill you. It's impossible."

"Yes, you can. You have to. If you don't, it's the same as refusing the job after you made the commitment." He grabs my limp hands and squeezes them hard. "Abaddon doesn't like it when we break our commitments. If you don't change your mind back before 3:12 tomorrow, the rest of your week of training will be forfeited. You won't have until Saturday anymore. You'll have to face Abaddon tomorrow, and you'll die." He lifts my hand to his lips and softly kisses the palm. "Please, Libbi. Please, don't make me take you to him. I don't think I could bear it."

"Okay, I've got it." Miss Lena hurries in clutching the first aid kit. "I had a devil of a time finding it. I had to interrupt Max's bath to ask him."

"It looks like you don't need me anymore." Aaron gently places my hands in my lap and stands. "I should go. It's getting late. Think about what I said, Libbi. Please?"

"I'm going with you." I try to stand but Miss Lena drops a

deceptively strong mitt onto my uninjured shoulder and holds me in my seat.

"I don't think so, Little Miss." She drags a chair in front of me and sits, replacing the paper towel with gauze from the kit. "I think you need stitches."

"No, I don't. It's fine." I shrug her hand off my shoulder. A tiny stream of blood rolls down my arm when the gauze falls away.

"No, it's not, Libbi." She presses the gauze against the gash and I wince. "I called your mother. She's on her way."

26

I hate to admit it, but Miss Lena was right. I needed stitches. Seven, to be exact. Damn you, Kyle.

Not that I don't deserve it. After all I've done to him, I deserve much more than a two-inch cut on the shoulder and seven stitches. But a trip to the emergency room with my mother in panic mode, firing questions at me like a CSI detective on Ritalin, doesn't help the situation.

"I don't care if Kyle's one of your best friends," Mom says while we wait for the nurse to come back with my discharge papers. She's much calmer now that the gash is stitched and covered with a bandage. "The boy threw a drumstick at you. He could have really hurt you. If he had hit you the wrong way, he could have killed you. I should call the police."

"Don't do that. He didn't cut me. The glass did." I twist the plastic hospital bracelet around my wrist. "He was just upset."

"That doesn't make it okay." She gives me an ominous stare.

"All you have to do is sign this and you're free to go," the nurse says as she yanks back the curtain of the little cubicle and hands my mother a clipboard and a pen. I'm old enough to escort souls through the Gateway, but I'm too much of a kid to sign my own discharge paperwork.

"Anyway, it doesn't matter. His actions sent you to the hospital, Libs," Mom says after she signs the papers and the nurse leaves. "I don't want you seeing him anymore. Not even if he only wants to apologize. I mean it." She shakes her head and mumbles as she gathers our things. "It's always the quiet ones."

I could argue with her, but I don't. It's pointless. She will never understand how much I hurt Kyle today. I shouldn't have pretended I was in love with him. I shouldn't have kissed him, no matter what my reasons for doing so were. It didn't make any difference, anyway. His mark didn't shrink at all. If anything, it grew.

Just like Aaron failed his stepfather, I've failed Kyle. I'm the one who owes him an apology, not the other way around.

Kyle deserves to know the truth. All of it. He might even need it. If the truth healed Sara's mark, maybe it can heal Kyle's too. Mom doesn't want me to see him anymore, but I don't care. She can't stop me. I have to fix this, if I can.

The only problem is Aaron and the fact that I have to kill him to take over as Grim Reaper. He shouldn't have kept that from me.

At first, the thought of watching powerlessly as my family and friends died convinced me not to take his horrible job. It was the appearance of Kyle's mark and the slim chance I could help him that changed my mind. If Aaron had told me from the beginning that I had to kill him, I probably still would have taken the job. For Kyle. And I would have kept Aaron at a distance. But now that I've allowed myself to get close, I know as surely as I know my eyes are green that I can't do it. I can't become the next Reaper if it means I have to kill Aaron, no matter what the consequences. He doesn't really want to die and I can't do it.

I've changed my mind halfway through training. That means I have until 3:12 p.m. tomorrow to change it back, or my training ends early and I'll die. But I won't change it back. Aaron may not want to, but he'll have to escort my soul through the Gateway. I'll have to confront the Blackness and Abaddon because I refuse to kill him.

And so, the countdown begins. Aaron is nowhere near as Mom and I drive through town, but I can still almost see the glowing red numbers of the digital clock in my head, counting off the milliseconds. I have seventeen hours to heal Kyle's mark before I die, for good. I just hope the truth is enough.

***

Mom unlocks and opens the front door, and the warm light of home spills onto the porch floorboards. Max sits at the top of the stairs with his chin in his hands. His face lifts when he sees me.

"You're home!" Max bounds down the steps.

"Did you think they'd keep me overnight or something? It was just a cut," I say as Miss Lena drifts in from the kitchen, a paperback novel in one hand.

"Max, it's almost midnight. I thought I told you to go to bed." Miss Lena glares at Max and then shrugs. "I'm sorry, Dina. I tried."

"He's fine." Mom hangs her keys on a hook next to the door. "He's just worried."

"Did you get stitches?" Max says it like getting stitches is some sacred rite of passage he can only dream of achieving. He bends forward and examines my bandaged shoulder with saucer eyes.

"Yeah," I say, matching his awed voice. "Seven."

"Wow! Can I see?" If Max's eyes get any wider, I'll have to scoop them up off the floor. God, I'm going to miss this kid.

"Not right now," I manage to squeeze through my tightening throat. *Snap out of it,* I tell myself. I can't cry now. "I'm not allowed to take off the bandage until tomorrow."

My cell phone sings in my purse. Mom crosses her arms over her chest, but doesn't say anything as I excavate to the bottom of my bag for the noisy little thing.

"It's late." Mom grips Max's shoulders and turns him toward the staircase, but her eyes lock on me. "I don't want you up all night."

"But tomorrow's the last day of school!" Max slogs up the stairs. "Libbi's staying up."

"No. I'm going to bed too." I follow him up the stairs and wait until I'm in my room, with the door closed behind me, before I read Kyle's text.

Kyle: I am so sorry I hurt you. I didn't
mean to. Are you okay?

Me: I'm fine. How did you know I was hurt?

Kyle: Max told me when I called the house.
I'm so sorry.

My bed squeaks as I sit on the edge and prop my elbows on my knees. My thumbs fly over the keys.

Me: It's okay. I understand. I'm the one
who should be sorry. Can you come over in
an hour when everyone's in bed? I need to
talk to you.

A full minute passes before I receive his reply.

Kyle: Okay.

***

I stand at the window and watch the sidewalk in front of the house for the glow of Kyle's soul. It hasn't been an hour yet, but I'm convinced he's not coming. He's probably decided he doesn't care what I have to say, that I'm not worth the trouble.

At twelve thirty, I shimmy my window open, cringing when it lets out the high-pitched squeak I should have remembered from the last time I snuck out of the house.

It doesn't matter what Kyle thinks of me. He needs to hear me out. And if he won't come to me, I'll go to him. I swing both legs over the windowsill and lean my head out. The last time I climbed out this window, the breeze had felt cool, crisp, and refreshing. Tonight, there is no breeze. The stagnant air settles on my skin like a thick, suffocating blanket.

My feet touch the shingles of the porch's roof and the light of my soul surges from about-to-blink-out dull to brilliant. The clock in my brain clicks on and tells me it's 12:31 and fifty-three seconds. Someone taps on my bedroom door.

"It's me," Aaron's muffled voice drifts to me from the other side of the door. I lean my head back into my room.

"I know," I say as loud as I dare with Max sleeping on the other side of the paper-thin wall. "Come in."

Aaron melds through the door and the room blazes with the light of his aura.

"I'm sorry for coming so la—" Aaron stops when he sees me half-hanging out the window. "What are you doing?"

"I need to talk to Kyle. I asked him to come here, but I don't think he will and I have to talk to him tonight. I'm running out of time." I wiggle my butt back on the ledge and twist so I can see him better. "I'm sorry, Aaron. I won't change my mind about this. I can't kill you. I refuse."

"You can't do that, Libbi!" Aaron rushes across the room, eyes wide with panic. "You have to kill me."

"No, I don't." I pull my legs back in. Aaron deserves an explanation without me hanging out of a window. "You don't deserve to die just because you wanted to talk your sister out of killing herself. I can't do that to you. I care about you too much."

"You have to!" Aaron grips my arms; his cheeks flush crimson. "Listen, you don't know me as well as you think you do. I deserve to die. More than anyone. I killed them, Libbi. My mother died because of my stupidity and I pushed my stepfather off Jumpers' Bridge. I killed him in cold blood and made my nine-year-old sister think she did it. And I made Margie help me, which marked her. I ruined their lives. I deserve to die. You have to kill—"

"Aaron," I whisper his name and he stops talking. The silence grows as I place my hands on either side of his face, keeping him from looking away. "I already know."

"What?" He searches my eyes, but I keep them steady, unflinching.

"The kitchen window was open at Sara's house. I overheard everything."

"You what?" He steps back and my hands drop to my lap.

"You didn't kill your mother, Aaron. Your stepfather did." I continue on, even though Aaron's face has drained of color and he looks like he might puke. "This may make me a bad person, but I don't blame you for what happened to that man. He did it to himself. And now that Sara knows she's not responsible for your death, she seems fine. And you said Mrs. Lutz's mark is so

213

light it probably won't affect her. So it seems to me everything's okay now."

"Hardly." Aaron snorts. "Weren't you paying attention? I killed two people. Charlotte and my stepfather. It wasn't an accident, Libbi. I knew what I was doing when I pushed him over the railing. I'm a murderer."

"I know, but that was a long time ago and I understand why you did it."

"No." Aaron shakes his head. "I deserve to die. You have to kill me."

The glow of a soul moves into my peripheral vision.

Kyle ambles down the sidewalk in front of the house. He nods when he spots me and cuts across my front lawn. I duck under the windowpane and lean out, holding my finger to my lips.

"Shhh…I'm coming down," I say to Kyle, then turn back to Aaron. "Maybe you should go. Kyle's outside."

"Why? It's not like he can see me. I'm invisible to him."

"I know. But maybe I want to talk to him alone. Okay?"

"I'm not going anywhere until you change your mind about this, Libbi." Aaron sinks into my bed, his forehead creased with concern.

"Fine. Stay," I say.

I don't have time to argue. If I wait too long, Kyle might get impatient and leave.

"But whether you stay or go, I won't change my mind," I say before I swing my legs over the windowsill and jump down onto the roof.

The old shingles crack under my feet. Little pieces slide down the incline and drop to the ground as I crabwalk to the closest wrought iron pillar and climb down. Kyle's already waiting on the porch swing with his back to me. The swing sways back and forth as he kicks the floor.

"Kyle?" I whisper.

He looks over his shoulder. There's no denying it. The mark has grown. A lot. The bubbling, goop-filled crack now hides his whole nose and right eye and half of his mouth. Above his mark, his bloodshot left eye shimmers.

"Oh Jesus," slips from my mouth before I can stop it. I barely miss hitting the armrest of the swing with my hip as I rush around it.

"Shit, Libbi." Kyle's fingers shake as he touches the bandage on my shoulder. "I am so, so sorry. Is it bad?"

It takes me a moment to reply, I'm so shocked by the change in his mark.

"Seven stitches, but I'm fine." The porch swing rocks back with my weight as I sit down next to him. He frowns and his eyes flick back and forth between my shoulder and my face. "Really, it's okay. They numbed me up pretty good. It doesn't even hurt anymore."

"I can't believe my drumstick broke the light. I thought I hit *him*." Kyle leans forward and grips his head in his hands. "I didn't mean for you to get hurt. I was just so angry, you know." His sad eye locks on mine. "You lied to me, Libs."

"I know I did. I shouldn't have, and I'm sorry. But I did it for a reason." I pick at the roof dirt under my fingernails. "If I tell you something that sounds sort of crazy, will you promise to listen and believe me?"

"What is it?" Kyle leans back and the swing lurches forward.

"Promise me you'll listen and believe."

"I'll listen…" he says, with a slight lilt at the end.

"Okay," I say when I realize he's not going to agree to believe me. I deserve that. "You did hit Aaron when you threw your drumstick. You hit him square in the back of the head."

"No. I missed him. Max said Aaron's fine, but the light is destroyed." His fingertips brush over the bandage on my shoulder. "And a piece of glass cut you."

"I know this sounds nuts, but the reason the drumstick broke the light is because it went through him. You can't hurt him, Kyle. Aaron's a Grim Reaper."

"A Grim Reaper?" Kyle scoffs. "You can't be serious."

"I couldn't be more serious." I stare at him, trying to convey exactly how serious I am.

"Your drumstick went through him. I saw it. It went directly through his face."

"That's impossible." His eyebrows scrunch together in a worried frown as his hands ball into fists. "What has this guy done to you? Drugged you or something?"

"Actually, that thought crossed my mind." I chuckle and Kyle's frown deepens. "There were a lot of things I thought about Aaron, but I know he's a Grim Reaper now. There's no question in my mind."

"A Grim Reaper, huh?" Kyle laughs and shakes his head. "Damn, this guy's good. How did he think up a line like that?"

"It's not a line. It's the truth." I sound like a petulant child, so I lower my voice and try again. "He collects the souls of the dead. I've helped him. He was teaching me how to do it."

"Okay. Fine." Kyle stands and the sudden movement causes the swing to twist on its chains. "Why would the Grim Reaper want to teach you how to collect souls, Libs?"

I stop the dizzying motion of the swing with my foot.

"Because I was supposed to take over for him and disappear. And in fifteen hours…" I swallow against the lump in my throat. "You'll never see me again."

Kyle's eyes grow dark and his lips form a thin, scar-like slash. "If this is some elaborate, yet lame, attempt at the 'It's not you, it's me' line, it sucks, Libs. Really."

"I'm not feeding you lines, Kyle!" My words echo down the street and I smack my hand over my mouth. That's all I need, to wake Mom or have one of the neighbors call the cops.

"Remember last week, when Jason totaled Salma's car? He was supposed to total me too. I was supposed to die that day, squished between Salma's Honda and Jason's truck, but Aaron saved my life so I could take over for him. I had to choose between dying and becoming the next Grim Reaper, and I chose to take his awful job. For you! All for you!"

"For me?" The eye I can see twinkles with dark humor. "What does any of this craziness have to do with me?"

"It's all about you. The reason I lied. The reason I kissed you." I lean forward and touch his hand. "You're marked, Kyle. And that mark means you're going to kill someone, soon. Probably yourself. I decided to take Aaron's job so I'd have the chance to change your mind. But nothing has worked. Your mark is getting worse."

Kyle's eyes widen with surprise. "What are you talking about, Libs? I don't want to kill myself." He slides his hand out of mine and crosses his arms over his chest. "Who told you this crap? Aaron? Did you ever think he might be trying to scare you?"

"He's not. And he didn't need to tell me about your mark. I can see it for myself." The swing's chains squeak as I stand up in front of Kyle. "It's right here." I run my finger down the middle of his face, outlining the crack in his soul. I expect to feel the sharp, jagged edges of the mark and the hot and slimy stuff inside, but instead I feel the hidden curve of his brow, the bridge of his nose, and his moist lips. Kyle leans his cheek into my palm and closes his eyes.

"Please, Kyle," I whisper. "Promise me you won't kill yourself."

"I don't want to kill myself and I never would. You should know me better than that," he says, and I believe him. But the mark still covers most of his face. Maybe he hasn't made the decision yet. Maybe his suicide will be impulsive. It wouldn't be the first time he's done something without thinking it through.

"Promise me," I say. "I need to hear you say it before I die tomorrow."

His eyes snap open and he stares at me. Anger and fear morph his face into a mask I've never seen on him before.

"Where is this guy?" he seethes. "Where does he live?" He yanks his single drumstick out of his back pocket and smacks it against his palm, like he can't wait for another chance to whack Aaron with it.

"Aaron?" I say. Stupid question. Of course he's talking about Aaron. "Why?"

"Because he's done something to you, Libbi. Drugged you. Brainwashed you. Something. He can't get away with that."

"Aaron didn't do anything to me, other than save my life and give me a choice."

Kyle seizes me by the arms and shakes me. I hear crackling in my ears.

"Snap out of it, Libs. None of this is real." He searches my face. His deep eyes swim with concern. "Come back to me."

"Let go of her." Aaron's voice emanates from the empty air beside us.

Kyle jumps back, releasing his kung-fu grip on my arms, and turns toward the deserted porch and Aaron's voice. The skin where he grabbed me stings. I'll probably have a bruise, not that it matters.

The air pops and crackles as Aaron materializes in front of us. The muscles in his jaw clench as he focuses on Kyle.

"What the—" Kyle backs into the siding of the house.

"Are you okay, Libbi?" Aaron's eyes remain locked on Kyle and his mouth barely moves.

"Yeah, I'm fine." I rub the sore spot on my arm.

"Good," he says. "Do you mind giving your friend and me a few minutes? If you're up in your room with the window shut, I should still be visible to him." I can't tell if his tone is threatening or not when he says, "Kyle and I need to talk. Alone."

"Really, Aaron, it wasn't a big deal." I hold my hands up and step between them. "He wasn't trying to hurt me. He wants to help, though he's still pretty clueless. You, of all people, should understand that."

"It's not that," Aaron finally looks at me. I don't see anger in his hard eyes or even concern in the tight pull of his lips. I see determination and the same fear I saw in Kyle's eyes a minute ago when I told him I'm going to die. "Just a few minutes. Please."

"Whatever you have to say to Kyle, you can say in front of me." I cross my arms over my chest and widen my stance.

"No, Libbi." Aaron takes my hand. "You have to go."

"I'm not leaving." I tilt my chin up in defiance and rip my hand out of his. "You'll have to make me."

"Fine." Aaron touches my uninjured shoulder. "I'm sorry I have to do this, but…"

My shoulder droops under the weight of his hand. Actually,

both shoulders droop, and so do my eyelids. I suddenly don't care about Aaron or Kyle. Or Haley, or Mom, or Max, or my death. All I care about is how comfy the porch swing looks and how much I need to sit down. No, lay down. No, sleep.

My knees buckle and I fall forward, vaguely comprehending Aaron's arms around me, sweeping me up. And then there's nothing but darkness.

Blackness.

27

Sunlight beats against my closed eyelids. I throw an arm across my face and yank the blankets over my head. It's too early to get up. My alarm clock hasn't shrieked yet.

And why is it so damned bright in here? The cogs in my brain turn slowly. I must have forgotten to close the blinds before I climbed under the covers last night. But that doesn't seem right. I don't remember going to bed.

My eyes pop open and I sit up, kicking my blankets to the floor. A stripe of sunlight streams through the naked window and bathes my bed in bright light. The blinds are in the same position I put them in when I climbed out the window to meet Kyle last night—all the way up.

The clock on the wall beside the window says it's 6:10 a.m., but I already know that. My internal Reaper clock is ticking away. Aaron's still here.

He snores softly in the rocking chair in the corner of the room. The purple flowered quilt my nana made for my eighth birthday covers him up to his chin. His crossed feet are propped on the white plastic laundry basket that he dumped and flipped upside down. I scan the laundry strewn across the floor for dirty underwear and bras and heave a sigh of relief that my unmentionables aren't visible.

I leap out of bed and shove him as hard as I can in the chest. The chair rocks back and his feet slide off the basket and thump to the floor. His red, puffy eyes snap open and he squints up at me through the sunlight.

"You asshole," I say just above a whisper. Mom has already left for work, but I don't want to wake Max. "You knocked me out last night. What the hell did you do to me?"

"Jesus, Libbi." He rubs his eyes with the palms of his hands and then blinks at me. "I relaxed you, that's all."

"That's all?" I shield my eyes from the sun and squint at him. "I told you never to use that power on me again. Ever."

"I'm sorry, but I had to." He goes to the window and lowers the blinds, plunging my room into the familiar early morning shadows. "I needed to talk to Kyle alone and you wouldn't let me."

"That's not an excuse to basically drug me, Aaron," I say. "And there's no reason for you to talk to Kyle alone. You don't even know him."

I know you don't know me or trust me…. The phrase invades my thoughts like the foggy remnants of a half-remembered dream. Where did that come from?

"Look, I thought if I talked to him, I could heal his mark. Okay?" Aaron rubs the sleep from his eyes lazily. "It's not like what *you* were doing was working."

Maybe that's true, but still.

"Well, did it work? Did it heal?" I ask nicely, despite the anger simmering in my chest.

"No." Aaron slumps on the end of my bed. "I don't think so."

"So you drugged me for nothing then."

"Not for nothing. What I had to say was important, whether it healed his mark or not."

This is important…. The ghostly voice speaks in my subconscious again. It sounds familiar, but the name of the speaker dances back into the fog before my brain can grab it.

I lean against my dresser and slide my hands along the grainy wood, trying not to let him see my fury. "So…what did you say to him?"

He meets my sharp stare and holds it. "That's between me and Kyle."

"Then it was about me."

221

Aaron narrows his eyes. "Some of it, yes."

"Was it about the decision I made?"

He doesn't answer, but his deep, blue eyes never waver from mine.

"I hope you realize it doesn't matter what you said to Kyle. I still won't kill you," I say. Aaron opens his mouth to reply, but I cut him off before he does. "It's not going to happen, Aaron, so get it out of your mind."

The bed creaks as he stands and strides across the room toward me. He pierces me with the fierceness of his gaze. I've never seen him like this before. So determined.

"I hope I can change your mind about that." His arms circle my waist, pulling me to him, pressing his chest, his abdomen, his hips against me, pushing me back into the dresser. Heat blooms in my stomach and my hands grip his back, hugging him closer despite my anger.

"I meant what I said last night." His lips brush over mine briefly and dance away. "I couldn't bear to take you to him. It would crush me to do that. I care about you too much, Libbi. I'd do anything to change your mind."

Do anything...

"Sorry, but you can't change my—"

He kisses me. There's more than lustful heat in his kiss. There's urgency in the way his lips move against mine and fear in the slight trembling of his jaw and something else I can't quite identify.

The radio in the next room screams to life, blasting some classic rock song my mother sings all the time. Time for Max to get up for school.

I ignore the obnoxious noise of his alarm and concentrate on the kiss, on Aaron's arms around me, on how well our bodies fit together, and the words spoken and unspoken between us. His fingers weave into the hair at the back of my head and his other hand slips under my shirt and over the curves of my hips and waist. There's urgency in that action too, but a different kind. It's the urgency of a longing that can never be fulfilled.

Now I remember the song playing on the other side of the

wall. It's the Rolling Stones' "You Can't Always Get What You Want."

The kiss ends when I chuckle at the irony, but Aaron still holds me close. He tucks his thumbs in the waistband of my jeans and stares down at me with sad eyes.

"Did you really think kissing me would change my mind?" I whisper.

"No. Not really." He sighs and his arms tighten around me. "You're too stubborn for that to work. I just wanted you to know how I feel."

"And how do you feel?"

"I don't want you to die today."

"You Can't Always Get What You Want" ends and the last few notes blend into the piano intro of Guns and Roses' "November Rain."

Max seriously needs to turn off his alarm. It's distracting.

"But you don't want to die any more than I do. I know you don't." I let my fingertips trail down his scarred chest. "If you tell me you do, I'll know you're lying."

"Listen to me." Aaron tucks a lock of loose hair behind my ear. "Before I met you, my life was not a life. It was an existence. So many years I've been alone, invisible and unable to do anything but watch as my baby sister sank deeper and deeper into depression. All because of me."

"It's not your fault."

"It *is* my fault." He lets go of me and backs away, shaking his head. "It's true. I saved your life so I could talk to Sara, to save her from the Blackness. But after that, I wanted to die. I just wanted it over." He combs his fingers through his hair and looks at me like he needs me to understand something important, but I don't.

"You don't want that now, though." I grab his hands and pull him back against me and hold him tight around his middle so he can't fly away.

"Only because of you." His fingers trace my jawline and I lean into his caress. "But that's the reason you have to kill me. My marks are forgiven because I'm a Reaper. If I die, I won't face the Blackness or Abaddon. When you take me to the Gateway, I'll get to go right to that light. But if you die today, Libbi, you will face them both, no matter how noble or romantic your reasons are."

My phone rings in my purse. *Chirp, chirp, chirp!* I have a text. It's probably Mom reminding me to do something. I ignore it.

"Then don't take me there." I grip the back of his shirt. "I will die. I get it. It's automatic. But who says you have to take my soul to the Gateway? I can just stay here with you, sort of like a ghost."

"No, you can't." Aaron shakes his head. "I begged Charlotte to let me keep my mother's soul the night she died. She flat out refused. She had tried it once, when her sister died. When Abaddon realized what she'd done..." I can feel Aaron's muscles tense against me. "Well, what happened to Charlotte and her sister was much worse than a few scars, believe me. Abaddon is Death incarnate, Libbi. He doesn't like to be cheated, even a little bit."

"Fine." I drop my arms from around him and push him away. "Take me to the Gateway when I die today. I don't care."

Chirp, chirp, chirp! I have another text.

"You're being stupid." He grabs my elbows. "You have to kill me. It's the only way."

"I'm not a murderer," I say.

...*do whatever it takes*...The dream voice speaks again. Where have I heard it before?

My phone chirps, and then it chirps one more time. Whoever it is must really want me to answer.

"I have to answer these texts before whoever it is blows my phone up."

He steps back and I walk around him, to my desk. I dig my phone out of my purse and check the messages. All four are from Haley.

I read the last one on the screen first.

Haley: Libbi! Answer me!

I scroll up and read the other three in the order they were sent.

Haley: Is Kyle with you? He's not home and I'm really worried about him.

Haley: He was acting weird last night. Have you seen him?

Haley: Answer me! I just found a note on his dresser. It says to tell you he's sorry about Max. OMG! What's going on?

I drop my phone. The announcer on the radio next door blurts out a loud "good morning" and promises "hit after hit from the seventies, eighties, and nineties." My heart flip-flops like a fish in my chest. I glance at the wall Max and I share and then back to Aaron.

I rush through my door and step into the hallway. Max's bedroom door is directly across the hall from mine. I take the few steps and bang on it with my fist.

"Max! Turn off your alarm. It's time to get up."

The radio answers with a corny advertisement for tires. I throw the door open and switch on the overhead light.

"Max?"

His bed is empty.

This is important...

His twisted, green camouflage blankets coil like a snake where he normally sleeps. In the divot where his head usually rests on his pillow is my Alaskan meteorite. It holds down a white sheet of lined paper. The ends of the page lift in the warm breeze wafting in from his open window.

...do anything...

"Aaron!" I yell over my shoulder. Before I finish saying his name, he's at my side.

"Where's Max?" he says as I cross the room and seize the note under my rock.

Whatever it takes...

I recognize the handwriting immediately; I've seen it so many times over the years. It always made me happy to see Kyle's sharp writing on a page, but today it fills me with dread.

Libbi,

Max is with me. If you want to see him again, bring Aaron

and meet me at Jumpers' Bridge.

Don't talk to anyone about this. If anyone other than you and Aaron shows up, Max will die. This is not a joke.

You were wrong, Libs. I'm not marked for suicide.

Do anything, Kyle. Whatever it takes... The ghost voice drifts from my memory again, but this time I recognize Aaron's soft, urgent tone. *Whatever it takes to keep her safe.*

The meteorite drops out of my limp fingers and bounces on Max's pillow. Without a word, I shove Aaron out of the way and he crashes into Max's dresser. I tear out of the room, Kyle's letter still clutched in my fist.

Down the stairs. Out the front door. Into the quiet, early morning heat.

"Wait! What does it say?" Aaron calls as he races after me.

It's a good thing he follows me. I can't run at the speed of sound without him. And I don't think I can drive right now. I wouldn't be able to concentrate on the road.

All I can see is Max.

And Kyle.

And Aaron.

The two of them conspired against me, as if I'm a helpless child who shouldn't make her own decisions. They decided last night, while I was under Aaron's relaxing power, to do anything to keep me safe. I guess "anything" includes hurting my baby brother.

I turn myself invisible on the front porch and take off running. Faster than I've ever run without holding Aaron's hand. It would be exhilarating, if I wasn't in such a panic.

Aaron catches up to me at the railroad tracks. He grips my upper arm.

"Wait, Libbi," he yells over the rushing wind. "Stop!"

I shake my head and try to rip my arm out of his grasp, but his grip tightens. I can feel him holding me back, slowing me down, and dragging me to a stop.

My feet reluctantly skid against the gravel and I whip around, fist balled and aimed for his face. Aaron ducks right before my punch can smash his nose through the other side of his skull.

"Let go of me." I twist my arm, trying to wiggle free.

"Not until you tell me what the hell is going on." Aaron grabs my other arm. His fingers tighten like mechanical claws on my flesh, holding me in place. Keeping me from getting to Max.

"Don't act like you don't know, Aaron." I glare at him. "You may think your relaxing power is the shit, but I heard you two talking last night. I remember what you said to Kyle when you knocked me out." I hit the middle of his chest as hard as I can with both fists and he grunts in pain. "Now, let me go!"

"What? What are you talking about?"

"You told Kyle to do whatever it takes to keep me safe!" I'm screaming now. My high-pitched voice bounces against the trees surrounding us. "He took him, Aaron! I was wrong. Kyle isn't marked for suicide. He's marked for murder, and he took Max!"

"I-I never told him to do that. I never told him to take Max." Aaron's grip loosens and his face goes slack. "I just wanted him to talk to you. I thought he might be able to change your mind if I couldn't."

"Well, it doesn't matter what you wanted. That's what he did." My muscles burn with the need to run. "He has Max at Jumpers' Bridge and he wants us to meet him there."

28

It always comes back to Jumpers' Bridge. A place of daring. A place of death.

Kyle leans against one of the steel girders at the bridge's midpoint, his feet crossed at the ankles. I make myself visible as I enter the bridge, and his head swivels to look at me. The boiling, black mark almost completely hides his face now; only one eye is visible. And he's alone.

I scan the length of the bridge twice and look over both shoulders, but Max is not here. Panic wells in my throat. What if I'm too late?

No. We would know if Max was dead. My head would feel like it was about to explode.

"I'm going to find Max." Aaron's warm breath tickles my ear. "Humor him."

"Where's Max?" My voice shakes with the fear and anger currently at war in my gut. I can't tell which emotion is winning the battle, but they're beating my insides into pâté.

"Libbi?" Max's quivering voice echoes around me, bouncing up from below. I peek through the breaks in the tracks at my feet. I suppose I only have the emotional capacity to be petrified of one thing at a time, because as I search the rolling water and jagged boulders far below, my fear of heights doesn't paralyze me.

Then I see him. Blindfolded, tied to a chair, and dangling from a rope under the bridge, like a fly caught in a spider's web. And now, I'm paralyzed.

Aaron slips around me, heading for Kyle. But the bridge is so long and Aaron is moving so slowly.

"Max is safe. For now." Kyle tilts his head toward the thick girder he was leaning against and the hidden safety railing behind it. A taut rope wraps the steel girder and disappears over the edge of the bridge. Only a thin, nylon rope keeps my brother from plummeting to the sharp rocks and angry waters below.

Kyle holds his hunting knife to the rope.

My feet finally unfreeze and I leap forward.

"Stay where you are, Libs," Kyle says. "Any closer and I'll cut."

I stop on demand. He's too far away. Even if I used the speed power, it takes time for it to build up. And by then, Max would be gone.

"Where's Aaron?" Kyle turns his faceless head from side to side, his one visible eye searching the expanse between us. "I know you're here, Aaron. I can feel that creepy vibe you give off. If you don't show yourself, I'll cut it. Right now." He plucks the rope like it's a guitar string and Max yelps.

Aaron has only crossed a quarter of the distance between us, not close enough to grab the rope if Kyle decides to cut it. He stops and sways on the balls of his feet, like he can't decide if he should keep invisibly moving forward or allow Kyle to see him. I psychically beg him not to take the risk and only breathe again when I hear the crackle I've come to expect when he becomes visible.

"Don't do anything stupid," Aaron says. "I'm right here."

Kyle jumps back when he sees him and jerks the rope. Max whimpers from the end and the sound strikes a shattering blow to the anger inside me. Fear has won the war.

"Pull him up, Kyle!" I sound hysterical, probably because I am. "This has nothing to do with Max."

"You're right. It has nothing to do with him." Sweat drips from Kyle's hair, and the hand holding the knife trembles. "It has to do with you. Both of you. I don't want to hurt him, Libbi, but I will if I have to." Tears pool in Kyle's visible eye as he points at Aaron. "Now, you, get up against that railing."

Aaron doesn't move. The muscles in his calves twitch, but he doesn't go to the railing.

"Now!" Kyle shouts.

"I don't know what you have planned, but it's probably not going to work." Aaron's quiet voice drifts back to me on the breeze, but he does as he's told. He slowly moves to the railing.

"Why are you doing this?" I say, trying to buy time as I inch forward. Tears obscure my vision and I let them spill over my lids.

"Ask *him*," Kyle says. "We both want the same thing. Don't we, Aaron?"

"I never wanted you to hurt Max," Aaron says.

"But it's working, isn't it? You want to die," Kyle jabs a finger at Aaron, as if to reiterate his point. "I don't want her to die. We both want Libbi to take over for you. You said the only way she can do that is if she kills you. You said you wanted her to push you off this bridge. And I don't care if that means I'll never see her again. At least I'll know she's here. Safe." His voice cracks. "And not with that thing you showed me in that Gateway."

"You showed Kyle the Blackness?" I say. "Are you crazy?" Aaron's stupidity is reaching epic proportions now. No wonder Kyle is stooping this low. He must be terrified.

"I had to. He didn't believe me." Aaron looks to me for forgiveness, or understanding, or both. "I had to tell him everything—that you have to kill me and how you refused—everything."

"How?" My eyes dance between the two of them. "I mean, I thought you couldn't use my abilities unless I was with you."

"You were knocked out," Aaron says. "I sat you in the front seat of your car and we drove there."

"It doesn't matter how I saw it. The point is, I saw it. I heard it growling. It's hungry, Libs. And if this"—Kyle lifts the rope in his hands—"is what it takes to keep you from being eaten by that thing, I'll do it. A thousand times, I'll do it."

"I don't think you will though," I say with as much confidence as I can muster. "What will you gain if you drop him? Because I can guarantee I won't do what you want if Max dies."

Kyle's hands shake but his one visible eye is firm and focused on me and I can't look away. "Do you really want to test that?" he says.

This can't be happening. The Kyle I know would never do something like this. He's kind, generous, and thoughtful. He's not a murderer. But I can't overlook the gaping hole in his soul or the black, evil gunk boiling inside of it.

He's marked for a reason. And if it's not suicide, then it's murder. I don't think he'd hurt Max on purpose, but what if he cuts the rope in an impulsive move to show me he means business. Would that count as murder in Abaddon's book? Something tells me it would.

I'm not about to take the chance with Max's life.

"Look, Kyle, there has to be a better way than this." My whole body shakes. "I don't want anyone to get hurt."

"There isn't. Aaron has to die." Kyle's voice is insistent. "Just walk over to him and give him a shove. I'm sure he won't fight it."

I glance over at Aaron. He stands at the safety railing with his arms crossed, staring down at the ancient railroad ties at his feet. His pained eyes slowly travel up to me.

"He's right, Libbi. If you push me over, I won't fight you." Aaron's jaw clenches with determination.

"See?" Kyle says. "He wants you to do it too. He told me last night."

"I can't," I whisper.

"Do it!" Kyle's voice bellows around me, shaking me with its force.

"Just push me, Libbi." Aaron's eyes fix on mine. "I'm ready. Please. It's all in your hands. You can save Max's life, heal Kyle's mark, and save yourself from the Blackness and Abaddon if you just push me over."

"There has to be a way to do all of that without killing you."

"Look at his mark." Aaron juts a finger at Kyle. "That crap is almost covering his face now. That's what my stepfather's mark looked like right before he murdered my mother. Kyle is going to cut that rope if you don't push me over. Right now!"

As if to prove Aaron's point, Kyle presses the knife into the rope.

"Kyle? Libbi?" I hear the tears in the high, quivering pitch of Max's voice. "This game isn't funny anymore. I'm really scared now. Pull me up."

I can't take it anymore. I care about Aaron and I don't want him to die, but Max doesn't deserve this torture. He's just a little kid. Tears of anger mix with my tears of fear as I narrow my gaze on Kyle.

I hate him. I hate him for doing this to Max and for putting me in this situation.

And I hate Aaron for pushing him into it, whether he meant to or not.

"Okay. I'll do it." I swipe my tears away with my palm. "I'll push him over. Just let Max up. Please, Kyle."

"Not until Aaron goes over the railing."

"Okay," I whisper. "Fine."

Kyle watches me take one step toward Aaron. Then another.

"Wait." Aaron holds up a hand. "There's one more thing." He twists the Scythe around his thumb and winces as the ring slides off. "You'll need this."

He holds the silver ring out to me. It looks sharp as sunlight gleams across the metal. Something shifts, no, *recoils* below the surface.

A trick of the light, I tell myself as I stretch my hand under his and he drops the Scythe onto my waiting palm. He grabs my hand and curls my fingers over the ring, squeezing me tight.

"Once you put this on, you will no longer be my apprentice. You will have all of my powers and you won't need me to use them anymore."

"I still need you." I choke on the words. "I'm not ready."

"Don't worry. You'll be a great Reaper. Smart, kind, compassionate. I believe in you." He brings my hand to his lips and kisses it softly. Then he turns his back to me.

Fine. It's better if I don't see his face when I shove him to his death. It won't spoil my memories of him. His strong, stubbly jaw. The way he runs his fingers through his hair when he's nervous. That stupid grin when he thinks he's being funny. His soft, full lips pressed against mine. His deep eyes.

I've seen his living eyes for the last time. The next time I see them, they'll be the eyes of his soul. Will they look the same? I doubt it.

I slip Aaron's ring into my pocket—it doesn't feel right to wear it while he's still alive—and raise both hands in front of me, palms facing his broad back.

I can do this. For Max. It will only take one hard shove to knock him over the railing and then gravity will take over. Aaron's not going to fight it.

It's what he wants.

He turns his head slightly and I can see the curves of his cheek and brow.

"Go ahead, Libbi," he says. "I'm ready."

I don't think I can do this.

But I have to.

What if I'm falling in love with him?

But it will be better for all of us this way.

Something flutters in my peripheral vision. My eyes follow the length of the safety railing to a pair of large, white wings spread in a fan. The blue heron I saw fishing at the river's edge once before jumps from the bridge and glides in a slow circle down to the river.

I'm about to turn back to Aaron and the horrible task at hand when something else catches my attention. Something attached to the safety railing. Thick coils of red rope wrap a figure eight around the bottom rung of the safety railing and a support beam. Several sturdy, metal clasps hold the rope in place.

Professional gear. Bungee jumping gear.

I pull my eyes up from the bundle of bungee cords at the base of the bridge to the top of the railing. Kyle's rope curves over the railing at a ninety-degree angle right above the bungee gear. His rope meets the gear and runs parallel to the bungee cord hanging off the bridge.

I let my breath out in a huge gust of relief. My fingers tingle with the release of tension. Max may be bound and blindfolded and dangling from a bridge, but he's safe. Kyle has him hooked to a harness.

I knew he wouldn't hurt Max. I knew it!

Well, maybe I didn't know for sure, but still.

"Where did you get the bungee equipment?" I back away from Aaron and meet Kyle's stare.

"What?" he says. His knife hand twitches.

Aaron leans over the railing, checking it out for himself. He nods, confirming my suspicions, but the look on his face is not joy at Max's safety. He looks disappointed.

"The harness you have Max hooked to," I explain, though the startled look in his eye tells me he knows what I'm talking about.

"I don't have—"

"Yes, you do," I say. "I saw it. Where did you get it?"

Kyle's shoulders slump with defeat and he sighs. "Matt let me borrow it."

"Matt? The lead singer of Red Motive Matt? He's a bungee jumper?"

"Yeah." Kyle shrugs. "Him and Tyler both. We've come out here every night this weekend, had a few beers, and they taught me how."

"You ass! You complete and utter moron! How could you do that to him? To me? Why?"

"Because I know you, Libbi. Aaron wanted me to talk to you, but I knew that wouldn't do anything but make you more sure of yourself. Once you decide something, you're too stubborn to change your mind."

Now that I'm not afraid Kyle will drop Max to his death, I run the length of the bridge, skipping the gaps in the wood as I do. I rush Kyle and shove him as hard as I can. He stumbles back and grabs the rope to stop himself from falling.

Max screams in terror with the sudden movement. He still doesn't know he's safe.

"It's okay, Buckaroo. You're safe. I'll get you up," I yell down to him, then I focus on Kyle. "Let him up, before I shove you over myself."

Kyle shifts his weight and turns to the steel support beam where the rope curls over the safety rail. He angles his head and looks at me with one sad, hopeless eye.

His plan didn't work. I didn't kill Aaron. I'm still going to die today.

And he's still marked.

Kyle bends his knees and yanks the rope. Hand over hand, he tugs the line, pulling Max up through the misty air. A flicker of red hair at the railing and I can't wait anymore. I run to my baby brother. Aaron rushes over too, and the three of us wrestle Max and the fold-up lawn chair he's tied to over the railing. We set him down on the wood ties.

The red safety harness loops around his arms, legs and waist. Kyle's long coil of rope weaves through the spokes of the chair and across Max's chest and belly, keeping Max and the chair in Kyle's control. A hunter green cloth wraps Max's head, covering his eyes.

"Oh God, Max!" I fall to my knees in front of him. "Are you okay? Are you hurt?" I tear off the blindfold as Aaron loosens the rope and harness.

"I-I'm okay," Max stutters. His wide eyes find Kyle. "Did it work? Did you help Libbi?"

"No, buddy. But you did great, though." Kyle shoves his hands in his pockets. "That was some superb acting."

"Max was in on this?" Aaron and I say together.

"What?" Kyle's visible eyebrow arches. "Did you think I'd kidnap an eight-year-old and dangle him from a bridge without his permission? What kind of a jerk do you think I am?"

"Actually, it was kinda fun!" Max grins, but then the smile melts away. "But it didn't work."

"No, it didn't work." Kyle frowns. "Libbi's still refusing to take over for Aaron. Aren't you, Libs?"

I nod. Now, more than ever, I refuse to take over for him. Not after all of this. Kyle was right. He knows my stubborn nature all too well.

"If that's how you feel," Kyle says with a curt nod, "then I have no choice but to try my other idea."

"What other idea?" I say.

"It won't work, Kyle," Aaron says at the same time. "I told you last night, I already have a replacement."

"I know what you said, but I have to try." Kyle's face pales paper-white as he turns away from us. "Just make sure you catch me, Aaron."

Before my brain even processes what's happening, Kyle sprints to the safety railing and leaps over into the misty void.

I don't think. I just move.

I run faster than I ever have with Aaron, whether he held my hand or not. I move so fast it feels like I disappear from in front of Max and reappear at the safety rail. My hands swing down and I catch Kyle's forearm.

His slick, sweaty skin slips in my palms and I dig my fingers into his flesh.

"Grab onto me!" I yell over the roar of the waterfall.

"No. Let me go." He kicks his dangling legs. One shoe slips off and spirals down, leaving a twisted path in the mist.

"I won't let you kill yourself!" My voice squeaks in panic.

"Let me go, Libs." He yanks his arm. "Aaron needs to do it."

"Aaron needs to do what? What the hell are you talking about?"

"Kyle thinks if I save his life," Aaron says behind me, "that he'll be a Reaper's apprentice, like you, and have the power to hurt me, like you do. Then we'd be able to kill each other and leave you as Reaper. But it doesn't work that way. I can't have two apprentices."

My arm muscles burn as my belly smashes against the railing. Kyle is so heavy. A hundred and fifty pounds of solid muscle. I don't know how much longer I can hold him. My fingers ache.

"See, Kyle? It won't work," I say through gritted teeth. "Grab my arm."

"I don't care if he thinks it won't work. We have to try," Kyle yells over the roar of the falls. "If you insist on dying today, Libs, I don't want to live either. Let me go."

"Help me, Aaron!" I twist and plead with my eyes.

"I want to help, but I can't. He's made his decision. You have to let him go."

"No!" I lean back and heave, but it's useless. I'm not strong enough to lift him. It would be easier if Kyle grabbed my arm and climbed, but he's trying to break loose.

"It's his free will, Libbi," Aaron continues in his teacher voice. "We can't interfere. It's against the rules."

"You said it yourself, Aaron. Screw the rules. And screw Abaddon." The words shoot out of my mouth in short, breathy spurts. "Sara had free will. We stopped her. What makes Kyle any different?"

"We changed her mind before she acted." Aaron stands at my side with his arms crossed, not helping me. "Kyle has acted, Libbi. It's too late for him."

"That's crap." My shoulders are on fire. My fingertips tingle and Kyle slips a little more out of my grasp. I'm losing the feeling in my hands.

"Please, Aaron. Help me. I'm going to drop him."

I try to lean back again, but I lose purchase and my feet slip out from under me. Suddenly, all of Kyle's weight is on my upper body, yanking on my joints, stretching the tendons and ligaments, separating the bones. The stitches in my shoulder snap, snap, snap as they rip open and I scream out in pain. Fresh blood drips down my arm, but I don't let go. I refuse to let him go.

Aaron's hands thrust down past mine and he seizes Kyle's arm at the elbow, relieving the strain on my upper body instantly. With the pressure off my shoulders, I can get my feet back under me.

"It's not going to matter if we save his life." Aaron grunts as he leans back and digs his heels into the wood, hoisting Kyle a few inches. "His idea won't work and he's already made his decision. Look at him. He's permanently marked. He intends to die today."

Kyle tilts his face up to me and I suck air in between my teeth. My grip loosens, but not because of his weight. The liquid, black stuff inside of his mark has stopped bubbling and boiling, but it's not the tranquil black sea I've seen before. This looks smooth and hard and absolutely permanent, like his face has been replaced by a layer of volcanic rock.

"That's not going to change," Aaron says.

"I don't care. We can't let him go now." I lean over the railing to get a better hold on Kyle's forearm and then I pull. "He would do the same for me."

Surprisingly, Aaron heaves with me. Then he releases one hand, and I think he's about to let Kyle go and make me do the rest on my own, but he doesn't. He repositions his hand under Kyle's armpit and lifts again.

"Let me go, Libbi!" Kyle screams and struggles as we haul him up. "Aaron has to do it. I have to be his apprentice, not yours! We have to kill each other." He twists and kicks and curses, but we manage to pull him up and over the railing anyway.

Once his feet clear the top of the railing, Aaron throws him down on the tracks and straddles him, pinning him down.

"Let me up!" Kyle's voice bellows from the black rock where his face used to be.

"Not until I know you won't try that stupid stunt again." Aaron leans forward and tries to clamp Kyle's arms to the wood, but Kyle is too fast. He twists away, balls his hand into a fist, and swings.

I hear the solid thwack of Kyle's fist against Aaron's face. Blood splatters from Aaron's lips and sprays the ancient ties.

"Ha!" Kyle laughs. "See! I can hurt you! I told you it would wor—" Kyle's body goes limp. His eyes roll and he flops back against the wood.

Aaron's soul surges with light and the hair on my arms prickles with energy. A puzzled frown crosses his face as he wipes the blood from his fat bottom lip and chin with his shirt.

The Scythe burns in my pocket. It vibrates and tugs against the fabric like it's trying to escape. An arc of lightning shoots out of the ring, right through my jeans, and circles Aaron's thumb. The light moves up his hand and arm, across his chest, up his neck to his face, leaving a jagged trail of radiance that fizzles out moments after the light passes. A glowing pinpoint of fire gathers in the middle of his forehead and grows brighter and brighter until it blazes with blinding intensity.

Lightning bursts from the pinpoint of light, connecting Aaron to Kyle. The smell of ozone permeates the air around us, and thunder rumbles. The bright circle created in the middle of Kyle's forehead pulses like a heartbeat. Kyle jerks, but he doesn't wake up.

"What the hell...?" I say.

"I can't believe this." Aaron stands, but the bolt of lightning joining him to Kyle doesn't break. It moves with him and continues to pulse light back and forth between them.

"What happened to Kyle?" Max whispers. "Is he dead?" He stands next to his chair, his face whiter than the mist. In all the excitement, I'd forgotten about him.

"I don't know," I say, trying to stay as still as possible. The arc of lightning still surges to Aaron from the Scythe in my pocket. Aaron may be brave enough to move around with a bolt of lightning blasting out of his forehead, but I'm not.

"I didn't think it could work on a suicide. Charlotte said they're too unstable." Aaron runs his hand through his hair and then gestures to me. "And I already chose you. I can't have more than one. Can I?"

"What?" I almost scream. "What the hell is happening?"

"You don't remember this..." He gestures to the light pulsing from his head. "But this is what happened right after I saved your life the first time, when you passed out on the lawn at school." Aaron looks at me with wide, astonished eyes. The bolt thrums one last time and then suddenly the link between them blinks out.

"We just saved Kyle's life, Libbi. That means I just offered him my job."

29

"**H**e's still marked." I point to Kyle's face and he moans like he heard me, but he doesn't move. "I thought Reapers' marks are forgiven."

"They are, once they accept the job." Aaron's brows furrow in thought. "Kyle hasn't accepted."

My heart and stomach switch positions and then switch back. That's it. That's how we can heal Kyle's mark. "We have to get him to accept the job!"

"I don't think he will." Aaron scratches his chin. "His plan was for us to kill each other so you could be Reaper. I don't think he's changed his mind about that..." His words trail off as if he has more to say, but he's holding back.

"Will someone please tell me what's going on?" Max walks up next to me. The color has returned to his cheeks, but his eyes are glossy and wide.

"It's complicated, Buckaroo." I squat in front of him and take his hands.

"Stop talking to me like I'm two, Libs. I'm almost nine and I'm sick of it." He crosses his arms over his chest. "Why did Kyle jump off the bridge? Why isn't he moving? What's going on?"

"It's hard to understand."

"I'm smarter than you think."

"What the hell?" Kyle jolts into a seated position. Aaron grasps his shoulders to keep him from getting up, but Kyle struggles against him. "Let go of me."

"Things are going to be really strange for you now," Aaron says and his words cause a shiver to drip down my spine like icy water.

"What's wrong with my eyes?" Kyle rubs his eyes and shakes his head. "Everybody's glowing. Did I fall? Am I...dead?"

"You're not dead. Libbi and I saved your life." Aaron lets go of Kyle and sits back, crouched and balanced on the balls of his feet. "There's nothing wrong with your eyes. You're seeing the glow of our souls. By saving your life, I've offered you my job."

"So I was right." Kyle sits up straight. "It worked."

"Yes, it worked. I didn't think it was possible, but you were right. You're my apprentice, along with Libbi." Head tilted and eyes narrowed, Aaron studies Kyle. I can almost hear the gears in his brain cranking. "Which means..."

"I can kill you now," Kyle says with a sly smile.

He leaps to his feet and lunges for Aaron, his clawed hands aimed at Aaron's neck. Kyle's fingers circle Aaron's throat, but before they can clamp down, Aaron disappears and reappears at the safety railing next to me.

"You're forgetting something important, Kyle. You can't kill me and expect Libbi to kill you. She won't do it." Aaron steps up onto the bottom rung of the safety railing and smiles. The wind billows his shirt and whips his hair around his face. "If you want your plan to work, we need to do it together. We have to kill each other. At the same time." He steps up one more rung, sits on the top rail, and pats the spot next to him, inviting Kyle to join him. "Why not push each other over?"

Kyle shrugs. "That'll work."

"No!" I step between them, but Kyle walks around me. I grab his hand, but he yanks it away. "Please. Kyle. Aaron, stop this!"

Kyle turns back to me. He touches my hair, my face, with trembling fingers. He wipes the tears from my cheek with his thumb.

"I love you, Libbi. I always have, even if you don't love me the same way." He kisses my forehead. "Keep an eye on Haley for me, will you?"

Max rushes over to Kyle and pushes between us. He grabs a fistful of his shirt and words gush out of him like a flood as tears collect on his lashes.

"You can't do that. I won't let you, Kyle. You're supposed to be my buddy. My big brother. You can't die. Promise me you won't do it."

"You don't understa—"

"What?" Max interrupts. "Am I too much of a kid to understand it? I wasn't too much of a kid to hang from a rope under the bridge."

Kyle looks to Aaron briefly, then to me, then back to Max. "If we don't do this, Libbi will die today and something really bad will happen to her. I know it's hard for you to understand, but this is the best way. The only way."

"That's stupid." Max crosses his arms and scowls. "Libbi's not going to die today. Are you, Libbi?"

I kneel in front of Max and restrain the desire to smooth his unruly hair. Max is tired of being treated like a child. And today, of all days, I think he deserves the unadulterated, non-kid-proof truth.

"No, Max. Kyle's right. As idiotic as their solution to the problem is, I am going to die today."

I tell Max everything. I tell him about being a Reaper's apprentice, and Abaddon, and the Blackness, and the terrible predicament we all face. Aaron chimes in when I'm not sure about something, and I think, not for the first time, that Aaron would have made a great teacher, if he'd had the opportunity to grow up.

Max scowls at his hands in his lap. Then he tilts his head up and his red locks flop into his eyes. He blows them away. "What if Aaron keeps his dumb job and you and Kyle run away together? Then no one has to die. And Aaron can't get in trouble with the Abaddon guy because he won't be able to find you. That would work, right?"

Max beams at us one at a time. Aaron scratches his cheek and the stubble sounds like sand paper.

"Good idea, Max. But, unfortunately, it won't work," Aaron

says. "I'll be able to find Libbi and Kyle wherever they are in Carroll Falls. And once Abaddon realizes there are three Reapers in the area and the time for training has passed, he'll come for them."

"We'll just leave Carroll Falls then." Kyle leans against the railing next to Aaron and slips his hands into his pockets.

"You can't." Aaron jumps down from the railing. "A Reaper can't leave his territory. I've tried. It's impossible. We're trapped here."

"*You* may be trapped in Carroll Falls, Aaron," I say softly. "But I'm not."

All heads turn to me.

"What do you mean?" Aaron says. "You're my apprentice. Of course you're trapped here."

"No, I'm not. I left town Sunday night to pick Max up from camp. I drove out Hell's Highway, right past the Gateway where you said the end of our territory is, with no problem." I shrug. "Maybe the official Reaper Rules don't apply to me until you die. Or maybe they only apply to whoever wears the Scythe."

Aaron touches his empty thumb and I feel the weight of the ring in my pocket. Heavy, like a shackle.

"So you and Kyle can leave town." Max grins.

I smile weakly, and Aaron takes my hand. His cold palms are slick with perspiration.

"Before you get too excited," Aaron says. "Even if you can leave the territory, we still have a huge problem: Abaddon. You will be seriously breaking the rules if you leave. Abaddon isn't confined to Carroll Falls. He will hunt you." Goose pimples stand his arm hairs on end and he shivers. "Facing the Blackness is better than what he'll do to you when he finds you. And he *will* find you. No offense, Libbi, but you're barely ready to be a Reaper. You don't have enough experience to train Kyle and keep out of Abaddon's sight. You wouldn't last a day."

The silence drifts around us on tendrils of mist. Aaron goes to the railing next to Kyle and gazes down at the boulder-strewn river. His knuckles blanch as he grips the green-painted metal.

Kyle glances over his shoulder at the long drop. He looks up at Aaron and then his visible eye locks on me.

"What about you, Aaron?" Kyle says, though his stare never wavers from me. "You've been a Reaper for forty years. Could you do it? Could you run and not get caught?"

"I can't leave town," Aaron says.

"But what if you could?"

"Maybe." Aaron folds his arms over his chest. "My chances are a hell of a lot better than yours. I know that."

"So what if Libbi is right and wearing the Scythe is what keeps you locked in town?"

"It sort of does make sense," I say as I pace the ties. "You've always wondered why Abaddon scarred you up like he did and told you to stay away from the border when he knew you couldn't get out anyway. It seemed like a gigantic waste of his time to come here just to teach you a pointless lesson. Unless he wanted to scare you into never trying it again, just in case you got the idea once you took the Scythe off and gave it to your replacement, for example."

"You know, you might have something there." Aaron nods and rubs his upper lip thoughtfully. His face is as pale and waxy as mine feels. "Once Charlotte gave it to me and I put it on, I couldn't get it off. Not until I was ready to give it to you. Even when I was in my Grim Reaper form, I couldn't drop it. It never left my hand. It was a part of me. Like a brand."

"Like a shackle," I say.

Aaron touches the bare spot on his right thumb.

"And now I'm free." The shock in his voice travels like a wave, punching me in the gut.

I don't trust my voice, so I nod instead. He's free. We can run.

"So what if you decided to pitch that thing into the river?" Kyle says. "Do you think you could keep us safe from him, if we all ran together?"

"Probably, if we kept moving." Aaron's voice rises with excitement. It's contagious. I can't stop the huge grin that spreads across my face. "I can feel when he's near, and if we jump from territory to territory, it'll be harder for him to catch us." Then his face falls and he says, "But I can't leave. Who will be Carroll Falls' Reaper? The town needs a Reaper. And the first time a scheduled death doesn't show up at the Gateway—which is in two hours, by the way—Abaddon will want to know what's wrong. He'll come here. No matter how much experience I have, that's not enough time to get some real distance. He'll catch us. Not to mention the Scythe is our connection to him. He'll know if it's not being worn."

"I'll wear it," Kyle pushes away from the railing. His eye remains steady above his black-rock mark, but his hand trembles slightly as he holds it out for the Scythe. "I don't want to leave Carroll Falls anyway. And if you think you can keep Libbi away from that thing, then I'll do it."

"Are you accepting my job, Kyle?" Aaron asks.

Kyle nods and my shoulders sag with relief. He's going to live and, as a Reaper, his mark will heal. But at what price? I certainly didn't want Aaron's job. I only took it for Kyle, and now Kyle has decided to take my place so I can run away with the object of his jealousy. It's so messed up I'd laugh if I didn't feel like crying.

"It's not as simple as just taking the Scythe. You need training."

"Then train me."

"And this is a big risk for you. Do you understand that?"

"Risk?" I say.

"Wait." Max speaks up from his spot by the steel girder. "What risk? Abaddon won't kill Kyle, will he?" The kid says exactly what I was too afraid to ask.

"I doubt he'll kill him," Aaron says and my shoulders relax. "He can't. He needs him to be the local Reaper. But he might hurt him. And I know for a fact he'll come after Libbi and me when he realizes we're gone. But I also know this is our best shot. And I think it's worth the risks. If Kyle's willing, all he has to do is say he'll be Carroll Falls' next Grim Reaper."

All three of us—Aaron, Max, and me—turn to Kyle with anticipation.

Kyle slips his hands into his pockets and gazes out over the safety railing to the tumbling water of Carroll Falls. He doesn't move or speak for several minutes.

"I'll do it," Kyle finally says to the waterfall. "I'll be Carroll Falls' next Grim Reaper."

A bubble of blue light blossoms in the air between Kyle and Aaron. It grows to surround them both and static electricity crackles around them.

Something pops like stone hitting stone and smoke oozes from a crisscross of cracks that form in Kyle's mark. A large chunk of the volcanic rock crumbles away from his face like a landslide and exposes his chin and mouth. Then another pop and his eye and cheek become visible. One more and the rest of the evil mark falls away from his face.

Kyle's lips curve in a smile and his warm eyes sparkle. Now that I can see it again, I can't believe how much I've missed that smile.

"Just remember, Aaron." Kyle's muffled voice sounds like he's talking behind glass. "If this doesn't work, I'm not like Libbi. I have no problem killing you."

30

Aaron's warm hand curls around mine.

"Are you ready for this?" His black hair lifts in the wind. The south forest sways and the leaves whisper around us. The trees are our audience and they know we're about to do something dangerous.

There's no clearing in the underbrush to mark the end of Aaron's territory on this side of town, but I know it's here. I can feel the electric charge in the air.

"I'm ready." I weave my fingers with his and squeeze. "Do you think Kyle's ready?"

"He may struggle a bit with a few things, but he'll be okay. He's a quick learner."

Once Kyle agreed to take over, the seven-day clock for his training began. Kyle had the same amount of time to train as me, but Aaron decided to cut it down to two very intense days.

Because Abaddon knows about me.

I was a scheduled death and on the Death Plan. After Aaron saved my life from Jason's truck, and after my almost-fatal asthma attack in the library, he had to go to Abaddon and explain why he didn't bring my soul to the Gateway.

But Abaddon doesn't know about Kyle. Kyle would have been an unscheduled death, and not on Abaddon's Death Plan. Aaron wants to leave town well before my seven-day training period is over so we have a good lead if Abaddon decides to check up on his newest Reaper and realizes it's not me.

Aaron and Kyle spent every moment of the last two days

together, going over the Reapers' powers and practicing. The first day, I tried to help, but I couldn't do much. My teaching skills suck and when it comes to reaping, I hardly know what I'm doing. When it became clear that my "help" was more of a pain in Aaron's ass, I stepped aside and spent my time with Haley, my mom, and Max.

Max and I told Haley everything. Kyle has been too busy with Aaron to talk to her himself. I'm not sure if she really understands or believes us, but she handled it well. Better than I would have, if I was in her situation. But I couldn't tell Mom. She wouldn't believe us, and she'd probably have me committed before she let me take off to God-knows-where with a guy I've known less than a week.

I wrote her a letter and left it with Max.

In it, I told her Aaron and I ran away together. That much is true, at least. I also told her that I didn't know if I would come back, but I promised to call and write. I hope that's not a lie. I don't know what will happen to us once we cross the border.

I'd be happy if we lost the Reaper powers and just became normal people, but Aaron thinks we'd be easier to find that way. He's afraid if we lose our powers, we'll become part of the Death Plan again and be on Abaddon's radar. But what I fear most is that we'll become ghosts, living shadows, invisible, unable to do anything, without even jobs to keep us occupied.

Aaron drops my hand and moves closer to the boundary of his territory. He reaches out, palm forward, fingers spread. Electricity snaps a blue starburst in the air in front of him and he recoils in surprise.

"You're sure you got through?" He glances over his shoulder. A bead of sweat collects on his brow.

"Yeah, I got through." I try to sound confident, but as I watch a thin tendril of smoke rise from the spot Aaron just touched, I'm not so sure. "I just hope I can get through with you."

We had decided not to test the barrier until we were absolutely ready to run. Aaron doesn't know how Abaddon knew when he tried to leave to see his sister. It could have been the Scythe, but it could also have been something else. Whatever it was, Aaron doesn't want to alert him of our escape prematurely.

One look at the scars crisscrossing his body and I don't blame him.

"Let me try." I reach one finger forward. Electricity sizzles and sparks where my finger touches the barrier. I steel myself for a jolt of pain as I push my finger through the wall of lightning, but it doesn't come. Electricity circles my finger, my hand, my wrist as they painlessly slide through.

"See." I smile and wiggle my fingers on the other side. "I told you I can get through."

"Well, there's only one way to find out if I can too." Aaron grabs my free hand. He lifts my fingers to his lips and gives them a quick peck. "Let's go, before I change my mind."

The trees surrounding us applaud as the wind rips through them.

I close my eyes and breathe. One breath in. One breath out.

"Okay. Let's go."

We lift our feet in unison and step out into the world.

ACKNOWLEDGEMENTS

There are so many people to thank I don't know where to start.

First, I'd like to thank my amazing agent, Lindsay Ribar, for taking a chance on me. Not only is she smart, sharp-witted, and talented as hell, she has the patience of the Dali Lama, and the ability to dish out tough-love better than anyone I know. I'd also like to thank Brenda Bowen for rescuing my little manuscript from the slush pile. And to all the staff at Sanford J. Greenburger, Associates, thank you!

A huge helping of gratitude goes to Georgia McBride and the staff at Month9Books for seeing potential in this story of mine and taking it on. I can't thank you enough. And much thanks to my editors, Kate Brauning, Jennifer Peterson, and Annie Cosby. For these women, patience is more than a virtue, it's a gift. Thanks are also in order for amazing cover designer, Arterismos, whose super-human ability to capture the feel of my story in image form blows my mind.

An Everest-sized mountain of thanks goes to my fabulous critique partners, Dorothy Dreyer and Anabel Gonzalez. Their good cheer and support kept me going more than they could possibly realize. Just as important are my tough-as-nails beta readers, Crystal Lee, Kara Taylor, and Marieke Nijkemp, without whom this story would be vastly different, and not in a good way. And I mustn't forget my first teen reader (other than my daughter), Caitlynn Weeden. Her excitement gave me the courage to keep on keeping on. Much love to all of you!

Last, but certainly not least, thanks to my kids (Hana and Caleb), my mom (Julia), my sister (Wendy), and niece (Briana), my friends, and my co-workers at Hanover Hospital, for all of your support, encouragement, and enthusiasm, and for believing in me when others didn't. You guys truly are the best!

Elizabeth Holloway

Elizabeth Holloway is a maternity nurse living in Southern Pennsylvania with her two teen children and their pets, Bambam the dog and Tinkerbell the cat. In addition to nursing and writing, she's also an avid reader, an artist, a karaoke singer, a music lover, and a kick-ass Pictionary player. Her debut YA novel, CALL ME GRIM, will be released from Month9Books in Fall 2014.

Preview more great YA titles from
Month9Books.

Visit www.month9books.com.

She will become the thing she hates,
to protect those she loves.

PREDATOR

JANICE GABLE BASHMAN

SARAH BROMLEY

One for sorrow,
two for joy.
A destructive girl,
a damaged boy.

a murder of
magpies